Annja sat bolt upright

When the yowl broke across the glen, it sounded like a banshee's screeching mixed with the cries of a wounded animal.

Ken was already out of his sleeping bag with his pistol in his hand.

"What was that noise?" Annja asked.

Ken shook his head. "I don't know."

Around them, the trees had gone still. The crickets no longer chirped. Even the roar of the waterfall seemed subdued. Annja searched the darkness for any sign of an enemy. As she did so, she gradually eased herself out of her sleeping bag. At least if they were attacked, she'd be able to defend herself.

Then she remembered what Taka had told them at the temple in Osaka. Hadn't he told them about the legend of the Kappa Swamp Vampire that supposedly guarded the mountain monastery? She closed her eyes and saw the sword.

"What's wrong?" Ken asked.

Annja opened her eyes. "I can't get my sword!"

Titles in this series:

ROGUE Angel

Alex Archer

WARRIOR SPIRIT

A GOLD EAGLE BOOK FROM
WORLDWIDE®

TORONTO • NEW YORK • LONDON
AMSTERDAM • PARIS • SYDNEY • HAMBURG
STOCKHOLM • ATHENS • TOKYO • MILAN
MADRID • WARSAW • BUDAPEST • AUCKLAND

First edition November 2007

ISBN-13: 978-0-373-62127-9
ISBN-10:   0-373-62127-2

WARRIOR SPIRIT

Special thanks and acknowledgment to
Jon Merz for his contribution to this work.

THe
LEGeND

...THE ENGLISH COMMANDER TOOK
JOAN'S SWORD AND RAISED IT HIGH.

The broadsword, plain and unadorned,
gleamed in the firelight. He put the tip against
the ground and his foot at the center of the blade.
The broadsword shattered, fragments falling
into the mud. The crowd surged forward,
peasant and soldier, and snatched the shards
from the trampled mud. The commander tossed
the hilt deep into the crowd.
Smoke almost obscured Joan, but she continued
praying till the end, until finally the flames climbed
her body and she sagged against the restraints.

Joan of Arc died that fateful day in France,
but her legend and sword are reborn....

1

The fist shot at her face much faster than she'd expected.

Annja Creed felt certain it would impact somewhere along the bridge of her nose, but at the very last second, her body seemed to take over and jerk her head out of the way. The fist sailed through empty air and as it went past, Annja saw the opening she needed. In the blink of an eye, she fired three punches into the attacker's midsection, scoring solid hits with all three.

"Matte!" The referee's voice barked out above the cacophony of the crowd's cheers. Annja stopped, and sweat poured down her face and into the folds of her karate uniform. The *gi* was stained with the sweat, dust and exertion of the past three hours.

She turned to the judges and waited. Two white flags went into the air.

Annja beamed but contained her joy over winning the match. Instead she executed a formal bow from her waist to the judges. Then she walked to her opponent, a twenty-some-thing punk rocker with tea-stained reddish-brown hair. He was still bent over, looking for the air Annja had knocked out of his lungs.

As she approached, he looked up and frowned. "How did you do that?"

Annja shrugged. "I thought you had me, Saru. But somehow my reflexes kicked in."

"Good fight. I may never breathe again, though." He tried to grin, but grimaced instead. His friends helped him off the traditional tatami mats.

Annja turned and went the other way toward the side where her gear awaited. One more match and she'd be done. But the last fight of the evening was looking to be nothing short of nearly impossible.

She gulped down water and waited for the next opponent to walk onto the mat.

When he did, Annja felt her stomach twist itself into knots. Nezuma Hidetaki was one of the most feared fighters that the Kyokushinkai had ever produced. A hard stylist, Nezuma liked to practice his punches against brick buildings. He'd split his knuckles so often that doctors had finally removed the remaining cartilage and simply sewn the knuckles together. Nezuma had calluses on top of his calluses and though short at only five feet six inches, his thighs were as big around as tree trunks.

He strode across the mat and stood in front of Annja with his arms folded across his barrel chest. "I will not be as easy as Saru was," he stated.

I didn't think Saru was easy, Annja thought.

She took another sip of water and then mopped her brow. The material of her *gi* top stuck to her skin. She flapped it, trying to get some air circulating so she'd be able to move without getting caught up in it.

Nezuma did some deep squats across the ring, warming up his body. As the reigning champion, he only had to fight one match—the last one.

Annja was already as warm as she was going to get. All that remained before her in this tournament being held in the Tokyo Budokan, was Nezuma. If she won this match, she'd be the lightweight champion in the Interdiscipline Budo Championship.

The judges looked at Annja and she nodded, then stepped onto the mat. Nezuma turned and bowed to the judges. Annja did the same.

Nezuma turned to Annja and gave her a curt bow. Annja bowed in the same style. If he's going to be rude, so be it, she thought. I can play that game, as well.

The referee stepped in between them and held his hand horizontally. He looked at both of them again, but Annja already had her eyes locked on Nezuma's.

"Hajime!"

Nezuma immediately stalked Annja, coming at her from the side, almost like a crab. Annja pivoted to her southpaw stance, bringing her guard higher than normal, aware that Nezuma preferred to attack with straight punches aimed at the head, trying to score immediate knockouts. He had successfully knocked out three of his previous opponents on his way to becoming the champion he was—the one Annja hoped to become.

Nezuma shot out a feint with his right leg, a flashing roundhouse kick aimed at her upper thigh. Annja stepped back out of range, letting the kick sail past her. Nezuma's follow-up was a straight blast aimed at her head.

Annja ducked and deflected the blow away to the inside and punched at Nezuma's exposed right chest. He brought his left hand in sharply and punched Annja's arm out of the way. Annja dropped back and away, clutching her arm.

Well, that hurt, she thought. She took a breath and gritted her teeth. Let's see how he likes this.

Against all her normal strategic thinking, Annja jumped and let a bloodcurdling shout erupt from her lungs as she folded her legs up and under her, aiming her left foot at Nezuma's head.

The jumping side kick caught her stocky opponent by surprise, and he barely missed losing his head to Annja's kick. Annja landed, aware that Nezuma was already punching at exactly the spot where she'd be landing. Instead of standing, Annja let the momentum drop her to the ground and then pivoted and swept Nezuma's legs out from under him. He went down hard and the judges scored it one point for Annja.

Just two more to go, she thought as Nezuma hauled himself to a standing position again.

He glared at Annja.

No way is he going to fall for that again, Annja thought with a smile. Still, it was worth it seeing the look of surprise on his face. Especially since she knew that Nezuma was a notorious misogynist who thought women belonged either in bed or in the kitchen, preferably both.

The referee barked at them to begin again, and Annja and Nezuma squared off.

This time, Nezuma didn't waste time by trying to find Annja's weak points. He simply flew at her with punch after punch. Annja backed up again and again, blocking them as they came shooting at her.

Nezuma attacked with a ferocity Annja hadn't experienced from her previous opponents. His punches came at her from different angles and levels. He punched high and low and right in the middle. Annja kept backing up, aware that the edge of the mat loomed closer.

Finally, Nezuma slipped one single punch past her and an instant later Annja felt it thunder into her lower abdomen and drive every last bit of breath from her lungs. Annja fell backward and landed hard on the edge of the mat.

She tried to flush her lungs but her diaphragm seemed to be spasming. Nezuma's face came into view, hovering over her.

"That makes us even again at one point each, Miss Creed." He smiled. "Now it really is anyone's match."

He helped her to her feet. "Just don't mistake this for anything but what it is, a long overdue lesson for all women that they need to stay away from *budo*."

"What a perfectly antiquated statement," Annja said. She smiled at Nezuma. "But don't worry, I'll make sure this doesn't sting too much when I lay you out on your butt."

Nezuma chuckled and walked back to his edge of the mat. The audience had hushed, aware that both fighters were even in points. One more score would decide the match. Annja could feel their eyes as they leaned in to watch.

She could hear the creaks of the old wooden folding chairs. The scent of sweat tinged the air, and Annja's thoughts went to what had brought her there in the first place.

After her last adventure, she'd needed a vacation. More than that, she'd wanted to test herself. And the martial-arts newsgroup she sometimes frequented had posted news about the upcoming tournament. It seemed a perfect time to do something for herself, so she made her travel arrangements from her loft in Brooklyn. Within twelve hours, she was hopping a flight bound for Tokyo.

Fourteen hours later, she arrived and went straight to her hotel and fell asleep, trying to get her system in tune with the time-zone change.

And now, here she stood, awaiting Nezuma's final attack.

Her nerves seemed poised at the edge of a very steep cliff, ready to jump at a moment's notice. Even the sweat seemed to be still wherever it was on her body.

Nezuma's eyes glistened like those of a ravenous tiger about to consume an antelope he'd pursued and had cornered. Annja's stomach still ached, but her breathing had returned to normal.

For the last time the referee stepped between them. Once more, he looked at them both.

Annja nodded.

Nezuma grinned.

"Hajime!"

The crowd roared and hopped to its feet. Shouts and cheers echoed across the cavernous room as Annja circled Nezuma. The Kyokushinkai fighter smiled and then roared as he launched a high roundhouse kick toward Annja's left temple. Annja stepped inside and started to drop to punch into Nezuma's groin.

This'll teach him, she thought.

But in that instant, Nezuma recoiled his kick and then shot his left arm out, clotheslining Annja across the throat in an aikido move known as *irimi nage*, the entering throw.

Annja felt the pressure on her throat and knew that if the throw finished, she'd be defeated.

Instead, she grabbed Nezuma's arm and used it to vault herself over like a gymnast. As she spun over, she kicked out with both feet at Nezuma's chest.

He sidestepped and shot a punch at Annja's head.

Annja ducked out of the way and the two of them broke apart again.

Sweat poured down both of their faces. Annja blinked through the salt and kept her guard up. Her arms felt like lead weights, dragging her down, but she was all too aware of how prizefighters often tire. Once the guard started to drop, the other fighter usually had no problem finishing them off. Annja was determined to not let that happen. Especially since she'd spent enough time listening to her self-appointed trainer, Eddie, harp on her about keeping her hands up where they could protect her.

Nezuma's guard had stayed perfectly in position throughout the entire fight. His arms looked like coils of tight sinew wrapped around steel girders. He still maneuvered on deeply bent legs, keeping his center of balance low and steady. Trying to unseat him would be almost impossible.

He screamed again and came at Annja with a series of stomping kicks aimed at her midsection. He looked as if he was taking giant steps across the mat, and Annja had to sidestep them again and again.

This is ridiculous, she thought. It's time I went on the attack.

She turned and launched a single roundhouse kick at Nezuma's head. He casually flicked it away and in that instant, Annja went low, driving her elbow toward Nezuma's stomach.

He blocked that, as well. Annja came up, driving up with an uppercut aimed at the underside of his jaw. Nezuma pivoted out of the way and then dropped unexpectedly to the floor. She felt the crushing instep of Nezuma's right foot sink into her stomach and then lift her up overhead. When it was fully extended, Nezuma retracted his right foot, but Annja kept sailing through the air, tumbling as she went like in some bad kung fu movie.

She crashed to the floor in a broken heap just as the judges raised their red flags.

Nezuma had won the match.

Annja got to her feet, determined not to lie there like a beaten fool. Even though her stomach ached as if someone had just used a spoon to scoop out her insides, she bowed to the judges and then to Nezuma.

"Next time," she said through gritted teeth.

Nezuma smiled.

Annja hobbled over to her bag and drank down some of the last remaining water in her bottle. The crowd at the *budokan* was still cheering Nezuma and he soaked up the adoration. He bowed several times and then left the mat. The spectators left soon after, filing out in the same orderly way as they had come into the *budokan*.

Annja sat there for another few minutes, catching her breath. She sucked at the bottle and realized that she was out of the precious fluid.

"Here."

She looked up and into the deepest, darkest eyes she'd seen on a man. He held out a fresh bottle of water and smiled.

Wow, Annja thought. "Thanks," was all she could say.

"That was some fight. You held your own against him remarkably well."

"Remarkably well? What's that supposed to mean?"

He held up his hands. "Please, I meant no disrespect. I certainly do not share Nezuma's viewpoint on the role of women in society."

"You know what he thinks about women?" Annja asked.

He smirked. "Nezuma has made no secret of his views on women and the martial arts. You can read about them in any number of magazines." He watched as the *budokan* emptied out. "Nezuma is an extremely adept opponent, however. But you made him work for that win. And that is something that doesn't happen too often. You should be quite proud of how well you fared."

Annja grimaced. "I'll save that for when I'm feeling better. Right now, my guts feel like they want to stage a revolt in my stomach."

He offered his hand. "My name is Kennichi Ogawa. I'm very pleased to make your acquaintance, Miss Creed."

Annja stared at him. "Nice to meet you."

"It's not often that this tournament attracts someone of your…professional stature."

Annja frowned. "You've heard of my work?"

"Certainly. You are, in fact, the reason why I am in attendance tonight." He waved his hand. "This is not my usual scene, I'm afraid."

"Not a martial-arts junkie?"

Kennichi shrugged. "There's a difference between sport tournaments and real martial arts. Most people confuse the two, but there are profound differences." He eyed her closely. "As I'm sure you know."

"Rules. In the tournaments there are always rules, even if the venue claims that anything goes," Annja said.

"Exactly." Kennichi nodded. "But on the street…"

"Anything really does go. Eye gouging, groin shots, knee breaks. Whatever it takes to survive."

He smiled. "You do know. And the mental perspective is also different. Fighting for survival can never be understood by those who have never struggled for their own life."

Annja gathered her towel and bag. "So, you took time out of your schedule to come here and meet me?"

"Yes, I did."

Annja mopped her brow. "Do you make it a habit to pick women up at martial-arts tournaments?"

Kennichi's eyes widened. "Does this look like a pickup?"

"I'm not sure yet." Annja slapped the towel over her shoulder. "I might need some time to think about it."

"Perhaps I might be interested in you for professional reasons."

Annja smiled. "Professional reasons."

"To be perfectly blunt, I'd like you to find something for me. Something old and quite priceless. Are you interested?"

"Do you need it found just this minute?"

He grinned. "Not quite this moment. No."

Annja nodded. "In that case, I'll head for the showers now. And after that, you can take me out for dinner. Then we can discuss your professional reasons and I'll decide then if I'm interested in your priceless artifact. Okay?"

"Uh…okay," he said.

Annja turned and walked away, aware that Kennichi Ogawa was standing stock-still behind her, very much surprised by the conversation that had just transpired.

2

The Spartan showers at the Tokyo Budokan weren't the kind of luxurious bath Annja would have preferred if she'd been home in New York City, but the scalding waters were good for relieving the tenderness of her sore muscles. She soaped herself up using the fragrance bar she carried with her, ridding herself of the body-odor stench that seemed a fixture in gyms all over the world.

Aside from her bruised ego and the purplish welts already covering parts of her battered body, Annja felt refreshed when she emerged from the changing area dressed in a gray turtleneck and black slacks.

Kennichi lounged by the front of the *budokan*, now almost entirely deserted except for the various ushers and cleaning crew. He seemed uninterested in the scenery around him. Annja could see his breathing was relaxed and deep, and every minute or so, his head scanned the immediate vicinity.

Despite his lackadaisical demeanor, Annja knew he was

completely aware of everything happening around him. She'd seen the same relaxed attentiveness before in some of the intelligence operatives she'd met during her various adventures. Still, she didn't figure Kennichi for a spy.

He looked up as she approached, his eyes giving her a lingering once-over. "You certainly clean up well."

"Thanks. Are you always so blunt?"

Kennichi smiled, showing a mouth full of polished teeth. "Are you wondering why I tend to be at odds with the relative obliqueness that most of my countrymen embrace?"

"I would have said it differently, but yeah, something like that," Annja said with a smile.

Kennichi led them outside, holding the door open for Annja. She felt the cool breeze wash over her and was glad she'd opted for the turtleneck. Kennichi guided her toward the parking lot.

"I was educated abroad. And personally, I've never really liked having to pry honesty out of people. I find it easier to simply say what I think or feel—within reason and tact, of course—and see where it leads."

"Interesting," Annja said. "Is that likely to catch on here?"

"I doubt it will ever be so. Japan's ways are ingrained deep into her psyche. Change is a very difficult thing to produce here." He pointed at the black Mercedes S550 parked alone under a street lamp. "This is me."

Annja whistled. "Nice ride."

Kennichi nodded. "I have a bit of a weakness for nice cars. As much as I try to wean myself, every year there seems to be something new that grabs my gut."

Annja slid into the leather interior. "Any other weaknesses

I should know about?" She couldn't help but feel intrigued by this man.

Kennichi eyed her for just a moment. "Maybe later. Right now, let's get something to eat. You must be famished after that grueling session you just logged."

"I could definitely eat." Annja rested her head back against the cushion. "It has been some kind of day."

He slid the car into gear and they moved off into the traffic. At a traffic light, Kennichi turned and smiled again. "First things first. Please call me Ken. It's easier than the mouthful that my name really is. And I'd hate for that to ever be a burden for someone."

"Okay. Where are we going, Ken? Steak and lobster? McDonald's?"

"There's a coffee shop in Kanda we can hit. They've got a very diverse range of food. I'm not sure what you normally eat after you fight your way through a horde of foes, so I thought it might be best to give you a smorgasbord of options. That way you can best decide what will replace the nutrients you lost earlier."

"Considerate of you," Annja said. "I appreciate that. Why don't you tell me about the object you're trying to locate?"

Ken held up his hand. "If you don't mind, I'd rather we wait until we eat first. Your attention right now is somewhat diffused. I need you a bit more…concentrated."

"I'm focused on you, Ken," Annja said.

Ken grinned. "I don't doubt it. But I think a meal in your stomach will do you some good before I unleash my family's woes on you."

"Family?" Annja frowned. "You're married?"

"I meant family in the lineage sense. Ancestors, descendants, that kind of thing." He glanced at her. "And no, I'm not married."

God, that must have come out like a schoolgirl crush, Annja thought. "Sorry, I didn't mean to—"

"It's no problem." He pointed. "We're here."

Ken parked the Mercedes in the tiniest parking lot Annja had ever seen. They both got out of the car. The front of the coffee bar proclaimed that it served pizza, Buffalo wings, hamburgers and an assortment of other American food items, all written in English. Annja's mouth watered at the thought of some wings. But she thought it might be better to stick to something a little less messy. Nothing said impressive on a first date than hot sauce smeared all over your face.

A line of Honda motorcycles that had been decked out with detailing and every latest gizmo available dominated the area immediately outside the coffee shop. At least ten of them vied for space in what should have only accommodated half their number.

Annja whistled. "Nice bikes."

Ken looked at them and shook his head. "If only their owners were that quiet. But come on, let's eat."

The hostess inside greeted them with a bow, and as Annja looked the place over, she couldn't help but marvel at how things in Japan could be so foreign and so familiar at the same time. Rock music blasted from the speakers, but not so loud you had to shout to be heard. Movie posters and surfboards were plastered on the walls. Diner-style booths with bright red naugahyde cushions and laminate tables reminded Annja of the 1950s-style joints she'd seen back home.

The hostess led them past a bunch of tables packed with Japanese teens adorned with body piercings and colorful spiked red hair. She felt their eyes roam over her body and now wished she'd worn something less clinging than what she had on.

More than the way they looked at her, though, she was alarmed by the way they checked Ken out. Several of them shifted in their seats, and Annja felt her own instincts buzz. Were they going to jump them? And if so, why?

"Annja."

Ken's voice brought her back to reality. He smiled at her and Annja smiled back. "Sorry."

"Forget about them. They're just *teppo*."

Annja frowned. "I've heard that word before—"

Ken nodded. "It means 'bullet'. It's what they call the kids who have just joined a Yakuza gang. They're low-level thugs who are used for intimidation. They extort money. Some of them run small-time prostitution rings or sell drugs on the side. And tragically, most of them are dead before they're twenty years old."

"That's horrible," Annja said. She'd seen enough of youth involved in crime to know the statistics could be devastatingly similar in the States, if not worse.

"Stupid, more likely," Ken said. "None of these kids have come from the lower class. They've all been recruited from the middle class. They have all their options open to them, but they choose instead to forsake the sacrifices their parents made simply because they think it's cool to be in a gang. It's very different in America, where the economics of poverty breed new generations of criminals. Here, it's a fad to be involved. And a stupid one at that."

A waitress on roller skates glided up to their table. Annja cracked the menu and ordered a hamburger.

The waitress smiled. "Would you like corn on that?"

Annja blanched. "Excuse me?"

Ken chuckled. "We put corn on a lot of things. Pizza, too."

Annja shook her head. "Just lots of cheese, lettuce, ketchup and mayonnaise. No corn. Oh, and I'd like a large glass of water."

Ken ordered a plate of Buffalo wings and a beer. "I miss the States and come here for my wing fix. If I could get Sam Adams beer here, I'd be really happy."

"Where did you go to school? That is why you were there, right?"

Ken nodded. "Georgetown for undergrad. Harvard for my master's."

"In what?"

"Partying, most likely. I was something of a nut in school." He smiled but then corrected himself. "My degree is in languages. Sanskrit, Tibetan and Nepali."

Annja leaned back. "Impressive."

"I had an ulterior motive for it. One we'll discuss shortly."

Their food arrived faster than Annja would have thought. After carefully checking her cheeseburger for any sign of corn, she took a huge bite. Tasting the juices and melted cheese run into her mouth, she moaned. "This is incredible."

"It's better with the corn," Ken said around a mouthful of wings.

"You've got sauce on your face, champ." Annja washed down her bite with a long sip from her water.

Ken wiped his mouth. "So that's what was stinging." He

took a healthy pull on his beer and then tore into the rest of his plate as if he hadn't eaten in a long while.

Annja devoured her burger and found the fries just as tasty. She and Ken ate in relative silence for the next few minutes until at last, Annja leaned back, wiped her mouth and sighed. "That was a great meal."

Ken finished his beer and gestured to the waitress. He glanced at Annja. "How about a beer?"

"Sure." Annja normally didn't drink alcohol after a fight, but she was full and relaxed and eating with a handsome man. One drink wouldn't be a bad idea.

Ken held up two fingers and then turned back to Annja, with a serious expression. "My family line is very old. Over one thousand years in fact. I'm descended from a long line of warriors. One of my ancestors was presented with a relic far back in Japan's history."

Annja glanced around the restaurant. "How far are we talking here?"

"A.D. 560."

Annja blinked. "You weren't kidding about a long family line. I never knew the name Ogawa stretched back that far."

"Ogawa is nothing so special. It's more the lineage itself that is important. But martial-arts lineages aren't normally named after people. They're instead named after an idea, concept or even a geographical location." He smiled. "Forgive me, I'm sure you know all of this already."

"Actually, my knowledge of Japanese martial arts is fairly rudimentary."

Ken nodded. "My family's lineage is known as the Yumegakure-ryu. It means 'hidden dream.' We were em-

ployed by the Regent Prince Shotoku Taishi during his reign
and by almost every ruler since then."

Annja frowned. "That's a lot longer than most historians
would argue records have been kept."

"Most historians are a bunch of academics who have little
common sense about the very things they claim expertise in.
They sit in dusty offices, using only books to make their
sometimes ridiculous claims," Ken said.

Annja grinned. She knew more than a few people who fit
that description exactly. "I'm something of a historian myself,
though. You think I fit the same mold as they do?"

The waitress brought their beer and Ken hoisted his in
Annja's direction. "I don't know too many academics who
would have the courage to fight for three hours in the *budokan*.
Kempai."

"*Kempai*," Annja said.

They drank together and then Ken rested his glass on the
tabletop and leaned forward. "Besides, you're an archaeologist. And you do your best work in the field. That's your real
value to me. I need you to help me find something that was
stolen from my family a long time ago."

"What is it?" Annja asked, feeling the excitement that
always accompanied a new challenge.

Ken leaned back. "My ancestors, for their service to Prince
Shotoku, were awarded a very special relic known as a *vajra*.
It means 'thunderbolt'. Prince Shotoku had the small sceptre
made specially for my ancestors, and legend has it that it was
also endowed with certain, shall we say, mystical qualities."

"What kind of mystical qualities?" Annja grinned as she
thought about how just a few years ago she would have

scoffed at the idea of mystical properties in relics. How times had changed.

Ken shrugged. "Probably nothing. After all, have you ever seen anything that defied rational thought in all your travels?"

Annja felt a twinge in her stomach. How would Ken react if she said, "Well, sure, I've got this magical sword that I can pull out of thin air if I get into trouble."

Instead she only smiled. "Go on."

"I suppose it might have been more a matter of what it represented—that it was given by a powerful ruler to my family so that we would continue to be a force for good and balanced thought against those who might use their power to prevail in an opposite direction. But its loss led to the eventual downfall of my family. Gradually, over many years, the Yumegakure-ryu began to die out. I am, in fact, the last descendant."

"Only you? There's no one else?" Annja asked.

"None. And now I have this incredible feat in front of me. I must find that which was stolen from my family and try to restore the Yumegakure-ryu to its former glory. It's a daunting task, which is why I came to you seeking help. I believe you can help me locate the *vajra*."

"But it could be anywhere," Annja said.

Ken shook his head. "I think it's still here in Japan. When it was stolen, Japan was still a very closed society. I doubt the thieves would have tried to escape the country with it."

"But since that time, Japan has certainly opened up." Annja shook her head. "It could be anywhere by now."

Ken shrugged again and took another sip of his beer. "Call it a hunch, but I think it's here."

Annja sighed. "All right. I'll help you."

Ken hoisted his beer again. "Excellent!"

Annja took a sip of her beer and then put her glass down. "Tell me something. I don't recall ever hearing the name of the Yumegakure-ryu in any of the various lineages that I do know about. If you were so well-known, shouldn't there be more written about your lineage?"

Ken shook his head. "We were well-known. Respected even. But history is written only by those who hold power when it is written. And the nature of my lineage was such that historians felt we did not belong in the annals of history. That we were, by nature, not honorable enough to be included."

"But other samurai lineages—even those that were less good than others—were included," Annja pointed out.

Ken smiled. "We weren't samurai, Annja."

"You weren't?" Annja frowned. "Then what—?"

"We were ninja."

3

Annja leaned back in the booth, feeling the cushions on her back. "Ninja? You're kidding, right?"

Ken's eyes never blinked. "Not at all."

"You were hired killers? Assassins? Those crazy dudes who wore black pajamas and disappeared in puffs of smoke?"

Ken simply grinned and took a swallow of his beer. "History has never been kind to *ninjitsu*. Hollywood has done even less for our reputation. We like to say we've suffered from a thousand years of bad press."

Annja frowned. Getting mixed up with a cult of blood-thirsty murderers didn't exactly thrill her. "So, you're denying that ninja were assassins?"

"I'm not denying anything," Ken said. "I'm merely asking you to reserve judgment until you know more about what *ninjitsu* truly entails. In this case, I'm asking you to not believe what history books say about my kind. Tough as that may be to discount."

"I've got an open mind," Annja said, although she didn't necessarily feel particularly open-minded just then.

Ken eyed her for a moment and then spread his hands in front of her. "*Ninjitsu* developed out of a need for specialists who understood unconventional warfare. The samurai code of honor—Bushido—explicitly forbade certain tactics for use in times of unrest. But the various warlords of feudal Japan also understood that these supposedly unorthodox techniques could help ensure their continued prosperity and success. So they would secretly employ ninja to help them achieve their aims."

"And murder people," Annja said.

Ken sighed. "Annja, the truth is there were certainly some ninja families who did hire themselves out to the highest bidder with little regard to the universal scheme of totality. In that case, yes, you could say they were thugs."

Annja could tell she was beginning to annoy Ken. "But not other families?"

"No." He glanced around for the waitress and caught her eyes. He spoke to her in Japanese.

The waitress bowed, a feat Annja admired considering she was on roller skates. I would fall on my butt if I tried that, she thought. She shook her head and refocused on Ken. "So tell me more."

"*Ninjitsu* is a fascinating system of martial arts. As you know, samurai who lost in battle were supposed to follow their daimyo—their lord—into death by committing seppuku, ritual suicide. Not all of them would do that. Some of them would wander on a self-imposed exile. They would set themselves up in small villages in the mountains of western Japan—Iga and Koga Provinces—and there they set about trying to live peacefully with the flow of nature."

"They'd become hermits?"

"Well, somewhat. Inevitably, the policies of the neighboring regions would impact their existence. Many of these villages developed into ninja clans as a way of preserving their way of life. They would carefully attempt to influence events such that their own lifestyle and that of their children would remain as unscathed as possible."

"Interesting." Annja could certainly understand wanting to protect and provide for future generations.

"Let me ask you this," Ken said. "If you could pinpoint one person whose death would save the lives of thousands of men, women and children, would you take the step and remove him or her?"

Annja frowned. "I don't know that I would ever want to make that decision. It seems like playing God to me." And yet, Annja was fully aware she had been forced to make such a decision many times since coming into possession of Joan of Arc's mystical sword.

Ken nodded. "I don't disagree with you. I would find it difficult to do, as well. But those were the types of decisions that ninja *jonin*—leaders of the clan—had to face if they were to survive."

"So, they would assassinate someone if it meant saving others?" Annja was suddenly sympathetic.

"Certainly. More often than not, however, they would take elaborate pains to set up networks of intelligence operatives who would keep their ears attuned to news and information. The ultimate goal was to be able to influence events as far ahead of time as possible to avoid war and destruction. This meant ninja had to be highly skilled at infiltrating enemy provinces, setting themselves up as regular people, reporting intelligence and, if the situation warranted it, sabotaging or assassinating key troops."

Annja leaned back, suddenly aware that the young thugs across the room had gone quiet. "Sounds like they might have been better than samurai to have on your side."

"A lot of people would foam at the mouth if they heard me say this, but many ninja were, in fact, samurai. There are plenty of crossover techniques and warrior *ryu* that include elements of *ninjitsu* and counter*ninjitsu*. It's quite fascinating."

"Well, this has been nothing if not enlightening." Annja leaned forward. "But I think we've attracted the attention of the young guns over there."

Ken looked up as the waitress brought over two new glasses of beer. "You think so?"

Annja could see the huddled conversation. One of the *teppo*, as Ken had labeled them, seemed more intent than the others. Annja figured him for the leader judging by the elaborate piercings, tattoos and amount of hair dye. "I guess we'll find out soon enough."

Ken grinned. "In that case, I'd better drink my beer."

Annja glanced at her own beer, but her stomach twinged. She'd already fought for three hours tonight. She wasn't sure she was ready for another bout right at this instant. "Shouldn't we get out of here?"

Ken shrugged. "Fact of the matter is if we leave, they'll follow us. If they're determined to cause trouble, it doesn't matter where we go."

"But we'll be outside."

"Yes, but I'm much more comfortable sitting here drinking my beer."

Annja shook her head. "You're an interesting guy, Ken. Anyone ever tell you that before?"

"Just beautiful archaeologists."

"You've known many?"

Ken finished his beer. "You're the first."

Annja smiled in spite of the rising tension in the room. She saw the waitress start to approach their table, but Ken glanced at her and barely lifted his index finger from the tabletop. The waitress immediately stopped and retreated.

"Well, before we begin, let me just say that you've been a most enjoyable companion for dinner this evening," Ken said.

Annja frowned. "Begin?"

Ken smiled. "Everything in the universe unfolds itself at the appropriate time. This situation is no different."

Annja wasn't sure exactly which situation Ken referred to, but she didn't have time to think about it. The thugs had finally made a decision and were sliding out of their booths, making their way toward Ken, who still seemed entirely unfazed by the thought of what might happen next.

The young man Annja had picked as the leader swaggered toward their booth. Ken kept his eyes on Annja and his hand on his beer glass.

The thug glanced at Annja and then at Ken. He barked out a quick sentence to Ken, who simply sighed. "My companion doesn't speak Japanese. Why don't you be polite and use English? I'm sure she'd appreciate it."

The thug frowned and glanced at Annja again before looking back at Ken. "You don't give me orders," he said in English.

Annja almost chuckled. Despite the thug's insistence he was in charge, he had already obeyed Ken without even realizing it.

Ken's eyebrows waggled once at Annja. "Is there something I can do for you?"

"You're sitting in our booth," the young man said.

"Really? That's fascinating. How come you weren't sitting in it when we walked in? After all, you've been here far longer than we have," Ken replied.

"You're in our booth." The thug put both hands on the table and leaned over Ken. Annja could see his shirtsleeves inch up, exposing a twisting snake tattoo that wound its way from the edge of his wrist well up the forearm.

Ken glanced at the snake and then at the thug. "You didn't use bamboo to get that tattoo, did you?"

"What?"

"Bamboo," Ken said. "You see, in the old days, truly tough Yakuza would insist that their tattoos be applied using slivers of bamboo dipped in ink. It was an excruciating process, by which the Yakuza would prove themselves as impervious to pain and able to withstand anything in their loyalty to their *oyabun*."

The thug sniffed. "Old days. Yeah, right."

Ken nodded. "That, however, looks like it was done using an electric pen like the kind they use in cheap parlors down by Jimbocho."

"What if it was?"

Ken shrugged. "Probably nothing at all, but it could mean

that you have less tolerance for pain than you like to think. It could also mean that you're not the tough guy you like to project. And furthermore, it might very well mean you aren't Yakuza at all, but simply a poser."

Annja's eyes widened. If the tension hadn't been palpable before, it was now at the point where she could have used her sword to cut through it. The thug backed up almost in total shock that Ken would say something like that to him in front of his group of followers. The loss of face was immense.

If we had a chance at walking out of here before, thought Annja, it's gone now.

The thug recoiled just enough to draw his right arm back, reach into his pocket and draw a slim stiletto. He stabbed it straight at Ken's heart.

Ken simply leaned back and let the knife go past him. Then he grabbed the thug's wrist with his right hand and tugged him forward. It happened so quickly the thug stumbled and lost his balance. As his face came toward the tabletop, Ken lifted his left hand and slammed the beer glass into the thug's face.

Glass shattered. Ken had slammed the glass bottom into the thug's nose. Annja heard the cartilage break. Blood flowed, staining the air with the smell of copper.

Ken let the young tough slump to the floor, but as he did so, he tweaked the stiletto out of his hand.

There was a moment of stunned silence as the gang looked from Ken to the floor where their leader lay. Then one of them gave a mighty cry, and all hell broke loose.

Annja blinked and almost missed Ken kick at the next-closest target, catching the young gun in the crotch. Ken used the kick to cover his slide out of the booth. Annja wanted to help him, but was unsure about what she was getting herself into. The last thing she needed was to land on the wanted list of every Yakuza member in Tokyo.

Ken seemed to have no compunction about doing so, however. Annja watched as he deftly evaded every strike and kick aimed at him by the gang members. One moment they would seem locked on to him, and the next, their strikes would pass through empty air. Ken would have somehow managed to get behind them or to their side and simply apply a few key strikes to take them down.

Annja watched one of them sneak up from behind and try to stab Ken in the back. She was about to shout a warning but as the stab came in, Ken sidestepped and the blade passed through air where Ken's kidneys had been a second before. Ken moved back and effected some sort of strange arm lock Annja had never seen before. In an instant, the thug was airborne, crashing into a group of other thugs, sending them sprawling across several booths and tables.

Ken had also somehow managed to contain the mayhem to their corner of the restaurant. Annja was aware that the rest of the crowd sat riveted by the action. In America, Annja theorized that the other eaters would have tried to get the hell out of there. Or at least recorded the entire fight on their cell phone cameras.

But in Japan, things were different.

Ken surveyed the scene. A quiet hush broken only by the low moans of the thugs he'd trashed fell over the restaurant. Ken stepped over to the thug leader he'd dispatched first and rolled back his sleeve some more. The supposedly elaborate snake tattoo ended halfway up the forearm.

Ken sniffed. "Just as I thought."

He stood and looked at Annja. "Well, now I suppose we should leave. While I'm not at fault for this, I do so hate police interaction. Japanese cops tend to be nothing if not ensconced in paperwork and bureaucracy. I have little time to waste on either."

Annja shook her head, trying to clear the images that had played out before her. "Are they dead?"

Ken chuckled. "Nope. But I imagine they'll be sore for a good few weeks."

The waitress skated up and presented Ken with a bill. He glanced at it and then frowned. "Fifty thousand yen for a table?" He sighed, but took out his wallet and removed a sheaf of paper notes. "Only here would the management take the time to calculate the cost of repairing all of this while the fight was going on so they could have the bill ready when it was done. Crazy."

He handed the waitress the pile of money and then nodded toward the door. "I think I'm more concerned about another itemized bill than these clowns. We'd better get going before the owner decides to charge me double for the glasses."

Annja took a breath and followed Ken outside. The cool air felt good on her skin. For some reason, she'd felt amazingly energized by watching the fight transpire. She'd wanted to join in but had held herself back out of fear of jeopardizing Ken. Somehow that sentiment seemed crazy now. Ken had handled himself unlike any fighter Annja had ever known.

"You're awfully quiet, Annja. I hope that didn't upset you too much. You seem somewhat accustomed to violence, though, so I didn't think it would be a problem."

Annja stopped short of Ken's Mercedes. "Just who the hell are you exactly?"

Ken grinned. "Hop in and I'll tell you everything you want to know. And probably plenty that you don't."

4

The interior of the Mercedes sat in darkness except for the lime-green luminescence of the dashboard lights. They cast a strange pallor over Annja's skin. Ken glanced at her, trying his best to determine if he'd already scared her off or not.

"That was some fight," she said finally.

Ken smiled. "I suppose so."

She looked at him, her eyes full of suspicion. "I've been in a lot of bad situations. Had people shoot at me. Been almost run over a number of times. Mountain climbing near misses."

"Perhaps I should be careful around you," Ken said, grinning. "If you're in the business of attracting danger, I mean."

Annja seemed to ignore him. "I've never seen anyone handle themselves like you just did."

"I'm nothing special," Ken said.

He could feel Annja's eyes on him, gauging and trying to determine if he was being falsely modest. The intense scrutiny lasted the better part of a minute. Ken felt himself shift under her gaze. She was certainly more intense than she had seemed on the television show he'd seen.

He finally took a second to look her deep in the eyes. "I'm not joking. My skills are nowhere near what they could be. I've been somewhat lazy in recent months."

Annja shook her head. "They certainly seemed more than adequate to get you out of trouble back at the restaurant."

He slid the Mercedes out in traffic. "Maybe. But I'd be a fool to grow complacent and believe they'd get me out of every situation."

"Why is that?"

Ken shrugged. "I tend to think that's what separates a true warrior from a wanna-be. A warrior will never stop learning. They'll quest ever on in search of perfection of technique even while knowing that perfection can never be attained."

"So it's the pursuit of perfection that defines rather than the goal?"

"Exactly." Ken braked at a traffic light. The night sky glowed with a thousand points of neon braced against the Tokyo superscrapers. Flashes of light, music and the sounds of traffic and people filled his ears.

"You're a ninja," Annja said quietly.

Ken shrugged. "I'd prefer to say I study *ninjitsu*. Ninja, you know it's got that certain stigma attached to it."

Annja shifted in her seat, adjusting the seat belt as she did so. "I've got a question. You told me that the Yumegakure-ryu was almost extinct."

"That's right."

"Well, if you're the last one left, how did you learn what you know—what I'm assuming is *ninjitsu*?"

"It's a fair question," Ken said. "The truth is, there are other *ninjitsu ryuha* still in existence. Very few. But there are some. And the man I study with is the grandmaster of three of the only remaining systems to date."

"He's here in Tokyo?"

"No. Outside of Tokyo, actually. There's a small industrial town to the northwest called Chiba-ken. He teaches there."

Ken could feel Annja's excitement rise a notch. It felt as if the car had filled with electricity. Annja looked at him, her eyes widening. Ken felt himself drawn into them, as if he could get lost in the secrets they contained. He shook himself slightly, trying to keep himself composed.

Annja touched him on the arm. "I'd like to meet this man."

Ken had known she would. He had studied enough about Annja to know that she would never turn down the chance to learn something new or at least explore something that supposedly didn't exist anymore.

"He teaches tomorrow night." He smiled. "If you like, we can go to his class then."

Annja leaned back in her seat and nodded. "So, I'll meet the last grandmaster of *ninjitsu*. Cool."

Ken chuckled. "Well, others claim they are, in fact, also grandmasters, but it's mostly false."

"How so?" Annja asked.

"The man you'll meet tomorrow night is the only one recognized by the Japanese government as being legitimate. He's been labeled a national living treasure, as well, since he helps maintain a piece of Japan's past and its traditions—even one as controversial as *ninjitsu*."

Annja grinned. "I've recovered a lot of treasures before. I don't think I've ever met a living treasure, though."

"He'll like you."

"How do you know?"

Ken looked at her. "Because you're beautiful. And he happens to love beautiful women."

Annja frowned. "Give me a break."

The light finally changed and Ken pressed the accelerator. "I didn't mean to upset you with that comment."

Annja shrugged. "Sorry. It's just I get tired of hearing that people either like or dislike based entirely on whether a person is attractive or not."

"I meant it only as a compliment."

"I know." Annja ran a hand through her hair. "Sometimes I think I hear it too often."

"Most people, they wouldn't mind hearing that said about them," Ken said.

Annja shook her head. "I don't hear it said about me often. Mostly I hear it said about other women."

Ken smiled. "That other anchor on *Chasing History's Monsters*. What was her name? The one with the sexy wardrobe malfunction."

"Kristie Chatham." Annja sighed. "She and I have differing views on how best to present a story to our audience."

Ken made a left turn, checking his rearview mirror. He didn't see anything there that concerned him. "In her defense, there's nothing wrong with being beautiful."

"But when it obscures the topic at hand, when the audience downloads a video to see a top pop off rather than the story, then that's a problem. At least it is in my book. I think I'm in the minority of opinion, though," Annja said.

. Ken laughed. "Probably so. But I find your journalistic integrity refreshing."

"Yeah?"

Ken nodded. "Yes. I can assure you there will be no time for the wearing of bikini tops on this trip to find the artifact. I think, therefore, you are reasonably safe."

"Great."

Ken wheeled the Mercedes down another side street. "We're almost there."

"Almost where?" Annja glanced out the window. Ken could see she had no idea where they were. He knew trying to gauge location at night in a foreign city was a daunting task.

"Your hotel, of course."

Annja frowned again. "You know where I'm staying?"

"Of course."

She turned and Ken could see her hands bunched up, almost as if she thought he might attack her. He held up his hands for a brief moment, risking taking them off the steering wheel for effect.

"I'm not stalking you, Annja. If that's what you're thinking."

"I might be." She kept her hands bunched up.

"You're cautious. I can certainly appreciate that. I try to be that way myself. Especially when I travel."

"So you understand why I'm about two seconds away from getting out of this car and never seeing you again."

Ken pulled over to the side of the road and unlocked the

doors. "You're more than welcome to leave. Although honestly, I hope you don't."

She looked at the door and then back at Ken. "Why do you know where I'm staying?"

"Because I'm careful about who I approach and entrust with confidential information." He looked in the rearview mirror again. "I like making sure people are who they claim to be."

"I don't claim to be anyone but an archaeologist. That's it." Annja pursed her lips. "If you've heard otherwise, you were misled."

Ken braced his hands on the steering wheel and stretched his back, relieving some of the tension he felt creeping into his muscles. "It's a force of habit. I've been dealing with people throughout my entire life who were often not operating in my best interests. Ulterior motives are a nasty business."

"Agreed," Annja said. She seemed to relax slightly.

Ken tilted his head. "But you are without guile. I can talk to you about the nature of my family's troubles. I can ask for your help and guidance and I feel quite comfortable doing so."

Annja waggled her eyebrows. "You never know, Ken. I might just be a plant."

Ken shook his head. "And there you have the reason I know where you are staying."

Annja sniffed. "You've had me staked out since I landed?"

Ken took a breath. "If we're being honest about things…it has actually been a bit longer than that."

Annja frowned again. "Just how long have you been around?"

"Would you believe three months?" Ken hoped his smile was disarming enough to distract her from the length of time.

Annja's eyes went wide. "Three months? You've been following me all over the world for the past twelve weeks?"

Ken smirked. "And you thought *you* were exhausted. I could do with a healthy spell of sleep myself."

Annja crossed her arms. "I can't believe it."

"I know what you're thinking. How could this Japanese dude actually follow me around the world without me noticing him? After all, I'm pretty aware. I can sense things to some extent."

Annja whipped her head around. "What's that supposed to mean?"

Had he just touched a nerve? Ken filed it away for the moment. "Only that you are, for the most part, an extremely aware woman. But even those who think they are aware usually have gaps in their defenses. Those gaps can be exploited. In this case, it enabled me to remain invisible despite your attentiveness."

"How?"

Ken shrugged. "Let's take your recent trip to Marrakech."

"You were there, too?" Annja shook her head. "I don't believe this."

"You stopped at a stall in the market to buy a mango. Do you remember?"

He watched her eyes track to the lower left. He could see her recalling the moment in her head. Vaguely, she nodded.

"It was pretty hot that day. The sun blazed overhead like a blast furnace. I thought I might melt under my robes. But luckily, you didn't stay that long and I was able to shed my garb and move inside to cooler environs."

"But where were you?"

"Across the way. You bought the mango and some dates, if I recall. I was at the stall with the cheap necklaces."

He saw recognition flash across her face. "That was you?"

"With makeup, but yes."

"Those necklaces were awful knockoffs."

"That was deliberate. I knew you would never waste any time looking at them. You'd be able to pick them out as bad forgeries from a mile away and therefore not waste any time on my stall. I could easily watch you without fear of you becoming suspicious about me. To you, I was simply another would-be con man trying to hawk some ridiculous goods to the naive."

"And that, I suppose, was the gap in my defenses?" He saw her smile in spite of herself.

Ken nodded. "You see? I was in plain sight, but so apparently not a threat or of interest to you that you simply didn't even catalog me except way, way back in the furthest reaches of your consciousness. True invisibility exists, but not the way that most people believe it would. By being obviously ridiculous without making a spectacle of myself, I faded from your mind."

Annja nodded and Ken felt that she just might have some appreciation for the techniques he'd learned so many years ago.

"It's actually pretty impressive," she said.

Ken smiled. "If I had meant you any harm, Annja, please believe me when I tell you I could have easily done something to you much earlier than this. There's absolutely no reason for me to make myself an obvious threat to you now. I'd be almost leveling the playing field by doing so."

Annja's eyes crinkled at the corners. "Almost leveling?"

Ken smiled again. "You're good. Don't get me wrong."

"But you're better. Is that it?"

Ken held up his hands. "I will plead the fifth, as you Americans say."

Annja smiled. "Yeah. Well, we'll see. Why don't you take me back to my hotel? I could use a good sleep."

Ken pulled the car away from the curb, relieved to have seemingly defused any suspicion that Annja might feel toward him. In her place, Ken would have felt exactly the same way. He might have even reacted more aggressively, taking out the potential threat rather than allowing it to continue to exist even for another few hours.

But Annja Creed was not like him. And that was why Ken felt sure she would make the perfect aide in his quest to find the sacred Yumegakure-ryu *vajra*. Her knowledge and ability would keep them in good stead.

And Ken also appreciated how utterly beautiful she was. What he liked the most was how unaffected she was by her natural beauty. Briefly, he wondered if she might think him handsome. Just as quickly, he pushed the thought out of his mind. He needed to stay focused if he had any hope of recovering the artifact before the others did.

"Are you going to tell me why the Yakuza is so interested in you?" Annja said.

The question jolted him. Ken struggled to come up with a response and instead chuckled. "So much for a segue."

Annja stared at him. Something had changed. Ken could see it in her eyes. There was a hard edge there, way back, but present nonetheless. "What happened at the restaurant, it was more than a chance encounter. Those thugs were waiting for you," she said.

"Are you asking or saying?"

"I'm saying. It's a fact," Annja said.

"Maybe."

"Were they waiting for me, too?"

"No." Ken shook his head. "Absolutely not."

They pulled up to the hotel and Ken put the car into Park. Annja sat facing him.

"Ken, you seem like a nice enough guy. But I need to know what I'm getting mixed up in here. I don't like the thought of tangling with the Yakuza or even wanna-be Yakuza. If they're interested in you and I'm around, that will make me a target of opportunity, as well."

"You don't strike me as being averse to danger. Some of your past adventures certainly contained far more danger than what I propose we undertake."

She shrugged. "I'm not necessarily averse to much. But I'd be a fool if I took all of this at face value." She placed one hand on the door handle. "You may not want to talk about it right now. That's fine. It's late and we're both tired."

"Thanks—"

She looked at him. "But we will talk about this. If you want my help finding this *vajra*, then you're going to tell me exactly what the hell is going on here. Otherwise, I will vanish and not even you will be able to find me again."

She opened the door and strode off to the hotel entrance. Ken sat still in the car and then after another minute smiled slowly.

Annja Creed, he thought, you might just be my dream woman.

5

Annja hunched over her laptop and started composing a post for alt.archaeology.esoterica—the newsgroup she favored so much for its candid information on many of the more obscure topics relating to history and relics. She hesitated, trying best to make sure she didn't come across sounding like a lunatic. After a moment, she sighed and typed:

Does anyone know anything about the Japanese martial art of *Ninjitsu*?
I've met someone claiming to be involved with this art and I'd like to know if they might be legit. Thanks!

She leaned back and crossed her arms. It could take hours before anyone would respond, giving Annja plenty of time to think over the night's events.

She decided on a long, hot soak in the deep tub that sat in the corner of her small bathroom. Everything in Tokyo seemed as if someone had pressed the reduce button on a copy machine, but the tub looked large enough for her.

Annja padded into the bathroom and turned the spigot. A rush of hot water blossomed and streamed into the tub. In seconds, steam filled the air and Annja realized she was suddenly overdressed.

Outside in her room, she stripped down. With her pants and turtleneck off, she ran her eyes over her skin, doing a basic damage inspection from the tournament. Nezuma's kicks had left some nasty welts. She could see purplish bruising above her ribs and on the backs of her legs. His punches had also left souvenirs. She frowned. Someday, she'd get him back. And the idea of him flat on his back while she stood over him as a proud victor definitely appealed to her.

She walked into the bathroom and stepped into the piping-hot tub. She knew the Japanese favored hot baths for their health benefits and the relaxation they provided. Annja gritted her teeth, wanting to enjoy the hot water but also aware that it felt as if she were burning the skin off her bones.

She withdrew her leg, emptied out some of the contents and then added cold water. After another minute, she tried getting in the tub again and this time found that she could stand the heat.

As she sank into the bath and let the water come up to her jaw, Annja closed her eyes and tried to breathe deeply, allowing the stress of the day to melt away. She was tired and the steamy heat made her feel even more so. As she replayed the day's events, she found herself focusing on Ken and his strange past.

Certainly she hadn't come to Tokyo to get involved in the hunt for some relic. Japan was supposed to be for herself only—away time from the stress and pace of her vigorous lifestyle. Not that fighting in a martial-arts tournament was the kind of prescription most vacation-bound folks would equate with rest and relaxation. But for Annja, it enabled her to play to some extent, without it being a matter of life and death. And since so much of her life lately had revolved around serious fighting, Annja also felt that any time spent practicing was time spent well.

"He is handsome, though."

Annja's eyes popped open. Had she just said that out loud? A smile flickered across her face. Apparently the hot water was doing its job by relaxing her to the point she felt comfortable speaking out loud. Annja sank deeper into the water and grinned just beneath the surface.

She tilted her head back and rested it on the edge of the tub, her eyes still closed as the heat enveloped her. The way Ken had moved in the restaurant earlier played across the screen of her mind. Annja slowed the reel down and tried to study how he had managed to thwart the gang without even appearing to break a sweat.

Marvelous, she concluded.

If Annja had even a small percentage of the same skill, Nezuma would be the one nursing not just bruises, but his wounded ego, as well.

If *ninjitsu* truly did exist still and Annja had a chance to see a class being taught, there was no way she'd turn down that opportunity. She didn't feel any particular obligation to one form of martial arts over another. She was far too pragmatic to get lost in the politics of that silly debate. Annja needed what worked; it was as simple as that. And if adding some *ninjitsu* to her arsenal helped her stay alive, well, bring it on.

A cool breeze suddenly blew over the room, scattering the blanket of steam that had hung about the tub like mist over a swamp.

Annja's eyes opened again.

Her stomach tensed.

Someone was in her room.

She could feel the air currents being disturbed. But she heard nothing. Whoever was inside the room, knew how to move in absolute silence. But movement—any movement—disturbed the air ever so slightly.

Annja wondered, could she move just as quietly and get out of the tub without them knowing?

She frowned. Not a chance.

The invaders must have known she was there. And depending on how long they'd been in the room, they might have even heard her say that line about Ken. It couldn't be Ken, could it? That was enough, she decided.

It was time to get out of the tub.

Instead of doing it as quietly as she could, Annja engaged a different strategy. She started to whistle.

"That felt good," she said as she stood and stepped out of the tub.

The door to the bathroom was closed almost all the way, except for a gap of about five inches. Annja braced herself behind the door in case they rushed the bathroom. But she didn't think they would. If they'd meant her harm, they would have already come into the bathroom when she was far too vulnerable.

She felt for the towel hanging on the hook and then mopped at her hair and shoulders.

Still whistling, she tried to figure how best to wrap the towel so she could fight if necessary.

The hell with it, she thought, frowning. If someone wants to throw down right now, being naked might just help my cause and give me a split second to get the upper hand.

So much for modesty. She almost grinned. Too bad the cameras weren't rolling now. This would earn her top ratings for *Chasing History's Monsters* in a way that bimbo Kristie Chatham never could.

Annja took a deep breath and flushed her system with oxygen. Adrenaline flooded her body as it readied itself for a fight. She flexed her fists and steeled her will.

And then stepped out of the bathroom.

Her room was empty.

Annja noticed that her stomach was more relaxed now.

Were they gone?

She shivered in the cooler air of the room. She felt certain someone had been here. And she'd been getting reacquainted with her long-lost primal instincts enough to place some trust in them when they warned her of danger. Somewhat. Annja was the first to admit that she still had a lot of trouble having one hundred percent faith in her instincts. Especially when her logical mind seemed ready to always mount a good argument for why she shouldn't.

Someone had been in the room.

But now they were gone.

Annja knelt and checked under the bed and at the base of the simple curtain framing her window. She carefully checked the closet, as well. Otherwise, there was no place to hide in the Spartan room.

She frowned again. A cursory glance around told her that they hadn't taken anything. Her laptop still sat open on the desktop, although the screensaver was bouncing around from a lack of activity. Annja's bags sat unopened next to her bed. And her cell phone and purse remained near the door.

Weird.

She padded back to the bathroom and toweled herself dry before pulling on a pair of sweatpants and a T-shirt. Then she walked around her room again before ending up at the window.

Annja's room was on the fifteenth floor of the hotel. From her window she could see the Tokyo skyline outlined in the dazzling colors of the neon spectrum. The city shone so brightly that Annja could pick out very few stars in the sky.

Her window wasn't locked.

I know I checked that lock earlier, she thought to herself. Being a native New Yorker, Annja was nothing if not security conscious. All doors and windows were always locked behind her whenever she was home. And that habit stayed with her no matter where she traveled.

But now, her window was unlocked.

She slid it back on the rails and found it could open wide enough to enable someone to get through it.

But who would be able to get through fifteen stories up from the ground?

Annja grinned and shook her head. She was being silly, imagining that someone would consider her such a prize that they would risk life and limb scaling the side of a high-rise just to get into her room.

Still…

She slid the window closed and locked it. The double latch

clicked shut, and Annja let the curtain fall back into place. She wished she had a fingerprint kit so she could dust the sill.

Annja sat at the desktop and brought her laptop out of its sleep mode. Once she clicked Refresh, she clicked the mouse and waited for the newsgroup page to reload.

"Wow." She already had one response to her query on the newsgroup.

Annja checked the name—Earl Sunday. He listed himself as a professor of Asian history at some college Annja had never heard of—probably some online institute that charged people a couple hundred bucks for a credit or two. Of course, that was no surprise. These days, anyone with some bucks could open a school and charge people money for a degree. And sometimes, they didn't even bother with the school part.

Annja looked at the post.

There is no such thing as modern-day *ninjitsu*. Ninja were used in Japan's past, but there is no evidence or verifiable records to suggest that so-called modern exponents of the art actually engage in authentic *ninjitsu* training. This, despite what many claim, is the truth. Furthermore, anyone claiming to be involved with *ninjitsu* should have their head examined. Ninja were nothing but cutthroat assassins who were only concerned about money. They had no honor and their historical significance is virtually nil. Japan would be far better off if there had never been such characters in her past.

Annja leaned back from her keyboard and shook her head. She guessed that being called wishy-washy wasn't a problem for Sunday. She also decided that he must be an extraordinarily inflexible person to post something so utterly rigid and devoid of anything useful to her.

"I'll bet he enjoys listening to himself talk." She frowned. "Jerk."

Annja hit the reply button and as the page refreshed, she saw four other people had posted responses.

Sammy23 in Baltimore posted this:

Ninjitsu does exist and if Sunday wasn't such a complete bonehead impressed more with the words he writes than actual fact, he might do better research before displaying his idiocy to the world. The art still exists and is taught in Japan and in many countries around the world by students who have returned from training with the grandmaster. *Ninjitsu* is a complex system of martial arts, broadly encompassing every facet of personal protection and survival. If you have the opportunity to study it with someone who knows what they're doing, I suggest you do so. Good luck!

Annja guessed Sunday had himself a bit of a reputation with *ninjitsu* enthusiasts judging by the similar tone of the other responses. In fact, by the time Annja was composing her thank-you note to those who had posted, ten more people had wandered over to blast Sunday. More so, they'd even reposted Annja's query on a martial-arts newsgroup, opening the floodgates on Sunday. Most people called him an academic who never bothered to go to the source and find out what *ninjitsu* was truly about. Someone even went so far as to call him an utter coward who would never have the courage to take a class with the grandmaster and find out for himself why *ninjitsu* was such a great system.

Annja typed her thank-you note and posted it. Then she shut the computer down and climbed into her bed. The pillows cradled her head and she sighed, trying to relax herself enough to fade off to sleep. Her eyes, however, simply would not stay closed.

Someone had been in her room. She just knew it.

And even though she no longer felt that she was in danger, she couldn't shake the feeling that her personal space had been invaded. It wasn't a feeling she enjoyed, by any means.

She glanced at the light sitting on the nightstand next to the bed. She should turn it off and go to sleep. But at the same time, she wasn't sure she wanted the room to be dark.

Annja closed her eyes and thought about the sword—her sword—and instantly it came to mind. She reached out for it and wrapped her hands around the hilt but didn't draw it out.

It was there if she needed it.

But why hadn't she thought about using it when she was in the tub? Why hadn't she immediately pictured the sword, and then come running out of the bathroom ready to slice and dice whoever stood before her?

It didn't make sense.

Unless she hadn't been in danger after all.

More questions that Annja didn't feel much like pondering. At least right then.

She turned out the light and settled back closing her eyes. Sleep was just what she needed.

The ringing phone sat her bolt upright as if someone had fired a gun in the room.

She clawed for the receiver and bounced it off its cradle. "Hello?"

"Good evening, Annja. I take it you're not asleep just yet?"

The last person she'd expected to get a phone call from in the middle of the night was speaking to her from God knew where. Knowing him, he could be in Antarctica or at a Starbucks coffee shop. Annja sighed.

"Hello, Garin," she said.

6

"It does sound as though I woke you. My apologies," Garin said.

Annja stretched out in the bed. Her toes touched the footboard. Still, she enjoyed the lengthening of her body. She exhaled in a rush and let herself go slack.

"It's late. I was headed off to dreamland when you called. What can I do for you? How did you—?"

"Please, Annja, let's not waste time on such trivialities. Technology being what it is today, and money always the most powerful enabler, it was no obstacle to uncover your whereabouts on your supposed vacation."

"So much for anonymity." Annja frowned. She was going to splurge and invest in a fake passport and credit cards one of these days.

"You feeling better after your competition?" Garin asked.

Annja sat up. "You know about that, too?"

"Certainly. Nice side kick, by the way."

Annja glanced around her room. "You're starting to annoy

me now, Garin. I don't like the thought of people poking into my personal affairs. In fact, if it keeps up, I'm liable to be pretty damned cranky the next time we meet. I don't need to tell you what that would entail."

"I can guess." Garin chuckled on the phone. "Which brings me precisely to that very point. We need to meet."

"Why? Last I heard you were on an extended journey to reclaim some degree of secrecy so Roux doesn't track you down and kill you for trying to kill him while he was trying to kill you for…whatever. I don't even know how you two keep score of that silliness."

"Yes, well, certain matters preclude me from worrying about my personal safety at this point." He paused. "It's important that I see you."

Annja shook her head. The darkness of the room embraced her. She felt a little cold and pulled the covers up higher. "I'm not leaving Japan yet. Possibly not for a while yet, in fact."

"Oh? Why not?"

"I'm involved in something here. Something that interests me a great deal. Not that such things are any of your business."

"Something? Or is it *someone*, Annja?"

"Mind your own business, Garin. I won't tell you again."

"As I recall, you owe me your life. That's not exactly the kind of grateful attitude I'd expect from someone like yourself."

"This conversation is boring me. I'm in Japan. You want to meet up, come and find me. Otherwise don't bother. I'm busy."

Annja hung up the phone and then unplugged it from the jack in the wall. That would at least guarantee that she'd be able to sleep through the night without Garin ruining her rest.

Unless he called her cell phone, too.

Annja groaned and clambered out of bed, padded to the small stand by the door and shut off her cell phone. Now she was cut off. Completely.

Unless Garin happened to knock on her door.

Annja stopped. Was it possible that Garin was the one who'd been in her room earlier? Had he sneaked in when she was bathing? But she knew Garin was enough of a jerk that he would pick the perfect time to do whatever he wanted to do and still grab an eyeful of Annja soaking naked in the tub.

"Bastard."

She climbed back into bed and pulled up the covers. In moments, she was fast asleep. And not once did she dream about Garin.

THE FIRST THING SHE SAW in the morning was the folded slip of paper someone had slid under her door during the night. How had she not heard that?

She sighed and got out of bed. Perhaps her run-in with Nezuma yesterday had dampened her senses as much as it had her body.

Unfolding the slip of paper, she read:

"Come down for breakfast in the lobby. G."

"So much for being halfway across the world from him," Annja said. "Figures."

Twenty minutes later she'd showered and applied the minimal makeup she normally wore. Dressed in jeans and a white blouse, she chose a pair of black flats rather than heels. Somehow, time spent with Garin always contained the potential for gunfire, car chases, explosions, bodies and lots of running.

Annja rode the elevator down to the lobby and when the doors parted, she could look right across into the restaurant. Garin was immediately noticeable. And not just because he stood a foot above anyone else in the area. Garin was damned good-looking. As she entered the eatery, he looked up and smiled.

He stood as she approached and kissed her on the cheek. "How is my favorite historical descendant?"

"Is that what you're calling me now?" Annja sat and ordered a cup of black coffee. "I would have thought you had other names for me."

Garin shrugged. "There are some, but I wouldn't use them in mixed company. You know, I'm nothing but a complete gentleman."

"How nice." Annja sat back and crossed her arms. "You look good for dodging Roux's repeated attempts on your life."

Garin waved his hands. "That gets rather mundane after all the time I've been alive. We've been after each other for so long it almost gets routine. Then we have our cease-fires and our détentes, and then something happens and we go at it again. Blah, blah, blah. Silliness."

"Yeah, those bullets are really overrated."

Garin leaned forward. "And not at all the reason I wanted to see you, my dear."

The waitress brought coffee and Annja ordered two eggs, toast, orange juice and melon slices. Garin ordered an aged Scotch whisky.

Annja grinned. "That's some breakfast you're getting."

He shrugged. "I'm on another time zone. And where I'm at, it's perfectly acceptable to have a drink to take the edge off."

"You just got in, then," Annja said.

"Something like that." He spread his arms. "Besides, I'm in phenomenal shape. For five hundred years old? You wish you'd look this good when it happens to you."

"I have no desire to live that long."

Garin frowned. "I said the same thing. Funny how fate just flips you the bird any time she feels like it."

"Such talk. Where were you before this?" Annja asked.

"I'm a man of many places and locales. I don't distinguish between them if I can help it."

Annja took a sip of her coffee. "I love the fact that my conversations with you usually entail a great deal of frustration on my part because you don't ever give me anything concrete to go on. You answer questions with questions and never confirm or deny anything. You're like a politician without an office."

Garin bowed his head. "Thank you for the compliment."

Annja laughed.

"The man you met last night." Garin smiled at her. "What is his name—Kennichi?"

Here we go, Annja thought. No middle ground, just right into it. "What about him?"

"Do you know who he is?"

"No, I liked the idea that he was a complete stranger. It made the unsafe sex all the better." She shook her head. "He told me his story."

"And you believe him."

Annja sighed. "I haven't really known him long enough to say one way or the other, Garin. We met, had dinner, he beat the crap out of some gangsters and that was it."

"Let's not forget what he asked you to help him do."

Annja narrowed her eyes. "Excuse me?"

Garin laughed. "You're not going to sit there and lie to me. Really now, after all we've been through, you're not going to feign ignorance to that question, are you?"

"My ignorance, as you put it, is genuine," Annja said, immediately regretting the poor choice of words.

Garin sniffed as if he'd caught wind of a skunk. "Your ability to lie convincingly needs much improvement, Annja. But if that's how you want to play this, fine. I'll do the talking and you can sit there and listen."

"That would be a refreshing change," she replied sarcastically. Annja leaned back and crossed her arms, waiting for Garin to begin.

His whisky arrived and he took it with a word of thanks in Japanese to the waitress who stared at him in awe. Garin waved her away as if she were a pesky fly, but Annja could already see that the waitress was enthralled. If the big man knew it, he showed no signs of being interested.

Garin sipped from the glass and seemed to savor it for just a moment before swallowing, and then looked right at Annja. "Ninja are very very dangerous people, my dear."

"So I've heard."

"You haven't heard the half of it. Yes, there are still families in existence. Anyone telling you different is a moron. But along with the overt families who teach the system to anyone who shows an interest, there are also more covert families who still engage in many shady things."

"Like what?"

"Remnants from the ultranationalistic groups like the Black Dragon Society that dominated the political scene in the latter part of the nineteenth and early twentieth centuries. Their subtle and terrifying manipulation of government affairs earned them lethal reputations that were well-deserved."

Annja cocked an eyebrow. "And they employed ninja?"

"Absolutely. Not the do-gooders that you read about today, but mercenaries who hired themselves out to the highest bidder. In this case, some of the ninja families had goals in line with their employers. The result was a marriage of sorts that cemented relationships and expanded empires. Much of what occurred in the last twenty years in Japan is due to the ground-work laid by these families immediately after World War II."

"What does this have to do with me?" Annja asked.

Garin took another sip of his whisky. "You may be inad-vertently helping the wrong side regain that artifact. If you're not completely certain of this man's identity, then by helping him, you could be undermining the rightful owner."

Annja looked up as her food arrived. She bit into the eggs and drank down some of the juice. "So, you're saying Ken may not be who he says he is."

"So, it's 'Ken' now, is it?"

Annja smiled. "Jealous?"

Garin ignored her. "I'm suggesting you make sure he is the rightful heir before you engage your rather impressive abili-ties toward helping him, possibly doing more harm than good."

Annja leaned back again. "What does this have to do with

you, anyway? I mean, why are you even concerned about this? Aren't you the guy who likes to let chaos unfold wherever it may be?"

Garin set his glass down and leveled a hard stare at Annja. "Don't ever simplify my personal philosophies like that, Annja. They aren't nearly as neatly labeled as you'd make them out to be."

"Fine. Whatever."

Garin finished his Scotch and the waitress immediately appeared with a fresh one. If she'd hoped to impress Garin, she was disappointed. Garin took notice of the fresh drink as if he had expected it all along.

He's so pompous, Annja thought around a mouthful of egg and toast. Still, she had to admit that what he suggested at least made some degree of sense.

"Why would anyone care about the relic anyway? It's just an antique."

Garin frowned. "With supposed magical abilities."

"*Supposed* being the key word," Annja said.

Garin smiled. "You don't believe it."

"I don't know what to believe. I mean, magic? Come on." Annja shrugged. "I just don't know if I can buy into that."

Garin shook his head. "Annja, there are times when that mind of yours truly does amaze me. Equally so, and regrettable even, are the times when your obstinacy nearly numbs me cold."

Annja set her fork down. "If you're going to insult me, I'll ask you to sit elsewhere."

"It's my table." Garin grinned.

Annja stood. "Fine, then I'll move."

Garin sighed. "Sit down, Annja." He paused. "Please."

Annja sat and resumed eating. If nothing else, she'd take pleasure in stiffing Garin for the bill. Not that he'd even blink. He had more money than he knew what to do with.

"I know the subject of magic is a touchy one. But honestly, the sword—"

"Is not connected to this at all and I'd appreciate you leaving it out of the conversation," Annja snapped and then stared at Garin. "Please."

"Very well. But you can't pretend it doesn't exist." Garin took a deep breath. "It's a part of who you are now."

"I don't pretend anything. But neither do I believe everything people say. You and Ken think this thing is magic. Fine. That's got no bearing on the fact that it's missing. I also don't expect it will matter when I locate it. Magic or not, the thing is lost and needs to be found."

"It does need to be found." Garin nodded. "As long as it's found by the right people."

"So you said."

Garin finished his second drink. The waitress reappeared. Now Garin looked her over. He spoke a few words to her and she blushed immediately.

Good lord, Annja thought. Tell me I'm not witnessing a seduction here.

Garin stood. "Be careful, Annja. That's all I'm saying." He strode out of the restaurant toward the elevator bank. The waitress dutifully followed behind him.

Annja gulped down the rest of her orange juice and then looked down at the table at the tiny slip of paper that had somehow materialized when she wasn't looking.

Garin hadn't paid the bill.

7

Annja spent the rest of the day exploring the small shops that surrounded the hotel. While the majority of Tokyo seemed encased in steel and glass, Annja was glad to see that there were still some small stores that carried all sorts of gifts ranging from handmade wooden combs to antique books and scrolls and everything in between. The toughest part of the day was trying to make use of the little bit of the language she knew to make herself understood. As it was, she still came away from her excursion laden with several bags full of unusual souvenirs.

As she jostled the bags and tried to maneuver the crowded streets, Annja couldn't help feeling that someone was watching her. Twice, she felt the feeling strongly enough to actually turn around and search the crowd for a familiar face. But doing so proved futile. The sea of faces that greeted her held no one she recognized.

"It's probably Garin," she told herself. Once he'd finished

with the waitress, he'd probably decided it might be amusing to stalk Annja for a while.

Annja frowned and continued her journey.

She grabbed a quick lunch at a noodle stand located by the train station. She'd heard that these small four-seat eateries could serve some of the best buckwheat-noodle soups in Japan and she wasn't disappointed. Fortunately, she had no trouble explaining what she wanted because the proprietor had taken the time to have an illustrated menu printed up. Annja merely pointed at the appropriate pictures and said thank-you when she was done. The piping-hot soup was served with a cold Asahi beer, which complimented the dish wonderfully.

When she arrived back at the hotel, the ever polite desk clerk bowed and then informed her that she had a message. Annja expected a piece of paper but was instead directed to a small phone in the lobby and told to press several buttons. Ken's voice purred in her ear.

"Please be in the lobby at six o'clock. Bring your training clothes."

Annja saw the large clock on the wall behind the reception desk read 5:40. She hung up the phone, raced upstairs and got changed. She hoped that Ken was taking her to see some authentic *ninjitsu* training.

At 5:58 she strolled off the elevator with her small carry bag. The hotel laundry had cleaned Annja's sweaty gear. Annja reminded herself to leave a decent tip for the maid service.

Ken leaned against one side of the lobby doors when she exited the elevator. He was dressed simply in jeans and a thin black nylon windbreaker with a T-shirt underneath. He smiled when Annja approached. "Good evening."

Annja smiled. "Hi."

"I trust you've had a nice day?"

Annja's eyes narrowed. Had Ken been the one following her? Was that what she'd felt? It would have been relatively easy for him to do so, especially in light of what he'd told her last night.

"Very nice," she said. No sense confronting him early on and ruining her chance to see the *ninjitsu* training. She noticed Ken's small bag at his feet and pointed. "Is that your stuff?"

He glanced down. "Hmm? Oh, yes. It will come in handy for where we're going."

Annja grinned. "Which is where?"

His eyes bounced back to hers. "Exactly where you think we're going. Please follow me."

He led her outside the hotel. The evening commute was still in full effect. Office workers streamed past while schoolgirls in uniforms that seemed to include microminiskirts hiked too far north to be anything but obscene giggled into cell phones and tossed their dyed hair in the direction of anyone who might notice.

Ken seemed to melt into the flow of people and Annja felt him take her hand, pulling her through the turbulent sea. His hand felt smooth but hard, like polished cool white marble, she decided. When they finally reached the train station, Ken let her hand go and Annja found herself wishing that he had held on to it.

Ken stood in front of the ticket machine and plunked several coins into it. The machine spit out two tickets and he handed one to Annja. "Come with me. Our train is downstairs and should be leaving soon."

They descended the stairs, passing more people. Ken led them onto an almost deserted train car. Two boys in their school uniforms and hair tousled into rat's nests slept in their seats.

Ken nodded at them. "They've been in school for many more hours than in America. After regular classes, they go to special after classes that are designed to help them get into college. Maybe they've been going for the better part of sixteen hours."

Annja frowned. "That must take a toll on them."

"It's all about getting into college over here. High school is the real grind. Once they get into college, they can relax somewhat. College is for making contacts that will help them the rest of their lives. But the competition to get in is fierce. Some kids, they don't make it. Every year there are a few suicides over it."

"Suicide?"

Ken shrugged. "It's not as bad as when I was growing up, but it can still get pretty crazy."

Annja shook her head. "But I saw schoolgirls earlier who looked like they didn't have a care in the world."

Ken smiled. "You saw some schoolgirls. There are plenty who stress just like these guys. But there are also plenty of other schoolgirls who don't. Some are actually prostitutes— some just don't care. Even the ones who graduate high school, if they've got the looks, can go get jobs with the airlines or marry a rich guy."

"Nice bit of equality over here." Annja frowned at the thought of wasting her life like that.

"Japan doesn't claim to be equal. Japan just is. That's what screws up so many foreigners who come here. They think they know what Japan is, what the society defines itself as. They take great steps to try to become Japanese, but it can never be."

"Why not?" Annja asked.

"Because Japan simply doesn't care. Our society is such that it take no pains to explain itself. It's as if the culture is one massive ball of who-cares-what-other-people-think. Japan couldn't care less if foreigners understand what makes us tick. We are enigmas unto ourselves. And Japan hides its true nature even from itself. The best way to survive in such a place is not to try to figure it out, but to simply accept. And if possible, manipulate that acceptance so you prosper."

"Manipulate it?" Annja shook her head trying to imagine how that might even be possible. "How?"

But Ken only smiled some more. "Well, that takes a bit of practice. But if you look at how we emerged from the ashes of World War II saddled with the strict regulations imposed by the Allies, and rose to become an economic powerhouse, that's one glimpse into how our leaders were able to do it."

"I thought Japan's economy was in trouble," Annja said.

"It is," Ken replied. "I think someone tried to figure us out and ruined what we had. But I'm not concerned. Something will happen to bring us around again."

The train chimed twice and the doors slid shut. Annja looked at Ken. "Where are we headed?"

"Out of the city. We're going to a small town about twenty minutes outside of Kashiwa."

The train streamed out of the station, and Annja marveled

at the smoothness of the ride. She felt a curious sensation; her buttocks were warm. She shifted once and then looked at Ken who smiled.

"They heat the seat here," he said.

Annja raised her eyebrows. "No wonder those guys are asleep."

Ken nodded. "It does seem to promote that, doesn't it?"

"I might fall asleep myself if I'm not careful."

"I'll wake you if you do. Don't worry."

But Annja had no intention of falling asleep. The city disappeared and an urbanized sort of suburb followed. Open fields clogged with rusted bits of farm machinery shot past her window. Smaller wooden homes replaced the high-rise apartment buildings.

Eventually, Ken nudged Annja, who jolted. "Huh?"

"You started to doze. Come on, this is our stop."

Annja followed Ken off the train, and her nostrils were immediately assaulted by a strange scent that seemed somehow familiar. "What is this smell?"

"Soy sauce. There's a big factory—one of the world's biggest companies—just on the other side of town. The air here is forever stained by it. You get used to it pretty quick, but I've been kind of turned off to soy sauce ever since I started coming here."

They ducked out of the station and turned left. Ken crossed the train tracks they just rode across and then turned left again. Annja saw a sea of bicycles parked in neat lines.

"Is this common?"

"Sure. People park them here all the time and ride the train into Tokyo proper."

Annja pointed. "But none of them are locked up."

Ken shook his head. "No one's going to steal them. There's no point to it."

Ken threaded his way through the small passage between the bike wheels and Annja twisted to do the same. She spotted some pimped-out bicycles and couldn't help but think that in America, these would have been stolen in no time flat.

They cleared the bicycle labyrinth and walked on. Ken smiled at Annja. "Tonight is likely to be very busy."

"Busy?"

"The dojo is small. Real estate prices being what they are, it was almost impossible for the grandmaster to find anything affordable that would still serve well as a dojo. Some of his senior students pitched in to help him buy this place. But it's still small by Western standards. Ordinarily, the size wouldn't be an issue but people journey here from all over the world. Numbers add up."

An open field that had recently been mowed sat on their left. Ken nodded at it. "This used to be full of tall reeds. We had a saying that we'd dump the bodies of annoying Americans into the swamp and let them rot there."

Annja didn't know if he was serious or not. "Did you ever really do that?"

"Of course not." Ken chuckled but then stopped. "Well, actually, there was this obnoxious fool named Pritchard Magoof. For him, we made an exception. He came over here as the student of a very accomplished teacher in America. And of course, he promptly let his ego explode and became rank hungry without having one ounce of technical skill. Now he mostly hangs around the dojo looking like a little puppy dog. We humor him, but he'll never amount to anything."

"Sounds like a real prize."

Ken's eyes narrowed. "Maybe if he's there tonight we'll let you train with him." He laughed. "Now that'd be entertaining."

Annja shook her head. "I'm not here to be anyone's entertainment."

"True, true. We have more important things to do than beat Magoof into smithereens. He'll do that himself anyway. Rumor is it's only a matter of time before he gets thrown out for being such an idiot."

They passed a ramshackle hotel. Ken pointed it out. "This is where the rowdy foreigners stay when they're over here making asses of themselves."

Annja frowned. "Forgive me for saying so, but it seems like you don't think too much of the non-Japanese who train with you."

Ken shrugged. "Honestly, I don't. Most of the people who come here to learn this art are too full of themselves to ever become truly good at it. There are exceptions and certain dojos that produce decent people. They are, unfortunately, the rarity rather than the norm."

"Is it really that bad?" Annja wasn't sure she was going to fit in with this crowd.

"Worse, actually. There are hotels in Tokyo that refuse to host foreigners associated with this dojo because in the past, those who stayed there trashed their rooms and partied and destroyed furniture. Maybe they'd never been away from home before—maybe they're simply immature fools. But whatever the case, they have marred the reputation of the school."

"And the grandmaster? What does he do about it?" Annja had images of this wizened old man beating the snot out of people who disgraced his name and style.

Ken smiled. "Nothing."

"Nothing?"

Ken stopped. "Annja, you have to realize that this art is *ninjitsu*. *Ninjitsu* is something entirely Japanese but at the same time it is something wholly un-Japanese. By virtue of its very nature, the art can seem to contradict itself constantly. What is expected is what never occurs. And the unexpected is routine. Only by accepting that you'll never know what to expect will you be able to glimpse what the art can truly accomplish."

"Expect the unexpected, then. Is that it?"

"Maybe. But it's more like don't expect anything. Because there's no rhyme or reason to any of what happens inside the dojo. Or for that matter, outside of it, either."

"That's a terribly confusing way to go through life," Annja said.

Ken nodded. "Remember, this is a martial art. *Ninjitsu* teaches you to be prepared for warfare. And there's nothing sacred in war. The moment you think you've got it figured out or that you know what's coming, a good enemy will use that against you and kill you."

"Good point."

"The grandmaster believes that it's his responsibility to convey that as best he can to those who wish to study with him. So he deliberately does things that seem completely bizarre. For those who get it, the lessons are priceless. For those who don't…well, who really cares about them?"

Annja smiled. "You're going to tell me that most of these people don't get it, right?"

"Yes. For the majority, this is just a fun way to show off. What they don't realize is they are showing off exactly how little they truly know."

"And the grandmaster's not concerned about them leaving with this information?"

"Nope. He knows that when he's gone, these fools will fade away. They've got no real skill to fall back on. The few who do sincerely study will know how to carry on. That's it," Ken said.

"It all seems rather Darwin."

"It is. Because it has to be. *Ninjitsu* has survived for so long, much of that time in secret, solely because it was carried on by the sincere. The idiots were disposed of long before they ever got close to being a threat."

"Buried in the swamp reeds, I suppose," Annja said.

Ken's smile twitched and he chuckled. "Exactly. Now come on, let's introduce you to the real art of *ninjitsu*."

8

The outer shoji rice-paper screen slid back smoothly on its runners. Annja could hear the raucous sound of laughter spill out from within the dojo about the same time as two bodies fell back on the small stoop and nearly crashed into her.

"As I said." Ken glanced at her. "Looks like it's busy."

They had to push their way into the dojo proper. Students of almost every ethnicity jockeyed for training spots on the tatami mat floor. Ken pointed to the right side to a small doorway.

"You can get changed in the bathroom."

Annja noticed that many of the students simply dropped their trousers wherever they stood, unconcerned about displaying their underwear or lack thereof. She frowned and found such displays tasteless and crude.

The bathroom itself was small, but spacious enough to get changed into her black training pants and top. When she emerged, Ken had already changed. He wore a heavy *gi*, and around his waist he wore a black belt that was fraying almost white in many areas.

"That looks like you've been wearing it for years," Annja said.

Ken smiled. "I have been." He nodded to the main floor. "Let's try to find a spot to train."

They stepped over the outstretched legs and arms of students engaged in limbering themselves up before class. At the far end of the dojo on a shelf looking down over the entire expanse, Annja could see a small temple.

"What's that?" she asked.

"The *kamidana*. It's the spiritual seat of power for the dojo. Special items are placed up there for the benefit of all students. Those are pictures of past grandmasters, special rice and plantings to help bless the environment."

Annja looked around some more. On the walls were racks with various weapons, mostly padded for training. "I've never even seen some of these weapons before."

Ken nodded. "We have an assortment of strange tools, taken not just from *ninjitsu* but from all Japanese martial arts. The grandmaster also likes to borrow the weapons from other cultures and apply the *ninjitsu* skills to their use. Makes for an interesting class. Painful, but always fascinating."

Annja looked at the students. "And all of these people are here to see him?"

"Well, some are here to train. Some are here to be seen. And some are here for grade."

"Grade?"

"Testing at the end of the class. For the fifth degree black belt—the *godan*—test. It's a very special test, or at least, it once was before every Tom, Dick and Harry came waltzing through on a whim."

"What do you mean?"

"You'll see the test at the end of the class and maybe later when we get something to eat, I'll explain it a little bit more." Ken nodded toward the door. "*Sensei*'s here now, so class will start soon."

Annja turned, possibly expecting to see some powerhouse of a figure striding into the dojo. Instead, she saw a diminutive man perhaps five feet tall, with a bit of a potbelly. His smile was huge, though, and he certainly seemed to be jolly. From what Ken had told her about *ninjitsu*, however, Annja suspected this was merely for show for those who needed a smile to reassure them.

The grandmaster walked past Ken, who bowed low and said something in Japanese. The grandmaster patted him on the arm and kept walking toward the *kamidana* shelf.

Ken nudged Annja toward the back of the room. Someone clapped and instantly, all talk ceased. All the students lined up. Annja got several frowns from some of the black belts who were forced to bow in to her left. She had no idea whether she'd just violated some unspoken rule or not, but tried her best to blend in.

In front of the huddled crowd that knelt on the floor, the grandmaster wove his fingers together and muttered something low and unintelligible. Then his voice barked out nine syllables and everyone around Annja shouted the same. The grandmaster and all the students clapped twice, bowed low, clapped again, bowed once more and then the grandmaster turned to face everyone.

From her right, someone said, "*Sensei ni rei*." Annja knew that meant bow to the teacher.

Everyone bowed and said "*Onegai shimasu*."

The grandmaster sprang to his feet and instantly started demonstrating techniques using a small knife. As he taught, someone with an Australian accent translated from one corner of the room for the benefit of the non-Japanese speakers like Annja. On the other side, someone else was translating into Spanish, of which there seemed a fairly large contingent in attendance this evening.

"Let's go," Ken said. He led her toward the front of the room and produced a small training knife from his *gi* pocket. His eyes twinkled. "Ready?"

Annja nodded and Ken came at her with the knife. Annja tried to remember what the little man had done to evade the attack and disarm his attacker. Ken's knife stabbed her in the stomach.

"Not quite," Ken said. "Try it again. But sink your hips first."

Annja did as he instructed and when he attacked again, Annja found the movement easier to perform. The knife stabbed past where her midsection had been seconds before.

"Now bring your hands up to guard against the back slash. My tendency will be to cut back in a real situation, so you need to be prepared for it."

Annja brought her hands up and saw how much easier it was to effect a disarm when they were properly positioned. After a few more tries, she and Ken switched roles with Ken assuming the defense and Annja attacking.

As she slashed in, Ken deftly evaded her attack and Annja found her knife had vanished, followed by her legs being swept out from under her. Unlike the other martial arts she'd experimented with in the past, this time when she hit the floor, there was no time to regain her breath. Ken quickly used her arm to rotate her around from her back onto her stomach, effectively pinning her before she could react.

"*Do gaeshi*. It means body reversal. Pretty cool, huh?"

Annja smiled. She could see how devastating it could be if applied with full force. "You could have broken my arm."

Ken nodded. "And once you were on your stomach, I would have broken your shoulder girdle, as well. Nasty stuff, but fun."

Annja handed him the knife. "I'm ready to try again."

Ken flew at her faster this time, but Annja felt her body relaxing as she dropped her hips and evaded the knife stab. This time she saw an opening for a punch and let her hands fly out after she'd disarmed Ken.

She heard him mutter, "Oof." And then saw him break into a wide grin. "Nice one," he said.

The class flew by quickly. Annja was sweating but enjoying herself so much, time really seemed to cease to exist. The nature of the class also impressed her. Unlike many other martial arts, there was no rote memorization of technique. The grandmaster seemed to stress the feeling behind the techniques more than anything else.

He would demonstrate techniques on various partners, always changing the flow, never staying the same. As he demonstrated, he would discuss what he was doing, how he affected the attacker's body so that a counterattack was almost impossible or at the very least incredibly painful.

Then he would look at the class and smile and shout, "Play!"

The only measure of time was a small but fancy clock high

on the wall above them. Every fifteen minutes it would gong. Annja found it annoying after a while, but Ken seemed to take no notice of it.

Finally, after a short break and another forty-minute stretch, the grandmaster clapped his hands. "*Godan* test."

Everyone scrambled for the back of the dojo. Ken led Annja to where they had bowed in earlier. Ken's voice was soft in Annja's ear. "Just watch. Say nothing."

From directly under the *kamidana* shelf, the grandmaster took what looked like a padded training sword wrapped in golden foam and held it above his head. He bowed to the *kamidana*.

Then he turned around.

Annja noticed that there were several students lined up to the right along the wall. The grandmaster nodded at the first one, and the student scampered out and sat with his back to the grandmaster.

The student closed his eyes. Annja could see he was breathing fast.

What?

Ken placed his hand on hers. Annja watched as the grandmaster placed the sword on the student's head and then lifted it high above. The grandmaster closed his own eyes. For what seemed an almost interminable amount of time, everything went still.

Then the grandmaster swung the sword down as if he intended to cut the student in half with it.

In the blink of an eye, the student launched himself forward and to the right in a shoulder roll. The sword cleaved air where the student's body had been a millisecond before.

The room erupted into applause. The student came out of his roll and bowed to the grandmaster, who nodded and pointed with a smile.

"Good one," Ken said.

Annja said nothing. She had no idea what was going on, only that the energy in the room seemed to go from still to incredibly charged and then back to still again.

The grandmaster resumed his position and nodded to another student.

The student came out and seated himself the same way the first one had. But this time, when the grandmaster raised the sword, the student rolled.

"Too soon," Ken whispered.

"Come back," the grandmaster said.

The student sat down. This time, the grandmaster's sword swung down, and with a sharp whack on the top of the head, the test was concluded.

"No. Come back later. Next."

Two more students attempted the test but they both got solid whacks on the head, as well. With each new student, Annja could sense the grandmaster's growing frustration.

Finally, the last student evaded the sword and the grandmaster's smile returned once more. "Good!"

Of the five who had tried, only two had passed. The grandmaster returned the padded sword to the rack beneath the *kamidana* and walked to the middle of the floor.

"Time to bow out," Ken said.

They repeated the process as when they had bowed in. The grandmaster turned to face everyone and smiled warmly. "Good training."

They bowed once more and then everyone leaped to their feet. Ken nudged Annja over to the side.

Annja shook her head. "That was incredible. Even though I have no idea what I just witnessed. Was it some form of psychic awareness?"

Ken smiled. "I'll answer all your questions later. Come on, you should meet *sensei*."

"But I—"

Annja turned and found herself face-to-face with the grandmaster. He smiled at her and bowed low. When he came out of his bow he said something to Ken, who chuckled.

"He says he is always happy to see beautiful women enjoying his training."

Annja bowed low and said to Ken, "Please tell him I am very happy to have been able to participate in this. It was unlike anything I have ever done."

Ken translated and the grandmaster nodded and then looked Annja over from head to foot. She found his gaze somewhat unsettling, as if she was being appraised, albeit in a nonsexual way.

Finally, the grandmaster spoke to Ken again. Ken translated to Annja, "He says the bruises are healing well, but that next time you should attack more often than you did yesterday. He also says you have embodied the essence of your *isshin-ryu* training well and the boxing you've been studying seems to complement it well."

Annja's eyes bulged. "He knows all that?"

Ken smiled. "*Sensei* sees more than what is apparent."

Annja bowed low and said thank you but when she came up from her bow, the little man was already gone.

Ken smiled. "Don't be upset. He's got a lot of people to say hello to tonight. He presses more flesh than a politician, it seems." He pointed to the bathroom. "Come on, let's get changed and find something to eat. I'm sure you've got lots of questions about what you saw in here."

"You could say that."

Ken nodded. "Good. I'll meet you outside in five minutes, okay?"

Annja took another look around the dojo. People had broken up into many little groups. Most of the Japanese, she noted, hung out with each other. Other bands of people shrugged out of their uniforms and got changed quickly before vanishing into the darkness.

Annja found her way to the bathroom and got changed.

She did have a lot of questions for Ken. She hoped he had just as many answers.

9

The night air of Chiba still smelled of soy sauce, but a stiff breeze from the east made it a little bit more bearable. Annja and Ken walked silently through the darkness. Annja was bursting with questions but felt that Ken was waiting until they were seated in a restaurant before he would open himself to conversation.

Twice, he seemed to have almost forgotten something and swiveled around so suddenly that he startled Annja. "Are you all right?" she asked.

He smiled. "Yes. I'm fine."

Down a side street lined with small shops specializing in bits of arcane martial-arts souvenirs they found a small family-owned restaurant with a hushed interior and nice comfortable booths. The laminate tabletops seemed almost out of place given they were somewhat removed from the more modern digs of Tokyo, but Annja chalked it up to yet another weird paradox that so typified Japanese society.

She stared at the menu in front of her and then looked at Ken. "I'm lost here. Any suggestions?"

He smiled. "Well, that depends. Do you trust me?"

Annja eyed him. "So far."

The waitress came over and Ken ordered for them. As they sat waiting, the waitress returned with two bottles of Sapporo beer and poured them into tall glasses. Annja watched as the head foamed up to the brim but didn't overflow the lip.

"Funny, I'd never considered myself much of a drinker before I started traveling," Annja said.

"And now?"

She shrugged. "Thing is, drinking is so common in so many cultures, especially with meals. Now, I don't think much of it any longer. It's strange the way we get uptight about things in America."

Ken hoisted his glass. "Congratulations on taking your first *ninjitsu* class, Annja. *Kempai.*"

Annja touched his glass. "*Kempai*. And my most sincere thanks to you for taking me to this tonight. It was, suffice it to say, amazing."

Ken took a long drag on his beer before setting it down again. "You have many questions, I assume."

"Not many. But I would like to know what I witnessed there tonight at the end of the class."

Ken nodded. "The *godan* test used to be almost the ultimate exam for a student of *ninjitsu*. The teacher would test the student's ability to sense the intention of a killer. In the old days, it was done with a live blade. It goes back to what I said earlier. The ancient traditions had methods for getting rid of the idiots before they could damage the system."

Annja sipped her beer. "Rather a final way to do so, though."

"Sure," Ken said. "I won't open it up to debate about whether it's right or wrong. But the martial arts have had to adapt to modern society, so nowadays we use a padded sword. Still hurts like hell if you get whacked, though."

"Okay, so, the grandmaster was doing what exactly? Was he trying to kill the student?"

Ken put his hands behind his neck and leaned back. "When he stands behind the prospective student, he summons his killer intent—he actually thinks about cutting the student down. As soon as he starts the attack, it is up to the student to pick up on that intention and then roll out of the way."

Annja frowned. "But surely it's possible to hear the sword coming."

Ken shook his head. "By the time the sound registers in your conscious mind, it's too late. There really is no way to guess at it. As you saw, the time between when the test starts and when the grandmaster cuts down varies significantly. There's no rhythm to it. You can't time it. You can't guess. The grandmaster says he waits until he feels compelled to move by the warrior spirits that inhabit the dojo. When they tell him to cut, he does."

"And if the student rolls out of the way?"

"They pass. Otherwise, as you saw tonight, they are told to go away and study the art more. Some of them will come back and try during the next class. They may pass then. Others still have many years to study before they should try it again."

"Did you take the test?"

Ken smiled. "Yes, a while ago now."

"And you passed?"

"Not the first time. I got bonked on the head, too. That's how I know it hurts." He chuckled. "But passing it is like nothing you've ever experienced before. I had failed the test and thought I knew what to expect the second time. When I suddenly passed it was because my body took over and got me out of the way of *sensei's* killer intention. I didn't pass because I suddenly thought, I should move now."

"So if you can get out of the way of your conscious mind, you'll do okay?" Annja thought about how it related to her trying to make sense of using her instincts rather than her logical mind. She wondered if it was more or less the same.

"Yes and no. It's not a turning off of your conscious mind as much as it is an awakening of your deeper primal instincts. Surely you understand that there lies within all of us the ability to summon incredible strength and sensitivity during times of duress."

"Sure. I can accept that idea," Annja said.

Ken smiled. "Well, the *godan* test awakens something that has lain dormant for a long time."

"It's fascinating," Annja said. "In all my years as a student of martial arts, I've never seen such a thing."

"That's because most martial arts don't teach these things. As time has passed, they have gotten further removed from what they were designed to do—teach warfare. *Ninjitsu* is almost unique in that regard."

The waitress reappeared bearing dishes. "What did you order?"

"Sashimi," Ken said. "Tuna, eel and sea bass. I hope you enjoy it."

Annja split her chopsticks and used them to pick out a slice of the red tuna. She dipped it in soy sauce and then plopped it into her mouth, chewing slowly to savor the taste. She smiled. "Delicious. How do you say that in Japanese?"

"*Oishi.*"

"Definitely *oishi*," Annja said.

The waitress brought over another tray laden with all sorts of special sushi rolls. She said something low to Ken, who bowed and then looked over at the counter where the chef stood and thanked him.

"Compliments of the house," Ken said. "The waitress tells me the chef thinks you are very beautiful and it's his honor to create these for us."

Annja smiled. "That's very nice of him." She looked at the chef and flashed him a smile. "I hope that's enough of a thank-you."

Ken chuckled. "You've made his day, I'm sure."

Around mouthfuls of food and beer, Annja asked Ken, "So, now that I've been formally introduced to the world of *ninjitsu*, when do we start our hunt for your ancient *vajra*?"

"Tomorrow. We'll start then if that's okay," he said.

"Not tonight?" Annja wasn't really serious and judging by how delicious the food and beer tasted, she'd need some sleep in order to be in top form tomorrow.

"Why?" Ken looked at her. "Are you in a rush?"

Does he know about Garin? Annja wondered. "No, but I thought you might be, considering it's been missing for so long."

Ken nodded. "There's always something going on to keep us from a schedule. I've found the less I hold myself a slave to one, the better."

"I assume you have a starting point?" Annja asked.

"Absolutely. But I won't tell you now. It's safer that you don't know."

Annja frowned. "What's that supposed to mean?"

Ken finished his beer and the waitress brought over another. When he'd taken a long drag on it, he put his glass down and smiled at Annja again. "Surely you know that any time there's a treasure to be found, there will always be other interested parties out there looking for it."

"Well, sure, I've run into opposing hunters before. The trick is to know who they are and then beat them to the goal. Sometimes it ends peacefully. Other times not so much."

Ken nodded. "Indeed. Sometimes, though, the opponents do not present themselves until long after the race has started. Sometimes, the most dangerous foes are the ones hidden in plain sight."

Annja looked around and noticed for the first time that they were not seated near a window. "You think there are people after us?"

"After you because of your association with me, no doubt. Or at the very least, interested enough in you that your safety might be compromised."

"I've only been involved with you for one day, Ken."

Ken fished another piece of sushi off the tray and ate it slowly. "Yes, and some people would consider your involvement as being twenty-four hours too long. I'm sure that steps will be taken to assess your risk level to the operation to recover my family's artifact."

Annja leaned forward. "And if they determine me to be a problem?"

Ken frowned. "I think you know the answer to that."

Annja finished her beer. Danger was an inevitable risk in her profession. And truthfully, she'd grown somewhat accustomed to it being in her life. If she was being honest, she almost enjoyed the thought of the adrenaline rush.

"What do you suggest I do to make sure I stay safe?"

Ken's eyes gleamed. "You might consider not going back to your hotel tonight."

"Not go back? Where would I stay?"

"With me. My apartment is quite large by Japanese standards. There's plenty of room and I promise I don't snore too loudly."

Annja smiled. The thought of spending the night with Ken wasn't an unpleasant one. He was as handsome a man as any Annja had ever met. But she didn't like the idea of abandoning her belongings at the hotel.

"You could always get your stuff in the morning," Ken said.

Annja blinked. "You read minds, too?"

"Reading minds isn't necessary if you understand how basic human psychology works. It's only natural to feel concern over your possessions. Me suggesting you leave them for the time being isn't going to alleviate that concern."

"Well, the offer is a kind one and I'm certainly tempted."

"But you'll pass." Ken nodded. "I expected you would. In fact, I would have been surprised if you'd accepted my offer."

"But you made the offer anyway." Annja shook her head. "Why?"

"Hey, I might have gotten lucky." His eyes danced. "I'm referring to the offer, of course."

"Of course." Annja smiled. She wasn't sure if the atmosphere, the exhaustion from the class earlier or the beer was having a numbing effect on her. Probably a combination of all three, she decided.

Ken pushed himself back from the table. "Did you eat enough?"

"Plenty. It was all incredible."

He nodded. "We should get going, then. Trains stop running at midnight in Japan, and if we stay any longer, we'll have to sleep on a park bench somewhere near Ueno Park."

"No, thanks. That doesn't sound inviting at all." Especially, Annja thought, if Ken was right about potentially dangerous people also being after the *vajra*.

Amid many bows and thanks, Ken and Annja made their way out of the restaurant. A light, misty rain fell as they wandered back toward the train station. Slowly, the lights in buildings and shops went out as the town tucked itself away for the night.

Annja shivered in the slight wind and then felt Ken place his arm around her. Something stirred in Annja and she turned to face Ken.

"It's late," she said.

Ken turned her back around and pressed her toward the station. "We might just make the last train back to your hotel."

They paid for their tickets and stood on the lit platform. Annja heard the sharp clanging of the approaching train and it whizzed past as it slowed into the station. On the car, only a few other passengers sat. Most were already asleep.

"I hope they know when to get off," Annja said.

Ken nodded. "Most of them come awake by instinct. But

a few will probably wake up in parts unknown. It could be an expensive taxi ride back to their part of town."

The train slid out of the station. The jostle of the car bounced Annja against Ken a few times and she did little to avoid it. It reminded her of the playful little bumps that had marked her high school love life.

But since then, her affairs had been few and far between. Usually only with very limited and very controlled consequences.

In truth, she didn't have time for much of a love life. Her career meant the world to her now. And with her constant expeditions to the furthest reaches of the planet, Annja had no illusions about maintaining a serious relationship.

Still, Ken was nothing if not enticing. And tomorrow would be the start of their journey. Annja was looking forward to spending more time with him. A lot more time.

Twenty minutes after they started, the train rolled into her station. Ken helped her up. "We're here," he said.

They climbed the steps and exited the station, which overlooked a plaza of shops that were now closed. A street sweeper hosed down the street and then vacuumed up any garbage. A few people hurried by on their way home intermixed with late-night drinkers en route to the nearby bars that stayed open well into the wee hours of the morning.

At the front entrance to her hotel, Ken stopped. "We're here."

Annja kissed him on the cheek, momentarily taken aback by her brash move. Where did that come from? she wondered.

But Ken seem unfazed by it. He merely smiled and bowed quickly.

"I'll see you in the morning. Have a restful sleep."

Annja watched him walk down the street until the shadows seemed to swallow him whole.

She sighed and then wandered inside.

Annja Creed, she thought with a grin, you need a good night's sleep.

10

Annja floated in a strange, lazy dreamworld of sounds and images. She saw faces from her past and faces she didn't recognize. She heard sounds and felt things that seemed out of place. All of them seemed to swirl together like melted ice cream in the hot summer sun.

She tossed. She turned. And still she couldn't get comfortable.

She thought about the *ninjitsu* class she'd seen this evening and how it seemed that someone trained well in the art might well be a truly formidable opponent if faced in combat.

Annja wasn't sure she wanted to test that theory anytime soon.

She thought about Ken. What in the world had made her kiss him on the cheek like that? It was just a peck, after all. But still. Annja wondered what she felt for him. Certainly he was attractive enough. But she sensed there was something else about him that drew her in. The mystery of his family, the missing piece of history and the quest to restore his lineage—she found it all so noble.

And she admired him for it.

Tomorrow, they would start their journey to find the *vajra*.

She turned over again, aware that her arm was going numb from sleeping on it too much. She propped herself up again.

Her stomach hurt, too.

Now that's weird, she thought. The last time that happened…

Her body tensed. Could it be? Was someone in her room again?

She cracked her eyes just a sliver, trying to pierce the darkness and discern anything that might indicate the presence of someone.

She knew better than to try to look at things directly in the dark. The human eye changed in low-light conditions, using the rods instead of cones to see detail. And since the rods were at the outer part of the eye, Annja glanced around looking at things out of the corners of her eyes to see.

But all she saw was blackness.

She felt a shift in the air. It tickled her face.

Someone *was* there.

What to do?

The other night, she'd been in the tub and naked. Now she was at least dressed. But she also realized that being under the covers as she was would be a hindrance to her movement. She'd have to toss the covers and then roll out of bed. A two-step process just to ready herself for combat with a person she couldn't even see.

Not good. Not good at all.

She watched the room some more. Now she could pick out

a black shape moving against the black backdrop of her room. There seemed to be no ambient light coming in from outside that she might be able to use to help her see who had invaded her room—potentially for the second time in as many days.

The shape moved to her desk.

He's looking for something, Annja decided.

But what?

Adrenaline poured into her system. She could feel her smaller muscles contracting involuntarily as she steeled herself for the possibility of combat. Would they simply search her stuff and then leave?

They.

Where had that thought come from? As far as she could tell there was only one person in the room. And yet...

No, there was one more. Somewhere Annja couldn't see. And trying to shift in the bed might make her a target again.

Her breathing had shortened now.

I have to move—I've got to find out who this is!

She flexed her hands, bunching up bits of the covers and readying her grip. She would whip the covers one way and launch herself out of the bed the other way.

But what if the other person was standing there waiting for her?

She bit her lower lip and almost cried out as it cut too deep. A copper taste flowed into her mouth.

She had to take the chance.

She steeled herself.

One...

Annja took a deep breath in.

Two...

She tensed.

Three!

She threw the covers at the shadow by her desk and swung her legs out off the opposite side. She flipped off the bed and then straightened up with her hands held high ready to fight.

Instantly she felt her legs being swept out from under her. She landed hard and tried to roll, but the small size of her room made that difficult. As she rolled, she felt one of her arms being pinned behind her.

A knee appeared on her shoulder, driving her face first into the carpet. Annja hit hard and exhaled to try to dissipate the impact.

"That wasn't a very smart thing to do, Miss Creed."

The gruff voice that spoke in her ear had a vague accent to it. Japanese? She couldn't tell. Annja tried to respond, but the knee holding her down along with the arm pin made breathing difficult. She coughed and some of the pressure released, but not enough that she could escape.

"What do you want?" she asked.

The voice seemed to float somewhere above her. "Where is it?"

"Where's what?"

"The *dorje*."

Annja frowned. "What the hell is a *dorje*?"

"The item he has hired you to find."

"Who? What? I don't know what you're talking about."

"Ogawa approached you last night at the *budokan*. We saw your meeting. You've been with him ever since. And we believe you already have the *dorje* in your possession. We want it."

"I don't know what a *dorje* is," Annja said.

The voice paused. "He calls it a *vajra*."

Annja sighed. "For crying out loud, we haven't even started looking for it yet. How can I possibly have it?"

She heard a muttered exchange of conversation between the man holding her down and the other invader. She tried to make out the language but found it impossible to do so.

After a moment, the voice reappeared in her ear. "We were told you had it in your possession already."

"Well, I don't."

"Why should we believe you?"

"Don't believe me—I don't care. Go ahead and tear my room apart. You won't find the silly thing." Annja was frankly tired of being held as she was.

She got no response.

"I don't know where you got your information from, but it's obviously a load of crap."

The voice came closer to her ear. "If we find out you lied to us, we'll be back…to kill you."

Annja heard a quick spit of speech again, and then the pressure on her shoulder and arm disappeared. Annja stayed where she was.

"Can I get up now?" she asked angrily.

Again, only silence greeted her question. Carefully, Annja got up off the floor. The room felt empty now. She walked slowly over to the lights and turned them on.

Her window was open.

Annja ran to it and looked out. She looked up, down and all over, but saw no one clinging to the outside of the hotel like a bug. Her room was far too high up, wasn't it? There'd be no way for someone to get out from this height. It didn't make sense. Unless, of course, they had parachutes or some other high-tech gear they could use to escape.

And yet, they'd been here. At least two of them.

And they'd very neatly vanished into thin air.

Annja sat down on the side of her bed and sighed. This trip had been nothing but eventful so far. She wondered what the next few days would hold for her.

Part of her wanted to call Ken. She wanted to let him know that other people were after his precious item. Garin had warned her of the same thing.

She frowned.

But Garin wouldn't be behind this, would he?

What would he want with an artifact like the *vajra*? What could he hope to do with it? Ever since Annja had found the sword of Joan of Arc, Garin had treated her with a vague, ambivalent respect. Annja wasn't sure if he thought of her truthfully as an enemy or what.

What she did know was that because the sword was back together now, Garin might not be immortal any longer.

But she had no proof.

She could call Ken. See what he thought about the whole thing. Maybe he knew for certain there would be others after her. He'd hinted at that earlier, hadn't he? That's why he had wanted her to stay with him.

Had Ken known about these guys?

Annja frowned. She couldn't see that happening. Ken seemed far too focused on retrieving the *vajra* to restore his family's name than anything else. Being in cahoots with some third party after the artifact seemed unlikely and completely out of character for him.

But Garin had also warned Annja that she didn't really know Ken that well.

Was it possible she was being totally naive?

Here she was questioning her own judgment. Not good.

She got off the bed and walked to the desk. The laptop sprang to life, and the screen saver vanished and left the search engine flashing at her. Annja sat down and poised her fingers over the keyboard. What am I looking for? she wondered.

She put her hands down and sighed. "This is ridiculous."

Instead of typing, she put the computer back to sleep, turned out the lights and crawled back into the bed. She needed sleep. A good sleep that would help her get up tomorrow and start the hunt with a rested mind.

There'd be plenty of time to discuss the wacky occurrences of the night with Ken en route to wherever he was taking her.

She settled her head on the pillow and took three deep breaths.

"It appears you weren't lying."

Annja's eyes snapped open. She tried to sit up, but a firm hand held her down. She could make out a set of eyes staring at her, surrounded by black cloth and face paint.

"Don't. You will only succeed in making me angry if you do that."

Annja stayed lying down. "I told you I didn't have it."

"We needed to see you weren't lying. But if you had been, the first thing you would have gone for was the *dorje*. You didn't do that. So, I believe you don't have it. That's good."

"So, you'll leave now?"

"Not quite. We want to propose a simple business arrangement."

Annja shook her head. "Forget it. I don't make business deals with people I don't know."

The man hovering above her paused. "Ask yourself if you really want to know who we are, Annja. Ask yourself truthfully. Are you prepared—really prepared—to know that kind of thing?"

Annja sighed. "What's the deal?"

"We know he's taking you west tomorrow. If you find the *dorje*, we want it. It's that simple."

Annja looked at the blackened face. "What do I get out of it?"

He appeared to smile. "Your life."

"That's not much of a deal."

"I could kill you now, if you'd prefer."

The way he said it was so matter-of-fact, Annja didn't doubt for a moment he could do it easily. She shifted slightly. "Fine."

"We'll be watching you. Don't renege on our deal, Annja. We'll know where you are, wherever you are. And if you betray us, there will be no escape from our vengeance. It doesn't matter where you go, we'll hunt you down. Remember that."

"All right."

"It's time for you to sleep now."

Annja felt a soft pressure on the side of her neck.

And then felt nothing.

Nothing at all.

11

Nezuma Hidetaki watched from the back of the black BMW M3 through heavily tinted windows as Annja Creed and Kennichi Ogawa walked into the train station near Ueno Park. He'd been tailing them since they'd left the hotel earlier that morning, using a network of low-grade idiots to do the grunt work while he stayed in his car and monitored their efforts.

But Ogawa was proving himself quite adept at nonchalant countersurveillance skills, purposefully backtracking several times, nearly catching one of Nezuma's men as he tailed too close by a video store in Kanda. A last-minute break spared the entire team from being burned, but one careless mistake had almost ruined the entire surveillance effort.

That man now lay in the foot well next to Nezuma. He was sweating tremendously and Nezuma sighed once before looking at him.

"You should have anticipated that he would backtrack.

You were told to expect such tactics. This man is not a fool."
He sighed. "I wish I could say the same for you."

The man's eyes widened. "Master, forgive me. It will not
happen again. Please, I beg you!"

Nezuma shook his head. The problem with the youth of
today was their rampant sense of self-entitlement. Not one
understood the need to work and work hard for what they got
in life. Youngsters these days deemed themselves worthy
without having to prove their worth. As a result, they were
sloppy and inefficient.

Not to mention wholly annoying, Nezuma concluded.

Nezuma blamed the plague of idiocy on a politically
correct generation of parents who rewarded failure as if it
were success lest they damage a child's self-esteem. He
sniffed. What bullshit. Nezuma knew that the only way to
build self-esteem was to challenge oneself on the anvil of life.
Only by failing and then trying again, failing more and then
eventually succeeding did you prove yourself worthy of
victory and all the spoils that went with it.

During his time in America, Nezuma had grown nauseous
at the sight of parents coddling their children and never letting
them discover the nature of risk. He had also seen an almost
complete lack of parenting—no discipline instilled in a mis-
behaving child.

God forbid they use the word *no*, he thought.

All of this left Nezuma with a pool of talent that would
have perhaps been better if he poured bleach into the mix. His
young guns were fools who thought a new Ducati motorcycle
made them impervious to seasoned veterans of battle. They
imagined their bravado alone would grant them respect.

And when they failed, they still expected to be rewarded. Ridiculous.

All of his employees were like this, except one. In the front seat behind the steering wheel sat the only person Nezuma trusted with his life—Shuko.

Her ebony hair hung in a tasteful bob, unmarred by the trendy tea-brown staining so common to others of her generation. At twenty-five, Shuko was Nezuma's finest pupil and most loyal servant. Adept with her hands and feet as she was with firearms and explosives, not to mention an almost superhuman ability to face risk and danger and overcome both, Nezuma valued no one as he did Shuko.

Her voice cut through the whimpering of the man in the foot well. "We should go soon if we hope to stay with them."

Nezuma nodded. "I would very much hate to miss my train."

"Master…" The young man in the foot well couldn't have been any older than twenty. He was weeping now. Mixed with the tears and sweat, the BMW would no doubt reek if Nezuma had cared enough about it.

He calmly withdrew the silenced Beretta .22-caliber pistol and aimed at the man's head. "Failure is not to be tolerated."

When he fired, the subsonic bullets barely made a sound. But they penetrated the skull and bounced about inside, tearing open the brain cavity and killing the man.

Nezuma sighed again, disassembled the suppressor and pocketed the gun. As he opened the door, a slight breeze gave him a healthy breath of fresh air and he sucked it in greedily.

Shuko slid effortlessly from the car, retrieved their bags

from the trunk and then closed it with a thump. Together, they walked across the street.

"Thank god I have you," Nezuma said.

Shuko bowed from her waist. "I am yours, master."

Nezuma smiled as the bright sunshine streamed down through the morning haze. They reached the other side of the street and entered the train station. Shuko sidled through the crowd and acquired two tickets for the bullet train heading west toward Osaka.

She handed one to Nezuma. "We should get aboard. The train will be leaving in a few minutes."

Nezuma took in a breath and let it ease out through his nose. "You're right, of course." He smiled. "But what about the car? We can't simply leave it there like that."

Shuko's eyes danced as she withdrew a slim white iPod from her pocket. She scrolled through the menu for a moment and then handed it to Nezuma.

Nezuma looked down. She had selected a song called "Demolition." Nezuma pressed Play.

Outside of the train station, the BMW M3 blew apart in a giant fireball that sent metal and body parts skyward for a hundred feet before cascading down to the ground in a fiery rain.

Nezuma clapped his hands amid the screams and chaos. He turned to Shuko. "Very impressive. Is it a new formula you've recently cooked up?"

Shuko smiled. "Something I've been working on for some time now. I'm glad I had a chance to field-test it before our trip."

"As am I." Nezuma kissed her lightly on the cheek. "You're marvelous and I don't deserve you."

"Master."

"But I will happily accept your service. God knows you're the only one I can count on to get things done properly."

The compliments seemed to run right off of her. "Our train."

"Yes, yes." Nezuma walked with her. "It would be rude, I'd imagine, to keep our friends waiting."

"What if the American woman spots you?" Shuko asked.

"I doubt very much she will. Besides, she is likely still sore from the other night. Probably more so than she will be willing to admit. But the pain will serve to keep her awareness dulled a bit."

Shuko frowned. "And Ogawa? He is far too dangerous to risk seeing us right now."

Nezuma followed her to the platform. "I don't think Ogawa knows the extent of our involvement, if he even suspects it at all. He seems far too interested in recovering the *dorje* than he does in discovering who is truly after the artifact besides him." Nezuma clenched his hands into fists. "His devotion to his family will be his final undoing."

They boarded the train and headed toward the rear compartment, passing a snack car and scores of other passengers.

Shuko said, "I was able to find out their seats are to the front. They are due to get off in Osaka."

"Excellent. We'll keep tabs on them anyway, just in case Ogawa has any surprises in store for us. It would pain me terribly to reach Osaka only to discover they had gotten off somewhere earlier."

Shuko smiled. "I don't think even Ogawa is foolish enough to risk jumping from a train traveling in excess of one hundred miles per hour through the countryside, over rivers and amid rocky terrain."

"Nor do I, but he is a ninja." Nezuma looked at her. "And they are a devious, cunning bunch, even if they have no honor. I will put nothing past him and I would urge you to follow suit."

Shuko bowed again. "As you say, master."

They settled themselves into their seats and Shuko immediately began reading the various books she'd brought with her. Nezuma insisted she maintain a steady diet of literature and current affairs.

When he'd met her, she'd been a homeless girl of sixteen, living under the bridges by Tokyo Bay. While others like her had readily sold their bodies for money, Shuko had maintained her dignity by refusing to do so. Instead, she scrounged for old computer parts and had taught herself how to make them work again. She was eking out the barest of existences when Nezuma came down looking for other young guns he could recruit.

His monthly forays always granted him unlimited access to the desperate and depraved. Nezuma set up pit matches between the liveliest fighters and watched as the skinny, ravenous youths tore each other apart for the promise of money, food and a job.

But on this foray, Nezuma found himself surprised in more ways than one. Just prior to the match, he'd seen a scuffle in the cardboard community that bordered the fight ring. The unmistakable sound of a slap on skin set his heart thumping.

The sudden barrage of kicks and punches and the body of a young man flying through the air and landing at his feet further shocked him.

In the dim light he saw Shuko bending back to work on her computers on a decrepit particleboard desk. He cleared his throat to make himself known. "What's your name?"

Nezuma had expected a deeper male voice to answer him, but he heard only a soft one honed to an edge by the poor economic conditions that had forged a raw spirit. "I am Shuko."

"The Claw?" Nezuma had stifled a laugh. "That's quite unique. Do you like cats or something?"

Shuko had turned to look at him. He could see the beauty in her eyes, hidden under the smudges of dust and soot. But there was something else in her eyes that moved Nezuma—honor.

"Cats have nothing to do with my name."

Nezuma nodded and took another stab at getting her to open up. "What did he want?"

Shuko shrugged. "What they all want—my body."

"Did he offer you money?"

She sniffed. "The little he had, yes. But I don't want their money for that. I am not a whore."

Nezuma nodded. "And do you know who I am?"

"You are the man who sets up fights and recruits the winners to work for him. I am told most of those you hire end up dead within a few months. This is because they are fools who are unused to the risks they so desperately seek."

Nezuma leaned against one of the bridge girders. "That is true. I have, so far, found no one who can handle the work I set before them. It is tough finding good help."

"The people you hire are morons," Shuko said.

Nezuma laughed. "Are you always so blunt in your opinion of others?"

"Only if it is deserved." She glanced at him again. "I am not opposed to giving respect to those who merit it."

Nezuma looked around. "Down here, I'm sure you don't find that very often, do you?"

"I don't find it at all." She flipped a switch and a cathode-ray screen came to life. Nezuma wondered where she was drawing power from and figured she must have rigged something to steal the juice from the grid. "Where did you learn to fight?" he asked.

She shrugged. "Here. There. Wherever. Usually when someone would try to take something of mine, I was forced to defend it and myself."

"It doesn't bother you—hurting someone with your skills?"

Her shoulders jumped as if she was chuckling. "Why should it bother me? It is one more tool I have at my disposal. My opponents never think much of me because I am a girl. That is their downfall."

"Will you fight for me tonight in the ring?"

She looked at him again. "On one condition."

"Name it."

"If I win, you take me away from this. If I prove myself capable, you teach me everything you know. I don't want to ever come back here. I want this place wiped from my memory as if it was nothing but a bad dream."

Nezuma knew then that she would beat anyone he matched against her. "You have my solemn promise, Shuko-san."

She stood. Nezuma could see the holes in her pants, the threadbare shirt she wore and the shoes with no soles. Shuko had turned to him at that point and bowed.

"Master."

Nezuma had bowed back, aware that he felt something that night for the first time—a certain respect. For Nezuma, it was the first time he'd ever felt this way toward a woman.

Shuko beat five men that night, damaging each one more than the previous fighter. She had used guile, cunning and deception along with a raw talent for decisive street fighting Nezuma had not seen in many years. She broke bones, ripped skin and gouged eyes. She sent two of the men stumbling out of the ring clutching at their testicles, which she had pummeled with a devastating series of upper cuts.

In the wake of the pit fight, Nezuma had driven them to Ginza to an exclusive health spa where he instructed the staff that Shuko should be bathed, manicured and pedicured, and given the haircut of her dreams.

While she was shedding the layers of dirt that had clung to her since her youth, Nezuma went shopping. He bought her an assortment of stylish clothes that enhanced what he believed would be her true beauty.

And when she emerged from the back room of the spa dressed and made up, Nezuma had barely managed to catch his breath. Shuko, for all her lethality and rawness, was utterly stunning.

She had bowed again, but when she came up, there were tears of happiness in her eyes. It was the only time Nezuma would ever see her cry.

"Thank you," was all she could choke out before she clamped the emotion down and seemed to rid herself of her past.

Nezuma took her to dinner, where they ate and discussed

12

"Are you feeling okay?"

Annja nodded, but she felt anything but all right. Not after having dealt with the masked invaders in her room last night. She had awoken this morning overwhelmed by the feeling that she had somehow betrayed Ken. But there had been something so completely overpowering about the shadowy people, she had felt she had no choice but to accept their demands.

The question she asked of herself was would she really give the masked invaders the *vajra*?

She frowned. No. And the next time she faced them, it would be on her own terms. She took a moment to close her eyes and make sure the sword was still where she could reach it if need be.

It was.

When she opened her eyes, Ken was staring at her. She found his gaze piercing and unsettling at the same time. It was as if one moment he could use his eyes to seduce, and the next to hurt.

everything from books and music to world affairs. Shuko wa
remarkably well-educated despite her background. Nezuma
would add to that education over time.

After dinner, where Nezuma watched the longing display
itself on every man who caught sight of Shuko, they drove
back to the large warehouse Nezuma owned on the outskirts
of Tokyo. Nezuma showed Shuko where she could sleep.

Over time, the bond between them became unbreakable
as Nezuma schooled her in martial arts, and every aspect of
killing he could think of. When he had no more to teach, they
went abroad, studying with arcane experts and borderline
psychopaths as they absorbed every skill that would add to
their ability to bring Nezuma's plan to fruition.

Then they returned to Japan, ready to unleash it.

He watched her reading and smiled. Shuko meant the
world to him.

But so, too, did the *dorje* Annja Creed and Kennichi
Ogawa were trying to find.

She tried to return his stare with the same level of intensity. "What?"

He blinked and looked away. "Well, that was certainly interesting."

"What was?"

Ken shrugged. "You obviously just went someplace else while you were sitting here. It was like one moment you were in your seat and the next you were a million miles away."

Annja tried to brush it off. "Obviously, I'm not if I'm sitting here with you."

"Physically. But there's more to life than just the physical." He grinned. "I mean, not that the physical isn't important, but—"

"I got it." Annja smiled. "I know what you mean."

Ken sighed. "You want to tell me what's bothering you so much? You've been distracted all day long."

Annja watched the landscape pass by outside their windows. The train must have been traveling in excess of a hundred miles per hour. According to their tickets, they'd be arriving in Osaka around one o'clock in the afternoon. The train rocketed along, and Annja barely felt a bump as it rode the tracks. She tried to recall the last time she'd felt excited about riding a train. Certainly, the United States had nothing near as advanced as the bullet trains.

She looked back at Ken hoping he'd given up on his line of questioning. But one glance at the expectant demeanor of his eyes told her he hadn't.

She sighed. "What's a *dorje*?"

Ken shrugged. "It is another word for *vajra*. Why?

Where did you hear that? Were you researching something on your computer?"

"I met someone who mentioned it." Annja felt her stomach twinge as she thought about it.

"Who's this someone?" Ken smiled. "Anyone I know?"

Annja shook her head. "I don't know if you know him. But he seemed to know all about you."

"Really." Ken's tone was level, but she knew he expected more information.

Annja turned herself around in the chair to face him. "I was asleep in my room last night. Someone broke in. Well, that's maybe the wrong word. They didn't break in so much as one moment they weren't there—the next they were. It was really weird."

"Go on."

"I don't think it was the first time, either. The other night I was in the tub and I could have sworn someone had come in while I was there."

Ken nodded. "Okay."

"But last night, I tried to fight them off. I thought there was only one, but there were two. And when I made my move, I got sucker punched basically. Before I knew what had happened, I was pinned down and totally at their mercy."

"You could have been badly injured or killed." Ken shook his head. "I'm glad you're all right."

Annja smiled. She appreciated the fact that Ken hadn't told her she shouldn't do things like jumping attackers. She also appreciated his concern, which seemed legitimate and sincere enough.

"While one of the goons held me down with some sort of armlock, the other one searched my room."

"What were they looking for?"

Annja's shoulders felt tight. "Your *vajra*, apparently."

"And that's where you heard the word *dorje*?"

She nodded. "The one holding me down demanded I give it to him."

"But you don't have it." Ken laughed. "Hell, *I* don't have it."

Annja glanced around the car. They'd told her they would be watching. What if they were sitting close by right now? She looked back at Ken. "I explained this to them. They seemed convinced that I already had it in my possession."

"What would make them think that?"

"Faulty intelligence. Maybe someone leaked word to them. I don't know."

Ken frowned and turned around. Annja gave him the moment. She felt there might be a few things he was keeping from her. Whether or not that was for her own good, Annja felt certain they would come out soon enough. Whether Ken wanted them to or not.

"It's possible," he said after another moment. "I'd be a fool to think otherwise. But like we discussed last night, there are bound to be other interested parties in the hunt. They all know the rumors of what the *vajra* can supposedly do."

"They're just rumors, though, right? I mean, no one really believes that it's magic, do they?"

Ken smiled. "Given the state of our world, rumors are enough. The way things are these days, all it takes is a piece of gossip or innuendo for people to derive hope and happiness and then use that to buttress their own insecure existence."

"I suppose." Annja didn't think the two people in her room had seemed all that insecure.

"And if they felt strongly enough about it, it wouldn't be too surprising that they might even undertake the hunt themselves to see if the legends were true or not."

Annja held up her hand. "But they wouldn't have access to the material I'm assuming you have access to. How would they hope to find it?"

"Blind luck? Who knows?" Ken stretched his legs. "Sometimes, that's all it takes. And blind luck mixed with hope can still be a powerful combination."

"I don't like the idea that others are out there looking for this, or spying on us, or any number of other things that might make this trip perilous." She sighed. "These did not seem like very nice people."

Ken smiled. "You're not worried about danger, Annja. You relish it. It's one reason I hired you."

"You've hired me?" She grinned. "I don't recall ever seeing a contract or even hearing a verbal agreement."

Ken shrugged. "So, I'm doing it now. You help me find this *vajra* and you can name your price. Okay? I have plenty of money and I'm sure I can offer you a fee that will more than compensate you for your time and efforts. Not to mention any of the risks involved."

"They ordered me to tell them when we find it." Annja watched his face for a reaction.

Ken's forehead creased. "The people who broke into your room last night?"

"Yes."

"I see." Ken frowned. "And what did you tell them?"

Annja held her breath. "I agreed to do it."

Ken nodded and grinned. "Good. Very good."

"Good? You're not upset?"

Ken chuckled. "Are you kidding? What were you supposed to do when someone's got you pinned down and able to kill you if they wanted? I wouldn't expect anyone to be stubborn and refuse in that situation. Talk about being foolish. No, you did the right thing—the only thing you could do."

Annja exhaled in a rush. "I'm glad you feel that way."

"Of course I do. Did they give you some sort of ultimatum?"

"They said they'd be able to find me anywhere if I tried to betray them. They'd find me and kill me no matter what."

Ken nodded. "So, the standard ultimatum 101, then. Good."

"You keep saying that. I fail to see how this is all so good. My stomach's been in knots ever since. I thought you'd hate me for it."

Ken shook his head. "Look at it this way—we know there is at least one other party committed to recovering the *vajra*. They're deadly serious, it would seem. That means they're definitely a threat. But, they're only a threat at the very end of the hunt, when you're supposed to contact them and turn the *vajra* over to them. That gives us an amazing array of leverage and advantage."

"How so?"

Ken spread his hands. "First of all, if they're watching us, they will be one more set of eyes watching out for us. If there are other parties looking, they may find themselves having to deal with these people you spoke to last night."

"Good point."

"Also, by knowing that they expect you to contact them at the end of the hunt, we can plan our strategy accordingly. We have the pleasure of choosing the exact spot and time for the showdown. You can't ask for anything better."

"Unless, of course, they watch us closely enough and then jump us when we actually have the *vajra*, instead of waiting for me to contact them."

"It's a measured risk," Ken said. "Did they tell you how to get in touch with them?"

Annja frowned. "Actually, no."

"So that probably means they'll have eyes on us the entire time. Maybe even right now." Ken said this last bit with a mock seriousness that made Annja want to grin despite the nature of their conversation.

Annja resisted the urge to look around the car. No sense alerting them. She looked at Ken. "You think it's possible?"

He shrugged. "I'm fairly good at detecting surveillance, but someone really good at it would have no problem shadowing us as long as they wanted to. And what makes it even harder is knowing there is more than one of them. They can swap off for short periods. Two faces instead of one. Makes remembering them all the tougher."

"Great," Annja said.

Ken shook his head. "Don't worry about it. I know plenty of ways to lose them if we want to."

"But we don't want to, do we?" Annja could see the plan forming now.

"I think we're better off knowing they're behind us. It's always nice knowing we've got our six covered."

"Even by enemies?"

"Even by enemies," Ken said.

Annja sighed. "If you say so. I guess I prefer to always have my enemies in front of me where I can see them. It makes it easier to attack them."

"Sure, who wouldn't? But we can't always choose our battles. So we make the best of them as they come and use our wits to even the playing field. If that's possible."

"So who do you think they are? These people, I mean?" Annja said.

"I have no idea."

Annja frowned. "Look, Ken, I was honest with you about this whole thing. And I can't shake the feeling that you're holding something back from me. You want my help, fine, but we've got to be honest with each other or this is never going to work."

"The search?"

"That," Annja said. "Or anything else."

Ken looked at her for a moment and then smiled. "You want to know about the Yakuza connection. I guess I don't blame you."

"Well, that attack our first night together didn't seem random."

Ken fixed another serious gaze upon Annja. "What would you do if I told you I'd hired them ahead of time to put on a show for you?"

"I'd call you a silly man and tell you I don't respond well to such idiocy or ridiculous displays of machismo."

Ken laughed. "Of course you would." He leaned closer. "I didn't, by the way. I just like seeing you react like that to crazy questions."

"So what's the real reason?"

Ken yawned and covered his mouth with one hand. "I sought the assistance of the Yakuza when I started my search."

"Whatever for?" Why would he climb into bed with organized crime? It was a crazy thing to do, Annja thought.

"The Yakuza have a great deal of leverage within my country. Even as the police attempt to crack down on them or politicians publicly condemn them, the Yakuza are as much an institution as any other here. Their history alone gives them something of an almost Robin Hood-type status. As such, they can get things done that are otherwise difficult within the constrains of Japanese society."

"But something like this?"

Ken leaned closer to her. "I needed permission to search on certain lands. I needed a lot of bureaucratic signatures and notes. All of which were hard to acquire even with my wealth. I had plenty of money to grease hands with but I had no idea whose hands I had to grease in order to get things moving smoothly."

"But for the Yakuza, that's easy knowledge. They're in the game, so to speak," Annja said.

"Exactly. They know who and they know how to do it without raising a stink. So I paid them to pay off certain individuals. It seemed like an easy arrangement."

"So, what's the problem, then?"

Ken frowned. "I should have known better. The problem is they gradually began to piece together what it was I was doing—what I was looking for. And when they realized I was after the *vajra*, they proposed a very different business arrangement than we had had initially."

"They wanted to have it for themselves."

"They'd heard the legends, too. And they probably figured that it would be a good idea to try to acquire it for their own ends." Ken smiled. "Obviously, I wasn't comfortable with that idea."

"I'd guess not."

"So, I told them no."

"And naturally, they didn't like that." Annja couldn't imagine saying no to the head of an organized crime family. Ken was either crazy or incredibly brave or even both.

Ken laughed. "That's an understatement. I was told I had to return it to them or they'd kill me."

Annja raised her eyebrows. "What did you do?"

Ken smiled. "The same thing you did last night, my dear. I said yes."

"So why attack you the other night? If you agreed to their demands, it doesn't make sense for them to beat you up."

Ken waved it off. "Probably just making sure I got the message. But the kids they used were simply for show. The beating wasn't the message—the idea of it was. Maybe it was just their way of letting me know they were taking this seriously."

Annja nodded. "Looks like we're both in trouble, then."

"Absolutely."

"Misery loves company," she said.

Ken smiled. "It will only be miserable for a little time. You see, by knowing we have two parties after the *vajra* now, we can start working on how to play them off against each other. Hopefully, they will cancel each other out, so to speak, with a certain degree of finality, if you catch my meaning."

"Sounds risky."

Ken nodded. "It is very much so."

Annja took a breath in and then exhaled. "This trip is starting to remind me of every other hunt I've ever been on."

Ken nudged her. "Yeah, but it's damned fun, isn't it?"

Annja looked at him. "It has the potential to be."

If everything works out, she thought.

13

"Annja."

Annja opened her eyes and looked at Ken. He was sliding his jacket on, his eyes surveying the train car casually.

Annja stretched her arms and legs. "Have we arrived?"

Ken nodded. "Yes, and it looks a bit overcast outside. I'm hoping it's not too rainy. You did bring a jacket, right?"

Annja sat up straight from where she'd been resting her head on the cushioned rest and wiped the sleep from her eyes. "I didn't even know I'd fallen asleep."

Ken smiled. "You sleep utterly silently, do you know that?"

"No. I assumed I snore like a congested heifer."

Ken laughed. "Whoever told you that was lying. Even when you reach the deepest part of sleep, you still are silent." He stood and reached for his bag. "That's quite a remarkable skill to have. Most people make some sort of noise. But not you."

Annja fished around in her bag and pulled out a black knee-length nylon rain jacket. She slid it on. "Well, nice to know I can impress even when I'm not aware of it." She glanced around. "Everyone's already off the train?"

"I thought it might be prudent to let all the other passengers disembark first. This way, we can spot anyone who might perhaps be more than casually interested in us."

Annja frowned. "Only until we get out into the station itself, though. I assume there will be a lot more people milling around there. A surveillance team can position itself accordingly."

"There will be places they can hide. But we can use crowds to our advantage."

Annja stood and flexed her knees. "Can we use them to find our way to a restaurant? I'm more than slightly hungry." She should have grabbed something at the snack car, but sleep came first. Annja had felt so relieved at being able to tell Ken about her room invasion that the stress release must have caused her to fall immediately asleep after they'd finished talking.

"Of course. I know of a good one that lies within a few blocks of where we're headed anyway. Do you like tripe?"

Annja blanched. "That's a cruel joke, right?"

"Actually, yes. The restaurant serves great food. You'll love it." Ken glanced out of the closest windows and nodded. "I think now would be a good time for us to leave. Otherwise, we'll find ourselves trapped here and on the way back to Tokyo."

Annja let him lead the way down the narrow aisles. When they reached the junction between cars, Ken slid the exit door open and stepped out onto the platform. Annja watched the way he shifted himself as he adjusted his coat, but in actuality used the movement to scan the platform. After a moment, he looked back at Annja and nodded.

"Seems to be okay."

Annja stepped out and felt the cooler, drier air greet her. "It is a bit chilly, isn't it?"

Ken hefted his carryall over one shoulder and led Annja down the platform. "Do you know Osaka was going to be one of the cities that the Americans dropped the atomic bomb on? It was only at the last moment that the decision was made to spare the city because of the enormous civilian and cultural damage that would have resulted. Your generals knew that by targeting a city like this, it would have galvanized the Japanese even more, resulting in greater American casualties."

"I suppose that makes it all the easier to appreciate the city itself." Annja wasn't sure if she felt comfortable discussing the war. Or any war, for that matter. To Annja, they all seemed a ridiculous excuse for politicians to pretend they were warriors.

"Indeed," Ken said. "For those who live here, it was certainly a blessing. Granted, Osaka is a bit more textile heavy now than during the war, but it still has a great deal of beauty to it. You just have to know where to look for it."

They reached the escalator going up toward the main concourse. Giant video displays and bright billboards displaying soft drinks and strange-looking snack foods surrounded them. Ken seemed strangely tense even though Annja could swear he was completely relaxed.

"You expecting trouble?" she asked.

Ken glanced at her. "Yes. I am."

Annja's stomach hurt immediately after he said that. She frowned. If trouble was imminent, she could probably bring the sword into play and quickly be done with anyone who wanted to cause them harm.

"I really don't think that would be the wisest decision at this point."

Ken's words broke her out of her introspection. "What?"

"Whatever you're planning, I would suggest not doing it. It might cause us more trouble than it would save."

Annja frowned. How did he know she was thinking about drawing out her sword? And how did he even know about it? Could he read minds? Could he see into her thoughts? That didn't make her feel very good. Annja liked having her mind to herself.

"If you're wondering, the answer is no. I can't read your thoughts. I can feel the subtle changes in the energy you put out, though. You broadcast your intention and I pick that up. I can only guess at what it refers to specifically, but sometimes I come very close."

At the top of the concourse, Ken turned to her. "I know there are aspects about you that you wish to keep concealed. I understand that desire. I respect it. But if you have something that might aid us, I'd only ask you to consider what its appearance might do for our situation. Will it really help or hurt our progress?"

Annja nodded. He was right. If she drew the sword in a crowded place like the train station, there'd be hundreds of witnesses. She and Ken would get hauled into the local police station for hours upon hours of questioning. When it was all done, they would have lost precious time that could have been better spent searching for the *vajra*.

The sword would stay where it was if anyone threatened.

Ken turned and kept walking. Annja caught up with him. "Does your ability to feel intention come from the *godan* test?"

"Yes. But in the wake of that test, a great many things happen, depending on the person who passes it. A sincere and good person by nature will find themselves on a very peculiar journey."

"What kind of journey?"

"One where you question everything about yourself. It's during this time that you must be completely and totally honest with what you are. If you are by nature someone who does things of questionable morality and then attempts to deny your true self, you will either devolve into a living hell or simply be unable to fully understand the wonders of the world in the wake of the test."

"And what if you're a good person?" Annja asked.

"If you're honest with yourself, there is still a trying period of self-exploration. After all, even the best of us have things we may not like about ourselves. By confronting, acknowledging and accepting those things, we remove their ability to cause us internal harm. It's a process of exorcising one's personal demons."

"That doesn't sound easy." Annja felt sure there were a few skeletons in her own closet that would put up a substantial fight if she tried to get rid of them.

Ken shook his head. "It's not. And the process can take a number of years."

"Years?"

Ken chuckled. "Enlightenment isn't an overnight transaction, Annja. Granted many people tout it as such, but truly

experiencing life-changing, honest-to-goodness enlightenment takes much longer."

"And what about after the process is complete?"

Ken shrugged. "Certain skills and abilities reveal themselves over time. Not in a grand fashion, but more as a natural
extension of skills already present."

"Just another way to see the world, eh?"

"Something like that, yes."

Ahead of them the concourse throbbed with people. Ken
nodded. "Osaka is a huge metropolis, second only to Tokyo.
Its train stations naturally reflect that."

Annja scanned the crowd but could pick out no one who
seemed particularly dangerous. "How in the world do you
sense the presence of danger in a place like this?"

"You wing it," Ken said. They moved into the crowds and
Annja stayed behind Ken as he threaded his way through the
bustling throngs of commuters, schoolkids and elderly people
on errands.

She stayed close to him. "You're not serious about winging
it, are you?"

Ken shrugged. "It's tough to pinpoint anything in such a
group. Probably the best way to avoid danger in this location
is to simply avoid walking through it in the first place. By
simply not being here, you avoid the danger."

"We don't really have a choice, though," Annja pointed
out.

"And that's what makes this so problematic." Ken indi-
cated to the exit. "Once we clear the building, we'll be better
off. If someone does choose this time to attack, we'll at least
have a better environment to handle them."

They managed to push through the final hundred feet without incident. Annja spotted a gaggle of schoolgirls loitering near the entrance, all glued to video iPods and cell phones. How times have changed, she thought. Back in her day, Annja would have either been working out or had her nose stuck in a book.

Outside, the overcast skies enveloped them in a moist mist that didn't fall as much as simply float in the air. Annja was glad she'd brought her raincoat. Ken zipped his jacket.

"Are we clear?" she asked.

Ken smiled. "Oh, not by a long shot."

Annja frowned. "But we left the station. No one tried to attack us."

"That's true," Ken said. "And ordinarily, that might make a person inclined to feel safe. But you must also view the position of the attacker in order to determine the relative level of safety."

"What's that supposed to mean?" Talking with Ken could be almost as annoying as talking to Roux or Garin, she decided.

"Would it make sense for an attacker to go after us in the train station?"

Annja looked back at the building. It had been far too crowded in there for anyone to make much of an assault. "I guess not."

"Short of someone trying to stab us as we walked past, opening fire or blowing the place up is a highly ineffective strategy."

"So what you're saying is we're still in danger."

Ken nodded. "As long as we're after this *vajra*, it's my belief we'll be in danger."

"Swell," Annja muttered.

Behind them, the doors of the station opened. Annja watched as roughly a dozen schoolgirls came sidling through the portal, all of them giggling and sashaying about on the concrete walkway.

"We should go now," Ken said.

Annja turned to follow him. The walkway sloped downward at an angle. Ken reached the bottom first and then glanced at Annja. "Can you run?"

Annja's stomach hurt again suddenly. "Why?"

Ken pulled her to the ground as a flash of metal cut through the air where Annja's head had been a second earlier. Annja glanced back and saw the schoolgirls rushing at them, screaming like a flock of crazed crows.

"Come on." Ken yanked her arm, and Annja let herself be pulled along down the main street as the schoolgirls chased behind them. Ken went flying past a bewildered police officer.

Annja looked behind her in time to see the cop put his hand up to stop the schoolgirls, only to have it hacked off by one of the girls who wielded a sword. The cop spun and went down, his arm spraying crimson on to the street.

"They just killed that guy!" she shouted.

"They'll kill us, too, if we're not careful." Ken ducked down a side alley and Annja followed. Trash lined the slick ground. They skidded to a stop.

The alley ended in a concrete wall that ran twenty feet high.

Ken frowned and turned. He didn't seem to be out of breath. "So much for that option."

Annja could hear the screams of the girls as they skidded to a stop in front of the alley. They saw Ken and Annja, the dead end they'd boxed themselves in, and smirked collectively.

"I guess we make our stand here," Ken said. He glanced around and found a length of wood on the ground. It was easily ten feet long, but Ken cracked it over his knee and handed half of it to Annja.

"Use this," he said.

"But they're just kids."

Ken shook his head. "They're killers. And if you think of them as kids, they'll kill you. They're all old enough to know better. Whoever hired them to attack us, hired them for a reason. If they come at us, you must think of them as enemies. Give them no quarter because they'll show you no mercy, either."

Annja hefted the wood in her hands. Compared to the swords, chains and assorted other blades she saw the girls handling fifty feet away, the wooden staff seemed woefully inadequate against their arsenal.

One of the girls hurled another throwing star at them. But Ken merely knocked it away with his staff. It skittered away, clanging on the damp ground.

Annja stood next to Ken and smiled. "This kind of thing happen on all your dates?"

He glanced at her. "Is this a date?"

"I was kidding, silly."

Ken smiled. "You can't say it isn't fun, though. Can you?"

"Ask me when this is over."

The girls screamed en masse and just as they were about

to charge, another sound filled the alley. It flooded the area like a grumbling thunderstorm and it took Annja a moment to realize someone was chanting.

"What the?"

Ken put a hand on her arm. "Wait."

The chanting grew louder and the schoolgirls looked nervous. From behind them, it looked as if a gray mist was coming for them, billowing into the alley. The chanting grew louder and more ominous and almost made Annja's ears hurt.

The effect on the schoolgirls, however, was more profound. As the mist enveloped them, they screamed in terror. Annja could see flailing limbs and heard sharp whacks and hits and strikes and more startled cries from within the cloud of mist.

After several long seconds, the screeching stopped.

The mist began to fade.

Annja could see the sprawled bodies of the schoolgirls on the ground. Their weapons were nowhere to be seen.

"What the hell just happened?" Annja asked, confused.

Ken tugged on her arm. "Come on."

They ran past the schoolgirls. Annja couldn't tell if they were dead or just unconscious. At the mouth of the alley they stopped. Ken pointed.

"Look."

Down the street, they saw the robed figure of an elderly monk leaning on a staff with rings atop it.

The monk stopped, turned and bowed low.

Ken returned the bow.

"Who was that?" asked Annja.

Ken shook his head. "I don't know. But he just saved our lives."

14

"Where'd he go?"

Annja looked back but the mysterious monk had vanished in a second in the sudden throng of people who had appeared on the street. Ken tugged on Annja's arm like an insistent child bothering its parent.

"We should get out of here before the police show up. A bunch of schoolgirls lying dead or unconscious in a crummy alley will certainly bring the authorities around by the dozens."

Annja followed him into the mass of people, marveling at how easily Ken slid through the gaps in space. They traveled for the better part of a mile. Finally, Annja pulled up short, which caused Ken to stop, as well. She leaned against a storefront and tried to catch her breath.

"Where exactly are we going?"

Ken gestured with his right arm as he tried to get out of Annja's grasp. "A small temple I know of. It's just up this way a bit farther."

Annja frowned. Something bothered her about all of this. Namely, there hadn't been much she'd been required to solve or figure out for Ken since this whole trip had started. All of the things they were doing he could have done without her help. So what was his reason for bringing her along on this jaunt?

She pushed off her resting point and followed him up another block and then down a side alley as he broke right. The area didn't look even remotely as if it would house a temple. Too many steel facades sprung up alongside them at every step. Bright neon flashed in *pachinko* parlors and video arcades hustled their wares. Internet cafés buzzed with people seated and surfing. And nowhere did it appear that a temple could find a home in this bustling modern metropolis.

But when Ken turned at the next corner, Annja found herself reconsidering her previous assessment. Sitting a half block farther on was the gate that marked the entrance to a temple. She could see the cedar beams and wooden shoji screen entrance, along with the blessed rope hanging down from the gate that marked this as a holy place. On either side of the door, two red Japanese maple trees were paired with small statues of an angry-looking god holding a sword and gnarled rope in his hands.

Ken stood before the structure and pointed out the figures to Annja. "Fudo Myoo, the god of warriors. His name means 'the immovable one.'"

Annja looked around. "And this temple is dedicated to him?"

"One of the few left in the country. For some reason, there aren't many who consider him a worthwhile deity to pray to in this supposed age of enlightenment and reason."

"But not you. You like to cover all your bases?" Annja asked.

Ken grinned. "Something like that. We're here to see a very old man who might just know how to find the *vajra*."

He stepped forward, knocked on the wooden frame of the shoji screen and called out a greeting in Japanese. From somewhere deep inside, a voice answered back and Ken nodded.

"Good. He's home."

They stepped up onto the wooden flooring and Ken pointed out the shoe cubby. Annja slipped off her shoes and stepped into a pair of small slippers that wrapped around her feet like tight socks.

Ken slid back the shoji screen and they stepped inside.

The first thing Annja noticed was how much larger it seemed on the inside than out. The ceiling towered over them and a large statue of Fudo Myoo stood deeper inside, bathed in dim candlelight. The fresh scent of incense wafted through the air and Annja found herself breathing deeply and feeling much more relaxed than she'd been before their encounter in the alley with the psychotic schoolgirls.

Ken stepped over to the smoky incense burner located by the back side of the Fudo Myoo statue and waved his hands through the haze. Pressing his palms together, he bowed several times and waved some more of the smoke over himself.

Then he stepped back and nodded at Annja to do the same. Annja felt a little strange about doing so, feeling that this wasn't exactly a deity she might worship. Still, being in the temple of any god, believable or not, she figured it seemed only polite to at least pay a small homage to them.

She waved the smoke on herself as she'd seen Ken do and

then bowed a few times until she felt more self-conscious than anything else.

When she looked up, Ken stood there smiling.

As did the diminutive monk standing next to him.

"Sorry, not exactly sure I did that right," Annja said.

"You did fine," Ken said. He turned to the monk. "This is Taka. He runs the temple here. All by himself mostly."

The monk bowed low and came up smiling still. "I used to have some help, but most acolytes these days prefer other gods to serve time with. I suppose this place just isn't flashy or fashionable enough."

Annja started. "Your English is perfect."

He shrugged. "I travel sometimes." He nodded to Ken. "Come. I have tea waiting."

Annja glanced at Ken and then back at Taka. "You knew we'd be coming?"

The elderly monk merely shrugged as he walked. "The future is not hard to discern if you listen to nature. Most events are clearly laid out if you only care to notice them ahead of time."

They walked down a corridor on cedar planking polished by years of feet scuffling back and forth in sock slippers. Annja marveled at the depth of the temple.

"It seems so small on the outside. And yet—"

Taka nodded. "It's much larger than it appears. In much the same way, Fudo Myoo's influence is much greater than is at first evident."

"Do you know Ken well?" Annja expected him to say they'd been friends for years.

Taka laughed. "We've only just met, actually."

"And you're not concerned about him?"

Taka stopped and looked at her. "Should I be?"

Ken looked at Annja. "Something wrong, Annja?"

She shrugged. "I just find it odd that you've never met him before and yet we're being welcomed as if we were long-lost family. I can't imagine the same thing happening anywhere else in the world."

Taka shrugged. "Perhaps Ken and I are more like long-lost family. Maybe that is why I feel compelled to have him and his guest in for tea and conversation." His eyes gleamed. "Or I might just be a lonely old man in need of some decent company. And you two are a welcome change from the real-estate developers who normally visit me."

Ken gestured around the temple. "I'd imagine they're offering you quite a sum of money for this place."

"Certainly, but what is money worth? Not a thing. They would pay me a fair price for the land and then tear down the temple only to build another club or *pachinko* parlor or apartment house. Man does not need any more of these distractions. He needs more temples." Taka shrugged again. "So I stay."

"The Yakuza don't bother you?" Annja asked. Ken flashed her a look and she blanched. "Sorry, please forgive my inquisitiveness."

Taka laughed. "It is not a problem, young lady. And yes, the Yakuza have stopped by. But while they are certainly to be despised for their criminal activities, they are one of the few groups in Japan who still have some degree of respect for the old ways. And when I told them I was not interested in selling, they accepted it with far greater humility and understanding than the new generation of developers, who cannot see beyond the limited life of their bank account balances."

They approached a small room set with a low table and three cups of steaming tea. Taka gestured for them to sit. "I've only just poured it, so it should be just about right." He lifted his cup and bowed to his guests. Ken and Annja followed suit.

Annja sipped the bitter green tea and smiled. "Delicious."

Taka bowed low. "My thanks." He took a sip and then set the cup down before turning to Ken. "Now, please, tell me why you are here."

Ken set his own cup down and regarded Taka. "I seek the *vajra* of the Yumegakure-ryu."

Taka nodded. "Interesting. I must admit I knew this would be your reason for coming here, but when I saw this happening, I did not believe it myself. It was the first time in many many years that I had questioned my faith. I see now there was never any need to do so."

Annja sipped her tea, waiting for Taka to continue. The spry monk took another sip of tea and looked at Annja.

"And you, young lady—are you also on this quest to recover the *vajra*?"

"Supposedly." Annja glanced at Ken. "Although honestly I don't know why I am. I've contributed nothing as yet that I would call either useful or even helpful."

Taka gestured to Ken. "She is an honest woman. And fully possessed of her own skill and wisdom."

Ken nodded. "It is one of the many reasons I asked her to come along. A valuable ally is a very difficult thing to find these days. She is unmotivated by the usual machinations of mankind."

Taka grinned. "Time will tell if your assessment is correct or not." He sighed and drank more tea. "You know the history of the *vajra*?"

"Mostly. I know that Prince Shotoku made a gift of it to my family over a thousand years ago," Ken replied.

Taka nodded. "Indeed. It was to be used as a force for good in the world of madness that descended upon Japan. During the Warring States period, the *vajra* was reputed to be one of the only things that helped keep the country from utterly destroying itself. As evil tried to gain root, the *vajra* countered its influence by helping those who fought for the good of the people. It was, needless to say, a very back-and-forth struggle. It was one of the darkest times for Japan."

Taka took another sip of tea before clearing his throat and speaking again. "In the wake of this darkest period of civil war, when only a few warlords remained powerful, peace at last seemed to be a possibility again. The Tokugawa family was rising to power and soon would usher in a period of hope and prosperity."

"And someone stole the *vajra* at this point, yes?" Ken asked.

Taka smiled. "That is how the story is told."

"I have tried for many years to figure out which of the warrior families might have been powerful and evil enough to do such a thing." Ken sighed. "I must confess I have been unable to figure out who would have been able to steal it."

Taka's eyes gleamed. "Perhaps you are looking at the wrong people."

Ken frowned. "What do you mean?"

Taka shrugged. "I mean you are assuming that it was an evil warlord that arranged for the *vajra* to be stolen."

"It wasn't?"

Taka shook his head. "Not at all. In fact, the people who took the *vajra* would contend that they did so because they were helping the forces of good, and not the forces of evil."

"But who would do that? There are no records of warlords mounting an expedition to steal the *vajra* from my family," Ken said.

Taka sipped his tea. "Your mind is still clinging to the thought that the *vajra* was stolen."

"But it was."

Taka shook his head. "Not at all. The *vajra* was entrusted to a group who could safeguard it more than your family could. Your ancestors were very wise, Ogawa-san. The Yumegakure-ryu was renowned for their ability to see the future and plan accordingly."

Annja finished her tea and set her cup on the table. "But who would they entrust such a special artifact to?"

Taka leaned over and poured more tea into her cup. "The only ones who were powerful enough in their own right to protect such a thing and still resist the warlords who might have tried to steal it—the *yamabushi*."

Ken frowned. "Mountain warriors?"

Taka continued. "Warrior monks who lived in secluded temples deep in the mountains to the west of Edo, the old capital. Their austere way of life, as well as their commitment to martial arts and devout ways, made them the perfect guardians of the *vajra*. Your ancestors knew that they would not be tempted to use the *vajra* for their own purposes. But your ancestors could not be so sure about their own descendants. Every new generation, after all, must find its own path—be it right or wrong. I imagine your ancestors believed it very likely someone born into the family would use it for their own gain and not the good of mankind as it was destined to do. They did the smartest thing they could, short of destroying it. They gave it to the *yamabushi* with strict orders for it to be hidden away and thereby protected."

Ken leaned back. "If that's true—"

"It is," Taka snapped. "I have little reason to lie about such things. What good would it accomplish?"

Ken bowed. "Forgive me, that was rude."

Taka smiled. "More tea?"

Ken held out his cup and thanked Taka when it was refilled. "The *yamabushi* still have the *vajra,* then?"

"I would assume so," Taka said. "I am certain it still survives. The *yamabushi* are nothing if not careful in where they hide such things."

"Then it would be up to me to go and retrieve it from them," Ken said.

Taka shrugged. "I suppose you could. But you must also ask yourself, why would you do that?"

"Because it belongs to my family. I want it back."

"But why?" Taka asked. "Certainly, the *vajra* still maintains some degree of influence over world affairs, even in the darkest hours of this century."

"But how do you know?" Annja asked.

Taka smiled. "For the easiest reason of all—we are still here, alive and in reasonably good health."

"I'd argue that the *vajra* should be returned to me," Ken

said. "After all, recent events like the rise of terrorism suggest that the forces of evil might be gaining momentum. If the *vajra* can be used to counter that momentum, then it is my responsibility to do so."

"We've also attracted the attention of other groups who want the *vajra*," Annja said.

Taka looked at Annja and then back at Ken. After a long moment he sipped his tea and then stretched. "Very well. You seem determined to get it back at any cost. And I am certainly not the one who should determine whether you should have it or not."

He stood. "Come with me. I will tell you how to find it."

15

Nezuma watched as police officers and investigators circulated around the alley near the train station in Osaka. Next to him, Shuko stood still, waiting for Nezuma to say something.

"Schoolgirls." Nezuma shook his head in wonder. "Now, that is an interesting turn of events."

Shuko frowned. "According to eyewitnesses, it doesn't even appear that Ogawa and the American woman fought them off."

"No? And just how did they get away?" Nezuma pointed. "And if not them, then who exactly disposed of this death squad with such creativity?"

"A monk," Shuko said. "That's what the police are jotting down in their reports."

"And they believe it?"

"The witnesses appear to be very reputable. A shop owner, a coffee-stand operator and a number of people using an Internet café across the street saw the entire thing unfold through the large windows."

Nezuma's mouth widened as he contemplated the information. "One monk against the better part of a dozen armed teenagers…that's some holy man."

Shuko looked at Nezuma. "This wasn't something you arranged, was it, master?"

Nezuma smiled. "Oh no. Not me. There'd be no reason for us to want them dead, anyway. We want them leading us to the *dorje*."

"That's what I thought."

Nezuma patted her arm. "And you know I would have definitely included you in the plans if I had intended to kill them."

She smiled. "Thank you."

"But this—" he frowned again "—this is the work of someone who is very interested in making sure the ninja never gets his hands on the *dorje* again. And that means we have a bit of a problem."

"How so?" Shuko asked.

Nezuma watched the police officers loading the bodies of the girls into ambulances. "They're not dead?"

Shuko shook her head. "Not a one. They were apparently soundly beaten and rendered unconscious, but they are otherwise intact. I'd imagine the authorities want to take them in for observation, but they should be released unless the police want to press charges for them having an assortment of bizarre weaponry in public."

"Whoever put these girls up to the task of killing Ogawa and Creed is a problem for us. I don't like other people interfering in our plans. And we can't afford them taking another shot at the ninja and his accomplice," Nezuma said.

Shuko nodded. "Understood."

"First things first, then," Nezuma said. "We go to the hospital and see what our wounded little lambs have to tell us about their employer."

"They may not talk," Shuko said.

Nezuma smiled. "I fully expect them not to. At first. But I'm fairly confident that once I explain the nature of things to them, they'll be more than happy to tell us all their dark and dirty little secrets."

"Had I known, I would have brought my chemistry kit with me."

Nezuma led her away from the accident scene. "Shuko, my dear, we're headed to the hospital. There are plenty of drugs there you can play with."

It TOOK THEM fifteen minutes to reach the nearby hospital by foot. Nezuma insisted that traveling that way would allow them to see if they had picked up any surveillance along the way. "If someone is after Ogawa, then there's a chance that they know about us, as well. I don't want any surprises," he explained.

Shuko trailed behind Nezuma as he walked to the hospital and they reconvened in the parking lot. Nezuma watched her approach from the opposite direction he'd taken, knowing that she'd probably backtracked on herself a number of times to make sure she had no followers.

"Nothing, master. I feel confident that we are clean," she reported.

Nezuma nodded and glanced at the hospital. The ten floors of the white-and-gray steel building sprawled across almost five acres of land. Nezuma knew that this particular hospital housed experts in a number of cancer specialties, as well as an infectious-diseases laboratory second to none in Asia.

But he was more concerned with catching up with the schoolgirls. They would be brought into the emergency room for treatment and observation. While there, the police would be around.

The key would be to get at them when no one else was around. Some sort of controlled environment, where Shuko could have time with them to get the answers they needed.

"If they've got trauma to their bodies, they'll want to make sure there aren't any broken bones."

Shuko smiled. "Radiology."

"Exactly."

They walked through the main doors of the hospital, and while Shuko inquired at the front desk about visiting hours, Nezuma glanced at the floor plan and noted where the radiology department was located.

Shuko led him to an elevator bank and they ascended three floors until Nezuma stopped the elevator. The doors parted and he glanced out. Seeing no one, he motioned for Shuko to follow him down the corridor until they came to a storage area.

Shuko ducked inside and reemerged with white coats and name tags. Nezuma made a note of his fake name and Shuko's. Then they walked to the other side of the hospital where another elevator bank carried them down to the emergency room.

Nezuma was feeling relaxed. He felt comfortable impersonating anyone and he knew that half the battle to pretending you were someone else was simply acting natural. If questioned, act with authority and that was usually enough to get by.

They spotted the police officers congregating near a corner of the emergency department. Each bed was sectioned off with curtains.

Nezuma nodded at Shuko, who slid behind one of the officers and then came back a moment later as he stood there studying a sheaf of papers on a desk nearby.

"The chart says she is scheduled for X-rays in twenty minutes," Shuko said.

Nezuma nodded. "Fast for a hospital this size."

They walked out of the emergency department and Nezuma led them toward radiology. Along the way, he grabbed a large brown envelope with X-ray screens from a clear plastic file holder outside a patient's room. Shuko helped herself to a clipboard and pen and appeared to be taking notes as they walked.

"There's no telling how many people will be in the department," Nezuma said. "Hopefully, there won't be too many."

"Incapacitate or kill?" Shuko asked.

"Just knock them out," Nezuma said. "And I'd prefer if w did this as covertly as possible. No sense having our fac televised. I have a reputation to keep up, you know."

"I understand."

As they approached the radiology department, they denly found themselves facing a group of doctors engag a spirited conversation as they walked toward Shuk Nezuma.

Nezuma started talking to Shuko. "Mr. Hanaguchi' films show that he has a stress fracture on his right possibly resulting from an overexertion during h fitness regimen. However, certain diseases cannot

out as the cause of bone weakening and fracturing, so I'd like to make sure…"

The group of doctors passed by without incident, not even pausing to say hello. To them it probably looked as if Nezuma was an older doctor discussing a diagnosis with a younger intern.

The doors to the radiology department slid open. Nezuma kept up his monologue with Shuko, who pretended to jot down extensive notes on the clipboard she carried. Nezuma noted to himself that she carried it just high enough to obscure her face. Nezuma himself was turned slightly toward Shuko and he had changed the timbre of his voice.

He could see a door leading back to the X-ray room. A lone nurse sat at the desk busy working on a computer. Nezuma kept talking as Shuko moved forward and then behind the nurse at the desk.

Within seconds, the nurse was unconscious. Nezuma helped Shuko move her and then he nodded at the doors. "Better check and see who else is here."

Shuko slid through the doors. Nezuma thought he heard a brief snippet of conversation, followed by a thud. Shuko reappeared and waved him back.

Nezuma took the nurse by her armpits and backed through the doors.

Shuko waited by an empty closet. The radiology technician was already bound and gagged. She tied up the nurse and then gagged her, as well.

Nezuma glanced at her. "How long do you think we have until they come around?"

"A half hour, no more. We'll have to be quick."

Shuko took the nurse's place behind the desk. Nezuma waited on the other side of the doors.

Five minutes later, he heard the approach of a wheelchair. He looked out through the doors and saw a lone schoolgirl sitting in the chair with her head bent slightly forward. Nezuma frowned.

He could see the girl was playing on her injuries. Every so often she would surreptitiously scan the area. He smirked. Whoever had hired them knew how to find talent.

He walked through the door and saw a police officer and nurse's assistant standing next to the wheelchair.

"What do we have here?" Nezuma asked.

"She won't tell us her name," the nurse's assistant said. "But she took quite a thump on the head. Dr. Tohno wants a complete X-ray of the skull to make sure she doesn't have anything to worry about."

Nezuma took the chart from the nurse's assistant and opened it, pretending to scan the information. He snapped it shut and nodded. "Very well. Let's get her in back."

Shuko came around from the desk and took the wheelchair. Nezuma held the doors for her. The police officer and assistant started to sit, but Nezuma smiled and said to them, "There's no need to wait. I'll have my assistant bring her back down when we're done."

The nurse's assistant frowned. "I'm supposed to wait for her. Apparently, she's been a bit troublesome."

Nezuma shook his head. "If she's got a knock on her head, she's probably got a headache that won't quit. That makes anyone cranky." He gestured to the police officer. "You look tired. Are you all right?"

The cop nodded. "I'm fine."

"Tell you what, why don't you two go and grab a cup of coffee upstairs? Come back in about forty minutes and I'll have her all ready for you to take back."

"Are you sure?" the nurse's assistant asked.

Nezuma waved at them. "Go. Enjoy."

They started to leave but as the doors to radiology slid open, the police officer stopped. "Doctor?"

Nezuma turned around. "Yes?"

"Can we bring you anything back?"

"Hmm? Oh, you know, that would be very kind of you. If it's no bother, I'll take a large coffee with extra cream, please. And my assistant is a real lover of the *chai* they serve there now."

The cop grinned. "My partner digs that stuff, too. Me? I can't see the attraction."

Nezuma smiled. "Thanks. I'd better get back there and start the X-rays. If she's as cranky as you say, I don't want her around here any longer than necessary."

He watched them leave and then slid back through the doors into the X-ray room. Shuko was standing over the girl. Her hands were bound to the wheelchair and her ankles were tied, as well.

Nezuma could see the fear in her eyes. She looked as if the entire situation simply didn't compute.

He bent down so she could see his face. "Hello there, my dear. You and I are going to have a nice little conversation. And if I like what you have to say, I'll even let you go."

He patted her hand. "But if you don't be a good little girl and tell me exactly what I want to know, then my assistant here is going to make sure your life becomes very painful indeed."

Shuko made a show out of sliding a scalpel under the girl's nose, just an inch from her skin. The girl's breathing increased. Nezuma could see the line of sweat that broke out along her hairline.

"Now, I'm going to take the gag out of your mouth and ask you some questions. If you scream, you will only do so for a mere second before we kill you." He chuckled. "I'd suggest you refrain from such activity."

Shuko stood poised to strike. Nezuma leaned closer. "Do we have a deal?"

The girl nodded.

Nezuma smiled. "Excellent. Let's begin."

16

He was a huge man by Japanese standards.

Towering over most people, he didn't so much walk as he did loom. His shadow fell long over the hallway he stalked down, and the people he passed only dared glance after him before turning back to their own worlds.

He detested the idea of impersonating anyone, but even he recognized the value of blending in. After all, he'd survived as long as he had based on his ability to remain undetected.

The hit had gone wrong.

Terribly so.

And the sudden appearance of a monk of all things meant that the plan had backfired in the worst way. Now he was left with the task of cleaning up the entire mess and ensuring that no one would be left alive who could link him to the attempt.

That meant doing things he would have normally preferred to employ someone else to do. He frowned. Doing so would have meant another loose end. A liability he simply couldn't afford.

His navy-blue uniform looked more black and reflected the dour mood that had come over him upon learning of the failed assassination. Not that he had expected it to go off well in the first place. Something like this was, after all, more of an experiment than anything else. But it had gone so utterly badly, that even he had been surprised.

He strode into the emergency department at the hospital and saw the relaxed group of patrol officers scattered all over the ward. When they saw him, they immediately snapped to attention, one of them going so far as to throw up a hasty salute.

"Who is in charge here?" he snapped.

Another officer stepped forward. "Shiraishi, sir!"

He looked around the room and glowered. "Your men are pathetic. They lounge about as if this were break time rather than a place of professional business. Get them looking sharp. I want to know all the latest information about what happened in that alley and I want to know it right now."

The patrol officer named Shiraishi turned and pointed at another officer. "You there—get the commander the latest reports."

Shiraishi turned back to him. "Can I get you something to drink, sir?"

"No."

"Very well. I was not informed you would be coming down to oversee this operation."

He barely even glanced at Shiraishi. "And since when is headquarters required to inform you that I am taking a personal interest in a case? Or are you now of the belief that you have the experience to run such things?"

"No, sir. I was merely commenting that I find it strange to see you here. Mostly, we never even see you at all."

"And you should count yourself lucky you do not. The more times I have to come out of my office to supervise something, the more likely it is that things have been done wrong. I am sent out to correct errors, Shiraishi. And I do not like finding them in the work of supposedly competent police officers under my command."

"No, sir."

"Where are those reports?"

Shiraishi turned and waved over the man he'd spoken to earlier. The officer ran up with a sheaf of papers and handed them to Shiraishi, who in turn handed them to him.

He glanced at them, scowling and grunting at the appropriate times and places. Finally, he took a deep breath and huffed it out.

"A monk."

"Sir?"

"A monk was able to disarm and render unconscious twelve armed schoolgirls?"

Shiraishi nodded. "It certainly appears that way, sir."

"What about surveillance?"

"Sir?"

"The video cameras, Shiraishi. Have you been able to pull anything from any of the local surveillance cameras?"

Shiraishi looked confused. "We weren't aware there were any in the area, sir."

He sighed. Of course, this dolt did not know about the

cameras. Most of Japanese society didn't know about them. But the government had secretly and very quietly put an extensive network of video cameras throughout Japan's major cities. The cameras were linked to huge computer banks that constantly ran facial-recognition software, comparing the thousands of faces that passed by them daily with the faces of known radicals and terrorists.

But Shiraishi didn't know that. He wasn't supposed to know that. And the dim look on his face told him as much.

He cleared his throat. "The Internet café didn't have video cameras? All that computer equipment and they're not the least bit concerned about getting robbed?"

Shiraishi shrugged. "I'm not sure, sir."

"Well, maybe it would be worth the time to send an officer down there to see if maybe he does have any cameras. And if so, could he potentially have a glimpse of our mysterious monk lurking through a frame or two?"

Shiraishi turned and dispatched two officers to investigate.

He glanced back at the report and then looked back at Shiraishi. "What about a composite sketch?"

"Sir?"

"Of the monk, Shiraishi. If you've got the witnesses this report claims, then maybe they could get together and come up with some sort of rendition we might use to track this character down. I wouldn't think it would be too difficult to spot a monk in robes wandering the city with a staff, would you?"

"No, sir."

"Get it done."

"Right away, sir."

He glanced around. The emergency department was fairly

empty. The evening rush hadn't started yet and most of the staff was relaxed. He looked back at the report, aware that Shiraishi was looking at him again.

"What are we doing about the Japanese man and the American woman?"

"We have officers out looking for them, sir." Shiraishi looked decidedly uncomfortable. "But they seem to have disappeared."

He grinned. "Who can blame them? If I'd just been targeted by a dozen schoolgirls, I'd make myself scarce, too."

Shiraishi chuckled. "I'd expect so, sir."

He frowned at Shiraishi and the latter's grin vanished. "Go and find them. If they're out there, they're most likely hiding. And possibly scared. Try to imagine how you'd feel if you had a bunch of giggling whores trying to kill you."

"Yes, sir."

He stood up and walked around the ward. Five of the schoolgirls were conscious and resting comfortably. Six were still unconscious.

One was missing.

He turned to Shiraishi. "Where is the twelfth girl?"

"Sir?"

He waved the report in Shiraishi's face. "Twelve girls. There are eleven here right now. That means one is missing unless I somehow managed to graduate without knowing basic math skills."

"Yes, sir. One is gone, sir."

"Where is she, Shiraishi?"

"Radiology, sir. They wanted to take an X-ray of her skull. To make sure she didn't have any lasting damage."

Lasting damage indeed. He turned and strode from the emergency department.

If he was in their position, it's exactly how he would have chosen to do it. Isolate and extract the information.

It was risky, of course. But then again, these people didn't strike him as being scared of such risks. They would no doubt understand that the risk would outweigh the benefit to getting timely and accurate intelligence.

Now the job was getting really complicated.

He needed to make sure the girl didn't talk.

He knew that soon enough, the other girls would silently make their way out of the hospital and dissolve back into their regular boring teen lives. It was why he had recruited them in the first place. It always amazed him exactly what he could purchase if the money was right.

Even Japan, with its supposedly rigid moral values and strict code of ethics, wasn't impervious to the whims of greed and lust. Offer enough money and codes, morals, and ethics went right out of the window, never to be seen again.

Or at least long enough to make sure the check cleared.

But this twelfth girl concerned him. Alone and isolated from the rest of her friends, she would no doubt crack under whatever strain they intended to put her under. She would tell them what little she knew. And while he'd been as careful as he normally was, there were a few choice tidbits she might know that could put them on the right track.

And the right track would mean he would be identified as having his hand in something he most definitely didn't want people knowing he was involved with.

He banked left at the elevators and kept striding down the

hall. The look on his face must have convinced everyone he passed that talking to him simply wasn't a good idea.

He didn't care about being remembered. The latex makeup on his face would come off easily enough with hot water and soap. He could vanish within seconds, just by using the restroom.

But the girl knew his true identity.

And that was dangerous.

Maybe he'd gone too far in recruiting twelve of them. But he didn't want to underestimate Ogawa and Annja Creed. With Ogawa's deadly skills as a ninja and Creed's skills as a resourceful and wily warrior, using less than a dozen could have been disastrous.

He grinned.

Not as if this had been a great day out by any means.

He saw the radiology department doors ahead. He frowned. Automatic. That meant a motion sensor nearby, which would trigger the doors and cause noise. Noise that would alert them to the presence of someone outside.

He shook his head.

He backtracked until he found a side door. It was locked but he removed an electric pick from his pocket and slid it into the lock. He pressed the trigger and listened as the rake caught the tumblers and then he twisted.

The door opened.

He knew how hospitals were laid out. And he knew they always had multiple entrances and exits to every department. It simply didn't make sense to build a hospital and not have other ways out in case of an emergency.

He hoped they hadn't taken notice of other doors leading into their area.

It was the only chance he had to catch them off guard.

The corridor ran fifty feet and then at the end he saw a small unmarked door. Looking up at the ceiling, he guessed that this had to be the back door. He tried the door and found it locked so he used the electric pick again.

This time, he gently pulled the door back, praying that the hinges wouldn't squeak and alert his prey inside.

The door opened without a sound.

He glanced around one final time, but found the area deserted. Smiling, he withdrew his pistol and from his left pocket, he produced a suppressor, which he screwed on to the threaded barrel.

He entered the radiology department.

Hushed voices reached his ears. He paused, trying to distill the nature of the room's set up. He expected to hear the girl's voice and he did. And the harsh whisper belonged to a man.

Interesting.

He nosed around the corner and took a quick glimpse.

The schoolgirl faced him in a chair. Her eyes were closed and she was bound hand and foot to the chair. Tears streamed down her face. He could see the fear and shock and despair in her features.

The man crouched close by, whispering in her ear. His back was to the back door, as was the lithe form of the woman standing nearby. Both of them were dressed in hospital staff clothes.

He was glad he'd opted for the police uniform.

The schoolgirl whimpered, muttered something about how

she didn't know who it was that hired her. This didn't please the man. He said something to the woman with him and she nodded.

The schoolgirl saw the scalpel and started sobbing.

He leveled the pistol on the point between the schoolgirl's eyes and squeezed the trigger.

As his gun spit once, the girl's head snapped back, a black hole punching its way into her skull.

In that instant, the woman pivoted and flung something at him.

He jerked back as the thin black throwing spike embedded itself in the wall.

He ran to the rear door and tore it open. Racing down the hall, he thought about how unfortunate it was to have to kill someone so young. All of the schoolgirls were eighteen years old, so legally, they were adults. But it did little to make him feel good about what he'd just done.

It was a necessary evil, and nothing more.

At the end of the corridor, he banked left, then right and then through the doors. In an instant, he was gone.

17

Nezuma regarded the dead schoolgirl's corpse and then looked at Shuko. "Did you see who it was?"

She frowned. "No. But he was huge. Too big to have been a Japanese, even though he looked like one."

Nezuma nodded. "You think he wore makeup?"

"Along with the police uniform, yes. It would be a good way to get in here and not have to answer any questions."

"I wish we'd thought of it." Nezuma nudged the schoolgirl's body back. "It's time for us to go. Our friends will be waking up soon and they'll make a commotion. It will be only a small matter of time before they're found. And then they'll find the body here. Once that happens, they'll lock down the facility."

"We don't want to be trapped inside," Shuko said.

"Definitely not."

Nezuma stood and stripped off the white coat and Shuko did the same. They exited through the front of the radiology department and kept walking as naturally as possible. They passed a nurse wheeling a patient toward radiology.

Nezuma risked a glance back and then nudged Shuko. "Faster."

"You don't think we would have time to go to the emergency department and find another girl we could question?" she asked.

Nezuma shook his head. "That doesn't strike me as very smart. The police will be all over the place. We'd never make it. And once that nurse back there walks through the doors of radiology, this whole place is going to light up."

They passed the elevator bank and Nezuma guided Shuko out through a side door. They kept moving purposefully toward the parking lot. "We need to get out of here. That nurse will remember two people and if we're spotted together, they'll know," he said.

Shuko walked away without being asked. They'd had to split up in the past and Nezuma wasn't concerned about her safety. Shuko could take care of herself. He'd trained her that way.

They would rendezvous back at the train station, hoping to catch Ogawa and Creed on their way to wherever they were headed. It was always a gamble, but Nezuma felt certain they would head out of Osaka soon. The *dorje* was not here in the city; that much he knew. He suspected it was probably concealed somewhere in the rural lands to the east, home to the ancient ninja families that had sprung up during feudal Japan.

Nezuma himself had spent plenty of time in those fog-enshrouded mountains in his past. His own hunt for the *dorje* had been an overwhelming obsession with him ever since he was a youth.

And now, he was close to acquiring it at long last.

He just hoped that whoever was trying to kill Ogawa and Creed would not get to them until Nezuma had the *dorje* in his possession.

Only time would tell if that would happen.

FROM THE SHADOWED DEPTHS of the delivery van he watched the man and woman split up. He marveled at how they both seemed to be in perfect rhythm with each other. There were no stutter steps or pauses for conversation and the discussion of potential what-ifs. The woman simply changed direction and it was as if they had no knowledge of each other.

He frowned. He knew the woman could certainly throw *shuriken* with unerring accuracy. It was only thanks to his lightning-fast reflexes that he hadn't caught the sharpened spike in his skull or worse, his eye. He might be dead if that had happened.

The man he knew well enough. He was a trained killer even if he did his best to obscure that fact every time he entered a tournament. He figured the woman then must be one of his employees or lovers.

He was well aware of how a teacher-student relationship could turn into something more. But somehow, he couldn't see the stocky Nezuma letting himself fall into such a situation.

But stranger things had happened.

He raised the telephoto-lens camera and squeezed off several shots of the woman as she made her way across the parking lot. Twice, she seemed to look up and around and he thought she might have sensed him. He'd leaned back, deeper into the shadows and then cursed himself. There was no way her eyes would be able to penetrate the darkness of the van's interior.

She glided up to the four-foot fence and climbed over it with such ease that he almost jumped in surprise. It was only when she stopped at a pay phone to make a call that he turned his attention back to Nezuma.

NEZUMA'S EYES SWEPT the parking lot.

Something didn't feel right.

With all these cars, he wondered if someone was watching him. He chalked it up as paranoia resulting from a botched job. His ears had already picked up the roaring alarm bells from inside the hospital. Soon enough, more sirens would join the cacophony of sound.

As long as we're gone, he thought, that's all that matters.

He knew Shuko would make her way back downtown and from there, take a circuitous route back to the train station. Undoubtedly, she would meander, doing her utmost to lose anyone who might be interested in following her.

And if they stayed glued to her, she would simply kill them.

Nezuma's stomach growled and he realized it had been many hours since he had eaten anything.

On the way to the hospital, he recalled seeing a comfortable-looking restaurant that advertised fresh seafood.

His mouth watered.

A nice meal might be just the ticket to restoring his confidence in the overall mission.

HE WATCHED Nezuma enter the restaurant and then set the camera down next to the laptop computer he had open on the back floor of the van. He connected the USB cable to the computer and downloaded the pictures he had taken moments before.

He opened his e-mail program and composed a new message. After typing in the simple one-word name, along with a subject and priority, he typed, "Identify woman and provide history."

He clicked the attachment icon and included the best close-ups he had shot. Then he clicked Send and waited.

NEZUMA WASHED DOWN the meal with a beer. The silver can was thoroughly icy and he loved the crisp taste as it followed the excellent fish tempura he'd eaten. He belched appreciatively and drank long from the glass in front of him.

His cell phone purred and he opened it up.

"Yes?"

"Master." Shuko's voice licked at his ear.

"Are you all right?"

"Yes. I am in a coffee shop across the street from the train station."

"Did you get food yet?"

"Yes."

"Good, then we'll be all set for when we have to move."

She paused. "That's why I'm calling. I think you should come here as soon as you can."

"Is something wrong?"

"Not at all. I have managed to find Ogawa and the American woman Creed."

Nezuma's heart raced. "Excellent work. How did you locate them so quickly?"

"I came directly here and waited. They came in a few

moments ago and ordered some food. They are at the train station now. I followed them. They purchased tickets aboard a train bound for Mie Prefecture."

"Where in Mie?"

"Iga."

Nezuma smiled. As he'd expected. "Excellent. I will be there very soon."

He clicked off his phone and gestured the waitress over. She presented him with the bill and he left a wad of cash on the table. Nezuma believed in tipping well for a great meal.

And Shuko's news was the perfect dessert.

HIS E-MAIL DINGED and he sat up, aware that he'd nodded off. He clicked the new-message icon and waited. The message filled his screen.

Woman's name is Shuko. No known other names. Reported to be the only member of Nezuma's clan he trusts implicitly. No history available from usual sources. She is extremely dangerous.

He grinned. That much he already knew. But she intrigued him. People weren't born without any history. Someone must know something about her. And he wanted to know what they knew.

The reply button beckoned. He clicked it and began typing up a new message.

"THEY ARE still there?"

Shuko nodded. "They just boarded the train about ten

minutes ago. But it doesn't depart for another twenty minutes. We have time."

"And our tickets?"

Shuko handed him one. "The train runs express to Ueno and thereafter makes a series of local stops. It's my belief that they will get off in Ueno, however."

Nezuma nodded and scanned the train station again. "That makes the most sense. If they are attuned to their environment and suspect surveillance, they will opt to ensure they have a chance at losing us. It's what I would do."

Shuko handed him a cup. "I bought this for you."

Nezuma sniffed it. "Tea?"

"Yes."

"That was thoughtful."

She bowed. "I thought it would help make us less suspicious if we are seen as more of a couple than as a team."

He glanced at her and smiled. "I enjoy the way you think, Shuko-san."

"And I will enjoy helping you finally acquire the *dorje* you have sought for so long."

Nezuma gestured at the train. "Let's get aboard. The sooner we find seats, the better. I don't want a crowd inhibiting our vantage points."

HE WATCHED from the concourse as Nezuma and the woman called Shuko boarded the train. His request for any information, even from questionable sources, came back with nothing.

He frowned. How was it possible for someone to have no history whatsoever? Surely there was something out there he'd be able to use to his advantage.

He would need to keep using his networks to scour for information.

In the meantime, he would keep tabs on Nezuma and his escort.

Perhaps fate would dictate that he and Shuko have a face-to-face meeting sooner rather than later.

He smiled at the thought.

And then bought a train ticket.

18

The Japan Railway train shuddered along the old steel tracks, twisting through the dense rural countryside of Mie Prefecture. Annja stared out the window, wondering about what Taka had told them prior to their departure from the temple in Osaka.

The old man had collected their teacups and led them down a hallway to another room filled with maps stuffed into a honeycomb of cubbyholes. He took one of the maps—more a scroll than anything else—and unfurled it on a low table. Crude line drawings showed a detailed overlay. Taka traced his finger along what might have been contour lines.

"The *yamabushi*," he said, "had a series of tunnels built into the very mountains of Iga itself. It was one such thing that helped them cultivate their aura of supernatural ability, much like the ninja."

Ken had pointed at the map. "And the *vajra* is hidden there?"

"Somewhere in there," Taka said. "The system of caves is supposedly very dense, with various traps and pitfalls to waylay the uninitiated. I doubt very much any of the *yama-bushi* still in the area would guide you to what you seek."

"I'm sure we'll be all right," Ken said. "As long as we know the general direction."

"There's more," Taka said. "An ancient guardian protects the *vajra* and the caves."

"What kind of guardian?" Annja asked.

"A *kappa*," Taka said. "Swamp vampire."

Annja had smiled. "Are you kidding?"

Taka shook his head. "Absolutely not. I'm merely telling you that it is rumored to patrol the area. You would be wise to keep its presence in mind. I don't imagine you'd like to run into one of those."

Ken had waved it off. "Superstitions are one thing. I'm much more concerned about the very real threats Annja and I have been facing since we started this journey together."

Taka held up one finger. "Superstitions, whether you believe in them or not, exist for many reasons. Not the least of which might just be that they actually do exist regardless of what you happen to think."

"A pesky, stout dwarfish creature with a bowl of sake on his head is not going to deter me from finding what is rightfully mine to return to my family's ancestral home. I wouldn't be much of a worthy inheritor if I allowed myself to be swayed by that now, would I?" Ken shook his head. "Thank you for your hospitality and for the information. But we should be going now."

ANNJA GLANCED at Ken, who was sleeping beside her. They had walked from the temple to the train station and purchased tickets for the local train that ran northwest of Osaka into the Iga countryside. Now, as the train shot past the trees, Annja turned back to the window and could see the mountains some distance away with puffs of gray-and-white clouds hugging their peaks.

"This is the birthplace of *ninjitsu*," he said.

She saw that Ken was now awake. "Is it really?"

He nodded. "The land here is rough. Not too many roads lead through it, even less in the old days. It made for a perfect refuge for those who practiced what many believed were dark arts. They called ninja 'sorcerers' in league with demons and various other evil creatures. In reality, the ninja used their enemies' beliefs to their advantage. Still, it's difficult to travel through this land without wondering if there really is some truth to the old legends and superstitions."

"You don't think we're going to have a run-in with a sake-drinking creature, do you?"

He smiled. "Like Taka said, you never know."

"I'd prefer to imagine the *yamabushi* might have better things to do with their time than invest too much in trying to make a legend come to life."

Ken nodded. "I'm more concerned about the traps inside the caves. We'll need some supplies."

"Those mountains look big," Annja said. "What's the weather going to be like?"

"Cold at night the higher up we go," Ken said. "We'll need extra clothing, flashlights, that sort of thing. You've done this before, right?"

"I'm no novice," Annja said. "As long as you can find us a store, we should be all set."

Ken leaned back. "We'll arrive in about forty minutes. We should get some sleep. Who knows how far we might have to hike to reach the entrance to the caves."

"That's if we find the caves," Annja said.

He grinned. "Just have some faith. I think we'll be fine."

Annja settled back and closed her eyes. She hoped Ken was right.

"I WAS VERY DISPLEASED to learn of the potentially lethal interference brought about by the Onigawa-gumi." Nezuma spoke into the cell phone while watching Shuko as she made her way back down the train car to where he sat.

The voice in his ear spoke for several more seconds. Nezuma sighed. "Well, let's hope there are no more complications. If the Onigawa cannot control themselves, then we may never learn where the *dorje* is hidden. And if that happens, we are right back to where we started, which is to say nowhere."

He disconnected and looked at Shuko. "Did you find them?"

"Two cars ahead of us. Both are asleep."

Nezuma nodded. "Good. At least they are none the worse for wear after that silly assault in Osaka."

"I take it the Onigawa-gumi played it off as nothing?"

Nezuma shook his head. "The Yakuza are fools. They have little appreciation for what the *dorje* means and how it can be used to further all of our agendas if it is handled properly. Kennichi's behavior has angered them substantially. They feel he has caused them a tremendous loss of face and mean to make him pay for it. Unleashing their child assassins was their pathetic attempt to make him feel like less of a man for being forced to deal with them."

"There's no evidence that he did deal with them," Shuko said.

"And the people you spoke to confirmed it was one man who took them all out?"

Shuko nodded. "They were quite specific, actually. They didn't call him a man at all. They said he was a monk. Complete with the ringed staff and everything. There was little doubt about what he'd done."

"And they report that there was some sort of strange fog or mist?"

"They say the alley filled with mist and the monk walked right into the midst of it, taking the assassins out as easily as drawing a breath. When he was done, he simply walked back out of the alley and vanished in the crowds."

Nezuma smiled. "That must have played well with the police."

"I imagine they have no idea what to do with the case," Shuko said. "Presumably, they will lose it in the bottomless pile of unsolved mysteries they have."

"Presumably," Nezuma said. "In the meantime, we are somewhat closer to our own goal of recovering the *dorje*."

Shuko frowned. "You really think she will hand it over to us?"

"Of course not."

"But you asked her for it anyway."

Nezuma brushed a hand along the length of Shuko's hair. She leaned into him and closed her eyes. Nezuma leaned closer to her ear and whispered, "She must be allowed to feel like she still has some measure of control over her own destiny. Otherwise, she will feel like a trapped animal and respond accordingly. That will not help us. By allowing her to still feel some semblance of power, she will play right into our hands."

Shuko looked into his eyes. "Have I always played into your hands?"

Nezuma glanced around the train car. They were almost alone save for five other passengers. Still, as much as he desired Shuko, he would not allow himself to falter.

He pushed her away. "The question has always been, who is playing into whose hand?"

She grinned and went back to looking out the window. "I suppose one day we will have to discover the answer to that."

"There will be time later," Nezuma said. "For now, we have but one thing to set our minds to."

She glanced back at him. "Only one?"

He smiled. "Perhaps later…at the *ryokan*, there may be time for us to briefly allow ourselves an interlude."

"I like interludes," Shuko said.

"As do I." He licked his lips, then looked out of the window at the passing countryside. "And when we have our hands on the *dorje* at long last, there will be many more such interludes."

Shuko nodded. "As long as we can keep the Yakuza from guessing we have recovered it."

"That will be the biggest task of all, I fear," Nezuma said. "Finding the *dorje* thus far has largely been uncomplicated. Kennichi, for all his skill, is still resolved to finding it. Since he doesn't know where it is, it makes it harder for him to elude our surveillance, as much as he might try."

"I'm not convinced he is trying," Shuko said. "And I must admit I find that suspicious."

"You think he knows we are on his trail?"

"I think he would be a pretty pathetic ninja if he did not assume he had other interested parties following him."

Nezuma frowned. "And yet he makes no attempt to discourage our pursuit."

"Exactly."

"I see why you are concerned. But perhaps his mind is as fixated on the prize as mine is. Perhaps he has allowed himself to be blinded by it."

Shuko shook her head. "You may be fixated, but you are still in control of your faculties. You still coordinate the recovery efforts rather than simply allow yourself to become blindly obsessed."

Nezuma shrugged. "Perhaps Kennichi is less skilled than we thought."

"Or he may be more skilled than we give him credit for. He may well be setting a trap for us to walk into," Shuko said.

Nezuma smiled. "There would be very little he could arrange that would take us by surprise. I have, after all, the finest partner one could ever wish for."

Shuko frowned. "I appreciate the compliment, master. But I would prefer to reserve judgment about Kennichi until we have the item we seek in hand. And he and the woman are both dead."

"I wonder how Miss Creed will react when she learns that it is I who has been taunting her at every stage of the game. Surely she will replay the ending moments of my victory over her at the *budokan* over and over. I imagine it will be enough to stop her in her tracks and enable me to finally strike her down dead."

Shuko smiled. "I will enjoy that."

Nezuma shook his head. "She should never have stepped into the ring. An American woman in the *budokan* fighting? It disgusts me to even consider it. I certainly hope she learned her lesson."

"Doubtful," Shuko said. "She seems far too stubborn for such a thing to sink into her mind."

"Death, then," Nezuma said, "is the only way for her to truly understand."

"And the Yumegakure-ryu will cease to exist, as well."

Nezuma nodded. "Kennichi Ogawa, the last descendant in that troublesome ninja family, will finally find himself out of options. He will go down fighting—I have little doubt of that."

"And then we will see what skills he truly does have at his disposal."

Nezuma looked at her. "I am glad you are with me."

Shuko bowed her head low. "As am I. Thank you for the opportunity to serve you once more."

"You are my finest pupil. It is only fitting."

"And if it comes down to it, will you permit me the honor of dispatching Ogawa?"

"Not the woman?" Nezuma smiled.

Shuko frowned. "The woman has offended you. It is proper that you administer the justice she so badly needs."

"And you take out Ogawa? That's a lot of history to kill, my dear."

Her eyes flashed. "You don't doubt my skills, do you?"

He laughed. "Of course not. If I had any concerns about your abilities, you wouldn't be here."

She leaned back. "I apologize."

He placed his hand on top of hers. "No need. We are both passionate about what we'll be doing. Soon enough, we'll be rid of the troublesome pair and be able to use the *dorje* to create the destiny we have dreamed of."

19

Annja welcomed the fresh air of Iga as she and Ken disembarked at the main city of Ueno. The station wasn't crowded and they were able to find a cab easily. As they slid in, Ken gave the driver some quick directions and they were off.

Ken pointed. "See that?"

Annja followed his line of sight and took a breath. A massive feudal castle rose out of the landscape. "That's amazing."

"Ueno Castle. It's been renovated and refurbished, but is largely the way it was hundreds of years ago when this part of the country was known as a thriving castle town. The walls are almost thirty yards tall."

Annja looked at the graceful white walls that seemed to spring up toward the sky. "It almost looks like a bird."

Ken smiled. "It's also known as *hakuho*, because it resembles a white phoenix taking off from a bed of green leaves." He looked behind them and continued to smile. "Would you like to stop?"

Annja nodded. "If there's time."

"I think we can make time. It's a nice diversion."

The cab let them off near the hundreds of steps that led to the castle's main entrance. Ken stood at the bottom and looked at Annja. "Race you."

Annja laughed. "You're kidding."

"Nope." Ken dashed up the steps. Annja gave chase and they were soon at the top. Annja gasped for some breath, but as usual, Ken seemed hardly fazed by the exertion.

"You must be in amazing shape."

He shrugged. "I suppose."

"Don't be so modest—it's really annoying," Annja said.

He smiled. "Sorry, I just don't think all that much about it. I train, but don't necessarily get maniacal about it. However I am is just a matter of what I've done and continue to do. No big deal."

Annja looked around. "It's even more impressive close up."

Ken paid for the tickets and they headed through the entrance. After a brief walk, they came into the main entry hall. A huge assortment of ancient Japanese weapons— swords, spears, daggers, halberds and more—decorated the area along with suits of samurai armor, giant *taiko* drums, masks, scrolls and even palanquins for carting royalty about.

Annja couldn't help herself. She had to look at everything. "What sort of weapon is that?" she asked, pointing out a long wooden pole with a curved blade at the end.

"A *naginata*," Ken said. "Traditionally, it was used by samurai women. There are still some amazing teachers of the art in Japan. The weapon itself it quite effective at dealing with mounted opponents, as you might imagine."

"The poor horse," Annja said.

Ken nodded. "Different times back then. I'm sure there was plenty of waste, regardless of species."

"How tall is the castle?"

"Five stories, but with the refurbishment work, they've reduced it to three floors only. You can see most of the city from the second-floor windows." He smiled. "Why don't we head up there now?"

Ken led them upstairs. A long corridor stretched before them. "Takatora Todo had this expanded to its present size in 1611. He was famous for his skills during the Warring States period. The castle still houses a lot of his personal effects and those of his family."

"When did they refurbish it?" Annja asked.

"Primarily in 1935, if I remember correctly. But I'm sure they've done other things over the years to make it accessible to everyone."

They reached the windows and looked out. Annja smiled. "Not a very big city, is it?"

"No, but then again, we are in the countryside. Ueno is a nice enough place to visit. But the surrounding area is where the real treasures lie."

"Literally," Annja said.

Ken smiled. "Apparently so, yes." He glanced down at the entryway and grinned. "Perhaps we should get going."

Why's he acting so weird? Annja wondered. "All right, but this time I'm going to win that race back down the steps."

Ken put his hand on her arm. "How about we take a different way out of here? That way, you'll get a chance to see everything about the castle."

Annja didn't like the tone of his voice. She closed her eyes for a brief second to make sure the sword was where she could pull it out if need be. It was and she nodded to Ken. "Fine. Let's go."

Ken led her toward a small sliding screen door with a small sign that Annja assumed meant something like Staff Only. It was dark and cool in the dimly lit space. Ken opened another door to a set of what looked like emergency steps that led down. He glanced back at Annja. "Are you okay?"

"Fine," she said.

Ken descended and Annja followed him. The space was extremely tight and at the bottom, she had to duck to get out of the staircase. Ken led her past airtight trunks full of weapons and armor. She could see a lit sign above a doorway in the distance.

"Exit?"

Ken nodded. "Yes. We'll leave through this door."

He pushed through it and the sudden daylight made Annja wince for a second. "Ouch," she said.

Ken held the door. "Sorry, they really ought to make that stairway a bit brighter. It's harmful when you go back outside."

They stood next to one of the tall stone walls. Annja glanced up but couldn't see any part of the castle from her vantage point. "Where are we?"

"A back exit. As you can see, it's tough to see the castle from here. And for anyone in the castle looking down, it's tough to see us while we stand here."

"Are we hiding?"

Ken looked around and then back at Annja. "We've had company with us since we left Ueno-shi."

Annja frowned. She had no sense of that. There'd been no warning. "Are you certain?" she asked.

"Absolutely."

"Who are they?"

Ken shook his head. "I'm not sure. It's a couple, though. A man and a woman. Both Japanese."

Annja sighed. "So, now what? Do we ambush them or what?"

"Hardly. That would be counterproductive to what we're trying to achieve."

"Yeah, but—"

"The best course of action," Ken said, "is to get as far away from them as possible. Right now, they should be in the main entryway. They'll go upstairs and look down and realize we aren't there anymore. That's when they'll get nervous about losing us."

"So, we'd better leave now. Come on," Annja said.

Ken shook his head. "No. We wait."

"What on earth for? We have a head start. We can get into the woods before they do and they'll never know where to look for us."

Ken leaned against the stone wall. "Have you ever done any escape-and-evasion training?"

"Uh, no."

He nodded. "One of the lessons I learned while I was going through that myself was how to discourage pursuers."

"And you're going to enlighten me."

"If you'll permit me, yes."

Annja leaned against the stone wall with him. "Fine."

Ken smiled. "It's only one option, but when there's a group

of people pursuing you, you can try to get behind them. You have to find a way to penetrate their line as they progress. Then once you're behind them, you have a certain amount of freedom. You can go back the way you came and go off in a different direction entirely."

Annja watched the sun start to dip behind the clouds to the west. "Is this what we're attempting to do now? Penetrate their line?"

"Yes."

"And you really think they'll freak out when they can't find us?"

"Absolutely. I don't think they know where we're headed. Otherwise they would have moved on us already."

"You think it's the Yakuza?"

Ken shook his head. "No. I think these are your friends. Not mine."

"The ones who broke into my hotel room?"

"Presumably."

Annja sighed. "Wonderful."

"You didn't really expect them to give you the freedom they promised, did you? They'd be fools if they did."

"I don't know what I expected."

"They need to keep tabs on you. This is how they'll do so. And they must be quite committed to the hunt since I've been doing little things throughout our trip to discourage potential tagalongs."

"Maybe they're good," Annja said.

"They are good," Ken replied. "I have no doubt of that. Now it will be a matter of seeing if they fall for my little ruse or not."

"And how are we going to be able to tell that?"

Ken led her away from where they'd been standing to a small pathway that ran alongside the moat of the castle. Annja could smell the hyacinth bushes and assorted other late-blooming flowers that sprang up this time of year. "Smells nice."

"Not in the moat," Ken said with a low chuckle. He parted some of the bushes and entered them.

"You're kidding."

His face reappeared. "Would you please get in here?"

Annja glanced around. Anyone seeing this would assume the two of them were engaged in some sort of sexual shenanigans. She grinned. Not that that would be such a horrible thing. "If my clothes get torn, you owe me," she said.

She ducked inside and followed Ken for a hundred yards or so through the dense foliage. When they emerged, they were on a steep embankment that overlooked the road leading to Ueno Castle.

Ken pointed. "There's the train station."

"I didn't realize it was so close. Why did you waste money on the cab fare?"

He shrugged. "It was necessary to see our pursuers. If we'd walked, it would have been harder to spot them."

"I can see the entrance to the castle from here."

"Exactly. But it's difficult for us to be seen provided we keep ourselves low." Ken checked his watch. "I would say any moment now we'll learn if we've been successful or not."

"There," Annja said. "A man and a woman just came flying down the steps toward that cab."

"Indeed."

Annja watched them climb into the taxi. The cab sat there

for a moment before shooting away from the curb. It rolled down the street toward them.

"Down!" Ken said.

Annja felt herself being yanked backward. Her back hit the ground hard and she lay there trying to catch her breath. Beside her, she could hear Ken breathing softly. After a moment, he rolled over to face her.

"You okay?"

"I think so."

"Sorry about that. I suddenly realized that they could see us if they were looking up as they drove past. Something they were probably doing anyway just to make sure."

Annja sighed. "It's not so bad laying here with the trees all around us."

"It is kind of nice."

She turned on to her side and stared at Ken. "Why did you bring me along to find the *vajra*?"

"Because I admire your ability to locate things."

"Is that all?"

He smiled. "Does there need to be something more?"

Annja sat up. "I guess not."

Ken sat beside her. "We should get going now. There are several small inns located a few miles from here. Any one of them will make a good place to hole up before we get started tomorrow morning."

"What about gear?"

Ken nodded. "There's a store on the way I know about."

"Will they know about it, too?"

"I doubt it. This isn't a store that advertises itself." He stood and held out his hand. "Come on."

20

The door was built of solid sheet metal and rusted through in the lower section. Flakes of it lay scattered about the ground. Next to the door was a single buzzer, which Ken pushed.

"Now what?" Annja asked.

"We wait, of course."

Annja glanced around the neighborhood. Waiting didn't seem to be a very wise idea. They were on the back side of Ueno, tucked down a side alley lined with topless bars and *pachinko* parlors. Already Annja had felt the eyes of scores of thugs checking her out.

"Seems a little odd that we're hanging out in this part of town. If we're trying to avoid the Yakuza, then playing in their neighborhood seems a bit silly," she said.

Ken shook his head. "The Onigawa-gumi doesn't control Iga. We're as safe as we can possibly be, given the environment."

"Wonderful."

Across from them, a group of five men stood drinking

from a single bottle. One of them finished it and threw it to the ground, where it shattered into a thousand pieces. None of them seemed particularly thrilled that they were suddenly out of booze.

"Ken…"

"Relax, Annja. They won't come near us."

"I wish I could be as sure as you seem to be."

Darkness had claimed the city as soon as they had walked there from Ueno Castle. By the time they found their way through the labyrinth of alleys and dead ends, the shadows had grown long and the last bits of sunlight had twinkled out.

One of the drunks yelled at Ken. Annja had no idea what he said, but she imagined it probably went something like, "Hey, what the hell are you doing on our turf?"

Ken laughed.

"What's so funny?"

"He said he'd let me live if I handed you over."

"Lovely." Annja felt herself getting angry. Plus, her stomach hurt. Neither of which boded well for anyone in her path. She closed her eyes and checked for the sword. It was where it should have been and when she reopened her eyes, she felt a smidgen better.

Another drunk said something to the other men. They all laughed.

"Great," Annja said. "Here we go."

The drunk took a single step forward and then fell flat on his face. The rest of his gang bent over laughing at him. They helped him up and together, they staggered down the alley toward the main street.

"I told you it wouldn't be a problem," Ken said. "Drunks in Japan are mostly harmless."

"Mostly?"

"Well, every once in a while someone gets into a bit of a stew. But mostly, they're just all talk and no action."

"Lucky for us." Annja glanced back at the door. "Are we waiting on someone to come down and open this or what?"

"Yes."

From inside, she heard a sudden clanging of locks and bolts. Ken turned around and grinned. "Ah."

The door swung open and a bright flashlight beam cut into the darkness. It flashed from Annja's face to Ken's.

A voice spoke English with a Brooklyn twang. "What do you want?"

Ken waved the flashlight away. "If you don't mind, I'm trying to preserve some of my night vision."

The beam vanished. "Answer the question or I shoot you both."

Ken sighed. "It's me, Jiro."

"Ken-san?"

"*Hai.*"

"Oh, wow. Sorry dude. I thought you were one of those drunks from down the way. They're always taking pot shots at my door. One of them ruined the rust I've been cultivating. You see that shit?"

Ken nodded. "Could we maybe think about coming in? We've still got to find rooms for tonight after we get what we need from you."

Jiro backed away from the door and Annja could see him for the first time. He looked all of about twenty years old with short, bristly, jet-black hair sticking out at all angles from his scalp. He was dressed in black jeans and a gray sweatshirt. From inside the building, Annja could make out the steady thumping of a bass line.

"Took you long enough to open the door," Ken said. "My companion was getting nervous about your neighbors."

Jiro eyed Annja. "Sorry about that. Got the tunes crankin' upstairs. I'm Jiro."

"Annja."

Jiro glanced back at Ken and said something in Japanese. Ken frowned. "That'll be enough."

Jiro backed away from the door. "This way, folks."

He led them down a short corridor to an old elevator. He pulled back the grate and stepped inside. Annja and Ken managed to fit, as well, but only just.

Jiro slid the grate shut. "Next stop, the store."

The elevator whined as it strained to reach the upper level. At last, Annja made out ambient light spilling out of the rooms upstairs. The elevator ground to a halt and Jiro opened the grate again.

"Welcome."

Annja stepped out and was met with stacks upon stacks of crates and boxes, all with lettering in a variety of languages.

"What is this place?" she asked.

Ken stood beside her. "You've been doing well for yourself, Jiro."

"Yeah, business is pretty decent."

The music was louder up there. Jiro found the remote and turned it down. "Sorry. I wasn't expecting anyone tonight."

Ken shook his head. "Didn't you tell me once that all of your customers drop by unannounced?"

"Well, yeah, but—"

"Here we are," Ken said. "And we need stuff."

Annja cleared her throat. "Are you going to answer my question?"

Ken pointed at Jiro. "His place, he should explain."

Jiro bowed. "I'm a bit of a collector. Other people rip stuff off and I take it in and resell it. I'm a distributor of sorts."

"You're a fence," Annja said. "You traffic in stolen goods."

Jiro frowned. "You make it sound so dirty."

"It is illegal."

Jiro sighed. "Man, just when I thought Ken might have scored himself a really cool babe, you gotta go and pull that holier-than-thou crap. Yeah, it's stolen, but so what? I'm just taking a small piece of the pie away from the big corporate suckholes who profit endlessly from cheap labor and tax breaks. They're the bigger thieves."

"And Jiro doesn't actually steal the stuff himself," Ken said. "He just sells it at a bit of a profit."

Annja glanced at him. "You're defending this?"

"Sure."

"I find that interesting given everything we've talked about in relation to good versus evil."

Ken smiled. "I told you I used the Yakuza for their connections. I told you I paid them a decent sum of money for their help. And they are as illegal as they come. Why are you so shocked that I would use other illegal channels to achieve my goals?"

Annja shrugged. "I just thought that you might steer away from this stuff."

Jiro leaned against a crate. "It's a little different here than back Stateside, Annja. Sometimes things are intertwined in such a way that it's almost impossible to separate them. And I happen to supply lots of people from a pretty broad spectrum."

Ken held out his hands. "And we certainly need his help."

"We do?" Annja asked.

"You know of any other stores in Ueno that are going to carry what we need at this time of night?"

"No."

"Neither do I. And besides, I always believe in trying to throw a few bucks to my friends if I can manage it."

"Just a few?" Jiro asked. "I would have left the door locked if I'd known you weren't going to make it worth my time."

Ken sighed. "We need stuff for hiking and camping in the mountains."

"Which mountains?"

Ken raised an eyebrow. "The ones around here."

Jiro held up a hand. "Hey, my man, you never know what people are going to ask for. I had a guy in here last month going to Kathmandu looking for some serious gear to handle the big stuff. How am I supposed to know what your plans are?"

"All right, just get us outfitted, will you? And try to make it compact. We don't need the five-star treatment, just the bare necessities."

"Well, that's no fun," Jiro said. "Wait here."

He vanished into the crates and Annja could hear him rummaging through a variety of boxes. "How's the training going anyway?" Jiro asked Ken.

"Well. How about yours?"

Jiro's head popped up. "Finally got my *shodan*."

"Congratulations."

"A black belt," Annja said, "what style?"

"Judo."

"Jiro's been training for almost twelve years now."

Annja lowered her voice. "It's taken him that long to get his black belt?"

Ken nodded. "Judo training here in Japan is very austere. They promote very slowly to discourage rank hounds from even signing up. But Jiro is quite accomplished at what he does. I've seen him take down men twice his size on the street without batting an eye."

A pair of black backpacks landed at their feet. Annja bent and picked one up. The ripstop nylon would repel rain and keep the contents dry. It was large enough to fit a change of clothes and provisions along with some rope. "Seems decent enough," she said.

"They're made in Egypt. Cheap knockoffs, but just as good qualitywise," Jiro said. "I wouldn't try to pass them off as L.L. Bean goods, but I don't think that's on your agenda anyway. Am I right?"

"Yes," Ken said.

Jiro vanished again and Annja turned to Ken. "You've known each other for a long time?"

"About ten years. Jiro supplies me whenever I go abroad. I met him when he was a pickpocket in Kyoto, eking out a living stealing wallets from tourists. I encouraged him to think a little bigger."

"And you got him into stolen goods?"

Ken smiled. "You have to admit it's a step up."

"I guess."

Jiro came around the corner with a box full of canned goods. "You guys like ravioli?"

Annja took a can and recognized the familiar smiling face of a well-known American brand of canned pasta. "Sure."

"You don't have any noodles?" Ken asked.

"Sorry pal, fresh out. I've got British rations in the back, though, if you want those instead."

"Not a chance."

"Wise move," Jiro said. "How about sleeping bags?"

"We'll need them," Ken said.

Annja started loading the backpacks with the canned ravioli. "How long do you think we'll be out there? These are pretty heavy."

"Hopefully no longer than a day or two." Ken shook his head. "I don't think I'll be able to stand ravioli after that."

"It's for a good cause," Annja said. "Just imagine how good it'll taste once we get it warmed up."

"Can't wait," Ken said.

Several jackets, sweaters and pants came flying out of the darkness of the crates. Jiro's voice called out, "I've estimated sizes, so don't yell at me if it's not a perfect fit for you guys. I'm not running a clothing store. But it should fit pretty well anyway."

Annja picked up some of the clothes and held them up. The dark parkas seemed well suited to the cooler climate of the mountains. She passed a pair of cargo pants to Ken, who slid them into a backpack.

Jiro came back with two sleeping bags. "You'll love these.

Latest generation from Canada. Specifically built to roll up small but balloon up and conserve heat. Plus they're nice and roomy. I've got a pair of hunting knives in here, as well, because knowing Ken, you guys aren't that far removed from trouble."

Annja smiled. "You've got a rep."

Ken shrugged. "I try to live it down, truly I do."

Jiro slapped the sleeping bags down and handed them each a knife. "All right, now the fun stuff really begins."

"Fun stuff?" Annja asked.

Ken sighed. "That's what Jiro says when it's time to figure out how much I owe him."

21

Shuko's naked body glistened with sweat. Nezuma could see every thin cord of wiry muscle wrapping itself around her bones, throbbing beneath her skin like some majestic hidden snake. Her eyes blazed.

Nezuma waited for her in the neck-deep waters of the *ofuro* steam bath. The temperature hovered just above one hundred degrees, and in contrast to the night air, the steam wafted about them both as Shuko approached the cedar-lined bath.

She lifted one leg to step over the edge into the water and Nezuma smiled with appreciation. She saw where his eyes were staring and moved her leg ever so slightly to conceal herself. She knew it drove him crazy.

Her leg slid into the waters totally without fear. She leaned forward and brought the rest of herself into the water. She stood before Nezuma and said nothing. She never did when they made love.

Shuko sank into the water up to her neck and dipped her

head back into the water. When she came up, her wet hair streaked down her back, framing her face.

It had taken them years before each was comfortable enough with the other to indulge in the sex they both knew they wanted. Nezuma had taken her to Paris one week close to Christmas and had shown her the Eiffel Tower. They had dined in the finest restaurant in Paris, drunk the finest wine and then gone back to his room, where he undressed her as if he were uncovering the most delicate and delectable treasure. She had exploded in pleasure the moment they connected.

Now, Nezuma could see her eyes drooping into the limpid state that he loved in all beautiful women. Shuko knew precisely how to use her sexuality to her utmost advantage. He had seen her do it enough times since their first encounter. Shuko could seduce men and women with ease. She usually seduced them in order to kill them or steal their secrets.

She drew closer to him, her moist lips brushing the surface of the water.

The ritual varied, but the goal was always the same—see how long they could stand being this close to contact before one of them gave in.

Shuko eased away from Nezuma with a teasing smile.

He almost broke into a wide smile, but forced himself to stay utterly impassive. It drove her crazy when he seemed unreachable like that, and it would escalate the tension and the enjoyment of the game.

"You don't like me?" she said.

"You know I do," he said finally.

Shuko moved toward him, but he stopped her.

And instead he brought both of his hands around her neck and squeezed.

Her eyes popped open, going white with terror.

She tried to speak, but Nezuma's grip was total and without any gaps. Air simply would not flow and enable the words to escape the python-like grasp he had on her throat.

He expected her to fight.

She did not.

He leaned close to her face. "It was your idea that we should leave Ueno Castle this afternoon and chase after our prey like a pair of fools."

Her head shook just a little bit. The color in her face deepened as she struggled to maintain consciousness.

"Now, we have lost them."

He could feel her pulse throbbing against the dam he'd created with his grip. Blood desperately wanted to get into her head while more wanted to get out of it. Neither would succeed as long as he held her the way he did.

"You know that I do not tolerate failure," he said.

Her eyes implored him. If she could have spoken, she might have pleaded with him for mercy. But Nezuma was not a merciful man.

Not tonight anyway.

"We could have stayed longer and possibly found them, but your carelessness and impatience made us look like fools. Worse, we looked like amateurs and lost our strategic ground to a ninja of all things."

He leaned closer and kissed her lips. They already felt cooler to the touch.

Pretty soon, he reasoned, she'd lose consciousness. If he

kept the pressure on after that, her brain would starve for oxygen and she would die.

"Let this be a lesson to you."

He increased the pressure on her trachea. Her body started to spasm. Her limbs flailed, thrashing in the water, spilling the contents of the *ofuro* bath over the side.

"No one is safe from my wrath. Not even the likes of you—a woman I truly love."

He released her.

Shuko gasped loudly and then immediately retched over the side of the tub, spraying vomit over the surface of the deck. She collapsed in the water, her hands on her neck, trying desperately to flush her system with oxygen.

She drank a little bit of the water and then spit that over the side, ridding herself of the last bits of vomit in her mouth.

"M-master…"

Shuko's breathing was shallow and intense.

"I apologize for my stupidity, master."

Nezuma smiled. "I know you do."

"It will not happen again."

"No," Nezuma said. "Because if it does, I will not release you from certain death. You will die by my hand."

He looked deep into her eyes and bared his teeth.

"Let's go to bed now. We have much to do tomorrow." He gathered his red kimono. "Hopefully, we can find some way to make up for the grave mistakes you made today."

22

"Nice place."

Ken looked around the expanse of the *ryokan* rural inn and nodded. "These places are what I love best about traveling out of the city. You'll find old-world charm and people who still strive to keep tradition alive in spite of the onslaught of technological advances."

Annja grinned. "Sounds like you've made that speech before."

"Never," Ken said. "I'll get us checked in."

"I don't suppose they have a vacancy sign out front?"

"Not really."

Annja stepped over the crushed-gravel walkway, aware that her footsteps made a lot of noise in the dark of night. To her left sat a heavy stone lantern with a candle burning inside that cast some light onto the walkway. But it was far from overpowering, merely a gentle flickering glow that helped her find her way.

Ken, naturally, walked right across the gravel barely making a sound. Annja frowned. "Show-off," she muttered.

He glanced around. "Huh? Oh, sorry."

"I don't suppose you give out free lessons on exactly how you're doing that without making a lick of noise?"

He stopped and pointed at his knees. "I keep my knees bent. And my footsteps are much closer together—a short stride."

"Is that it?"

He smirked. "My feet also don't lift and stomp down on the rocks. They roll over them. It's a sort of rolling footwork that compacts the stones together before too much weight is applied and causes the action to make a lot of noise."

Annja tried lowering herself on bent knees and kept her feet closer together as she rolled across. The stones still made noise when she tried it.

"It does take a great deal of practice," Ken said. "And leaves are even tougher."

"Swell," Annja said. "I guess I flunk out as a ninja-in-training, huh?"

"Maybe you can get some gravel installed at your apartment in Brooklyn."

She pointed. "Now, there's a thought. A bad one, but it's a thought.nonetheless."

Ken smiled. "I'll go ahead and check us in while you practice." He moved on, leaving Annja alone in the darkness.

Bend my knees, she thought, frowning again. I was bending my knees. And then the rolling footwork. How the hell did he do that? She bent her knees again and tried allowing her feet to come down almost in an arc with the heel touching first and then the rest of the foot as she rolled across the stone.

This time, the noise was greatly reduced.

"Hey, cool—"

She stopped.

A breeze had scampered across the area, rustling tree limbs and leaves. She shivered and realized she felt tense. She turned and looked out into the night. The ambient light from the lantern wasn't so bright that she couldn't see into the darkness.

All around the inn the mist-enshrouded mountains of Iga loomed. The birthplace of *ninjitsu* was what Ken called it. She shivered again as another breeze laid its hand across her shoulders. Imagine the history of this place, she thought. Imagine what it would have been like traveling through here at night hundreds of years ago when this region was controlled by the ninja.

Annja frowned. She was letting her imagination run away with itself. She was, after all, a scientist, and even though Ken had certainly proved that ninja still existed and Annja herself had trained in some of their amazing techniques, she was letting the superstitions about them get a hold of her mind.

And that was dangerous.

Still, it was somewhat spooky being out in the night like this when everything else was completely silent.

Where was Ken?

She moved up the path and found the entrance to the inn. From inside, much brighter light spilled onto the gravel walkway. She saw Ken talking to the innkeeper, a gaunt old man wrapped in a dull gray kimono.

As Annja approached, the innkeeper looked around Ken and frowned when he saw her. He muttered something to Ken, who barked back at him.

Annja could feel the tension immediately escalate. "Everything okay?"

Ken looked back at her. "Give me a moment, would you?"

"Sure." Annja backed out and waited just outside the entrance. She made a note to start studying Japanese when she returned home. Whatever Ken was saying to the innkeeper, it didn't sound particularly friendly.

Had Garin been right about him? Was Ken someone Annja should be wary of? Was he up to something bad? Her instincts offered no warnings.

Ken ducked back outside. "I apologize."

"Everything all right?"

Ken glanced away. "I'd rather not discuss it."

"It sounded serious."

"Stupid is what it is," Ken said.

"I'd like to know."

He sighed. "All right. The innkeeper was a bit upset that you weren't Japanese."

"Excuse me?"

Ken nodded. "I know, I know. It's ridiculous, right? In this day and age, the idea that someone would be racist or xenophobic is truly appalling. It turns my stomach, believe me. But unfortunately, once you leave the cities, in parts of Japan, just like in America, you run into hicks who can't figure out if the earth is round or not. This guy happens to be one of those special morons."

"A Japanese hick." Annja grinned. "Who woulda thought?"

"Not me," Ken said. "Or I certainly wouldn't have taken you here. However," he sighed, "it is late and I'm not so sure we can make it to another *ryokan*. They tend to close early and if we don't take what we have, we might not have anything."

Annja nodded. "And I expect we'll be out for a few days in the woods anyway, so I suppose we ought to have one final night in comfort, so to speak."

"Exactly."

"I've dealt with worse," Annja said. "And I'm sure you have, too."

"On a highway in Mississippi outside of Keesler Air Force Base a few years back," Ken said, "I was walking with a good friend of mine who happens to be African-American. We were walking toward the riverboat-gambling area and a pickup truck full of rednecks rolled by hurling racial epithets at us."

Annja shook her head. "What did you do?"

"Well, my friend wanted to fight them then and there, but they were driving too fast for us to catch on foot. However, as providence would have it, we were invited to a party at a local motel and what vehicle should just happen to be in the parking lot but the very one full of those inbred, narrow-minded idiots."

Annja grinned. "I take it you enlightened them as to the error of their ways?"

"Believe it or not," Ken said, "I did very little. The real dervish that night was my friend who stood all of about five and a half feet tall but had a spirit a mile high. He sent three of them to the hospital."

"Sounds like a good friend to have."

Ken smiled. "There have been several times since that night that I have dearly wished he was around."

"Get the room," Annja said. "And don't worry—I won't send the old man to the hospital unless I absolutely have to."

Ken ducked back inside and returned moments later. "We're all set. Follow me."

Annja entered the *ryokan* again and found the innkeeper suitably sheepish this time. Whatever Ken had told him had apparently reduced his hostility exponentially. The innkeeper gave Annja a stiff bow and welcomed her. With one hand holding a candle he beckoned them to follow him down a narrow corridor.

On either side, Annja could hear the soft snoring noises of other guests. She and Ken had left their shoes in the entranceway and on stocking feet they made no noise as they traversed the hall's shiny wood flooring.

At the far end, the innkeeper turned left down another corridor and at last knelt before a shoji screen door and slid it back on its runners.

Inside, a young woman dressed in a floral kimono knelt and was placing small plates of food and bowls of rice on a low table. She looked up and bowed at the sight of Ken.

"Dinner?" Annja asked.

Ken nodded. "I took the liberty of ordering for us. I hope you don't mind."

"I don't think I could have read the menu anyway."

"I'm sure you'll like the dishes. They're basic staples, but hearty and will give us some energy for the morning."

Annja ducked inside the room, which was warm. Ken pointed. "There's a heater under the table. Keeps this place warm."

The young woman said something to Ken, who nodded. She exited the room and returned a minute later just as Annja was seating herself at the table with her legs tucked under her.

"Sake," Ken said. "Have you ever had it before?"

"Once or twice."

He smiled. "I prefer it warm myself but some of my other countrymen swear by it being served cold. I find that nauseating. But warmed to 98.6 degrees Fahrenheit, it is truly a spectacular drink."

The young woman poured the rice wine into small cups and bowed toward Annja. Ken hoisted his cup toward Annja. "*Kempai*."

Annja smiled. "*Kempai*."

She tilted the cup toward her lips and took a sip of the drink. The warm liquid flowed into her mouth and then down her throat with such smoothness that it surprised her. The sake warmed her on its way down and only after she'd swallowed it did it hit her with its dreamy effects.

She put the cup down and saw the waitress instantly refill it.

Annja nodded at her. "Is she trying to get me drunk?"

Ken smiled. "I think you'll make a lovely couple."

"You wish." Annja shook her head. "Seriously, why is she refilling it for me? It wasn't empty."

"Japanese tradition," Ken said. "You aren't supposed to let the cup get empty. If we're alone, we're supposed to refill each other's cup every time we take a sip. It's considered bad form otherwise."

"I'd rather not start our journey tomorrow with a hangover," Annja said.

Ken said a few words to the young woman, who bowed and left the room. Ken turned to Annja. "Let's get some food in us before this stuff makes us crazy."

He took the covers off the plates and Annja breathed in the scent of the freshly cooked food. Ken pointed out the various dishes.

"*Tonkatsu*, pork cutlet, sashimi, tuna *maki, soba* and rice with vegetables." He looked up. "As I said, nothing too special, but hearty enough."

Annja grabbed a pair of chopsticks. "Is there any particular way to go about this without insulting anyone?"

Ken laughed. "Just dig in. I'm starved."

Annja tore into the food, not realizing she'd been keeping her hunger in check until now. The last time they'd had anything of substance was on the train ride to Iga and that was but a snack. Now the home-cooked meal seemed like just the thing for Annja and she tasted every dish. "This is amazing stuff."

Ken nodded around mouthfuls of rice. "Another benefit of staying at a *ryokan*. Some of them house tremendous cooks who really know what a hungry traveler needs to feel welcome."

"Even if they are racists."

Ken laughed. "Even if."

Within a few minutes, the food was gone. Annja and Ken had polished off the entire dinner, and when the soft knock at the door came followed by the reappearance of the young woman in the kimono, Annja was already leaning back on her haunches, marveling at how much she'd managed to put away.

She sipped her sake, aware of the calming effects the liquor was having on her. "That was marvelous."

Ken looked at the young woman. "*Oishi*."

She bowed low and said what Annja took to be thanks. As she exited the room, she turned and said a few words to Ken, who smiled and bowed.

"What?"

Ken grinned. "She apologized for her father's old-fashioned ways. I believe she overheard my exchange with him about you not being Japanese. She's very embarrassed that he would say such things."

"If I had a buck for every time I've heard kids express horror at stuff their parents have said, I'd be rich," Annja said.

"Who wouldn't?" Ken replied. He leaned back. "I'm exhausted."

"So where do we sleep?" Annja said.

Ken held out his hands. "Right here."

"Here?"

"Of course."

Annja frowned. "Oh. It's just I thought we'd have separate rooms."

Ken shook his head. "I thought I told you—this was the last room they had available."

"You didn't tell me that, actually."

Ken looked away. "I'm sorry. If it makes you uncomfortable—"

"No, no, that's fine. I mean, it's okay, I understand." She looked into his eyes and he smiled at her.

"I promise I won't try anything," he said.

"I know," Annja said.

She didn't know if the sake was having an effect on her or if she was simply enjoying her time with Ken, but part of her hoped he would try something anyway.

23

Annja slept enveloped by the warmth of the bedding on the tatami-mat floor, listening to the crickets outside and the occasional breeze ruffling through the trees and shrubs. A lone fountain in the rear of the *ryokan* bubbled over stones, dribbling down a meandering waterfall. She breathed deeply, dreaming of perfect peace and quiet, lulled into a state of complete relaxation by the sake and exhaustion.

Somewhere in the vagueness of nocturnal time, Annja's subconscious noticed something. A brief glimpse of disharmony spotlighted against the backdrop of natural rhythm.

Ken's hand suddenly snaked over her mouth. His voice was a harsh whisper in her ear.

"Stay still!"

She came awake immediately wanting to fight him off. So this was it—what Garin had tried to warn her about—that Ken was an evil man, after all. He'd wanted her along on this trip for some reason only to now spring a deadly trap on her. She would die in this rural inn in a country not her own.

Her limbs were pinned. Ken knew how to keep her from moving.

"They're outside," he whispered.

She frowned and stopped trying to move. Ken let her go and as she turned over slowly, he pointed toward the shoji screens. Annja could see nothing beyond their opaque paper. Certainly there were no shadows cast against them like in some bad Hollywood movie.

But Ken seemed insistent. He let his other hand move toward his backpack. From within, he withdrew a small pistol with a sound suppressor attached to it.

Annja frowned. When the hell had he found time to get a gun? She reasoned Jiro must have supplied it to him during the gear-shopping expedition.

Ken brought himself into a seated position with the gun held at the ready. His breathing had deepened rather than shallowed like Annja's had. He looked firm and resolute, committed to using the gun.

Annja closed her own eyes and saw the sword where she needed it to be in case things went to hell. She opened her eyes and saw Ken looking at her. He barely nodded.

Annja nodded back.

Ken pivoted and shot a single round through the back wall of their room into the corridor. Annja heard a grunt and then the sound of someone toppling to the ground in a heap.

Ken knelt by the door and slid the shoji back on its runners. He ducked low and peeked around the corner, only to jerk his head back a nanosecond later as a metallic object whizzed past his head and buried itself in the door frame.

Annja looked. A throwing star blackened in soot stuck where Ken's head had been just a second before.

Ken rolled back. "Whatever you've got access to, now would be a good time to bring it out."

Annja closed her eyes and reached for the sword. She saw herself closing her hands around the hilt.

The walls of their room exploded as figures leaped into the room. Annja jerked her eyes open. The sword in her hands deflected the downward cut from one of the black-clad invaders. His sword clanged off the broadsword Annja held.

She ducked and cut horizontally, slicing into the midsection of her attacker. She felt the blade cut deep and heard the muffled cry of pain followed by the sharp tang of copper flooding the room as her blade bit into his flesh.

Ken's gun spit three more times, catching more attackers. He spun and maneuvered to try to get closer to Annja.

She rolled to her feet and came up with her sword held vertically in front of her. Another attacker materialized from outside, stepping calmly into the fray. He sized up Annja and her sword. He brought his hands up, and Annja heard the sound of a chain unfurling.

The links bit into her hand, wrapping themselves like a metallic snake. The invader jerked his hand back, and Annja felt one of her hands come away from the hilt of her sword.

Rather than try to fight, she inexplicably went with the energy of the attacker's pull and turned her body, cutting straight down with her sword. She cleaved his arm off and he screeched, rolling back out into the night.

Ken was firing now with regularity. She heard his gun spit rounds into more attackers.

"How many are there?" Annja shouted.

Ken didn't answer; he just kept shooting.

And then his gun went dry.

"I'm out!"

Annja spun and dropped her blade down, deflecting another throwing star that had been hurled at her. The *shuriken* clanged harmlessly to the corner of the room.

Two more attackers flew into the room, each armed with *katana*. Annja saw the curved swords gleaming in the vague moonlight. Their breathing misted the room as the cooler outside temperatures mingled with the warmth of the *ryokan*.

Annja regarded them both. "I might need some help here."

But Ken was engaged with three attackers of his own. Annja could hear him fending off their attacks with just his body. She thought she heard another startled gasp. Ken had apparently dispatched another one.

Annja's attackers spread out in a vague arc in front of her. The presence of her sword must have given them reason for pause, but she knew it wouldn't hold them off for long. Whatever they were determined to do, they would try regardless if she was armed or not.

One of them dropped his lead foot back and drew his sword high above his head. The other dropped the tip of his low, aimed almost at her foot.

Annja kept her sword held vertically in front of herself.

All she could do was wait.

From where he held his sword high above himself, the attacker on her left cut down straight at her head. Annja felt her body jerk itself to the left, dodging to the outside of his cut. She realized they wanted her to dodge to the inside, where the second attacker would have easily cut up and into her.

Instead, Annja allowed her sword to dip and deflect the downward cut. She spun and then cut back down above the attacker's arms. Her sword chopped into both his arms, slicing into them. His sword dropped to the *tatami* mats below, staining them crimson. Annja flipped the blade and cut back up, catching her attacker in the throat. His body slumped to the floor.

The second attacker regarded her coolly now. He knew she was no amateur.

Another body rolled off to the side, his head at an odd angle. Ken had taken out another attacker.

But Annja couldn't afford to concentrate on him right now. Not when the second swordsman looked as if he was ready to kill her for all the death Annja had managed to wreak on the invaders.

He circled her and Annja moved with him. The room was tight but somewhat maneuverable as long as she didn't lift her sword high overhead. She had to watch her footing, though. More and more bodies littered the room and she could easily fall or trip on any of them. The blood on the floor also made things slippery.

The second swordsman kept her between himself and Ken.

Annja frowned. He knows how to use the environment to his advantage. He doesn't want to risk getting between me and Ken.

Smart.

She started moving the other way, trying to position him between her and Ken. But he changed his posture and stance with the sword. If she tried to continue to do so, he'd be able to cut her badly and possibly kill her.

Another grunt sounded behind her. Ken must have polished off his third attacker.

Annja could see something in the eyes of her attacker. He was furious that Annja had killed his partner, but he must have also seen that he was now alone. And it would soon be two against one. Not two amateurs, he would have realized, but two very competent fighters.

He sliced up at Annja from the lower right, trying desperately to cut her from the waist to her head.

Annja leaped back and let her own sword arc down and up, redirecting his cut. She knew in a second she would clear his blade and be able to cut horizontally across his chest, ending this battle for good.

But as she did so, he leaped back and away, suddenly bringing his own sword high overhead.

Annja ducked and rolled as the blade cut through the air a hair's width from her head. She came to a stop ten feet away, nearly bumping into one of the corpses on the floor.

The swordsman sliced at her again, and she barely had space to bring the blade up and block the cut. The sharp clang of steel echoed in the room.

"Annja!"

Ken's voice reminded her she wasn't alone.

It must have also reminded her attacker, who suddenly backed away. For another long second he stood silhouetted in the gaping hole of the wall and then in a flash, he was gone.

Annja stepped forward, ready to pursue, but felt Ken's hand on her shoulder.

"No."

She looked at him. "Why not? We've got to get him."

"That may be exactly what he wants. He may be waiting out there for you to come through that hole and go after him. He'll cut you down easily then."

"So, what now?"

"We wait."

"For what?"

"Morning."

Annja slumped to the floor, leaning on the heavy sword blade. Ken squatted next to her. "You did amazingly well."

"Thanks."

He stared at the sword. "I must confess I knew you had some secrets, but this is not what I was expecting."

Annja smirked. "Don't ask, okay? It's too long a story to get into, and I'm not even sure how to tell it."

He smiled. "Fair enough. Later though, okay?"

"Maybe."

Ken stood and walked to one of the corpses. He rolled him over and started searching him.

"You hoping to find something?"

Ken nodded. "Yes. I'd like to know who they were."

"Aren't they ninja?"

Ken frowned. "These were no ninja. They had no skills in *ninjitsu*. Just bad imitators dressed in cheap clothing and using crummy weapons." He pointed. "You see that *shuriken*?"

Annja looked at the throwing star that had embedded itself in the door frame. "What about it?"

"You see how many points it has? That's what they sell in Hong Kong flea markets. That's not a legitimate Japanese *shuriken*." He stood. "No identification on this one."

He checked the other bodies but found nothing.

"Well, it seems they were smart enough to know not to have any identifying features on them in case things went wrong," Annja said.

Ken nodded. "Just makes this all the stranger."

"You did say that we were bound to attract the attention of other interested parties. And that some of those parties might not want us to find the *vajra*."

"Yes. I did."

"Surely this proves your theory out."

Ken sighed and sat down on a clean spot on the floor. "I just wish it didn't. We've already got enough troubles as it is on this jaunt."

Annja could hear anxious noises coming from elsewhere in the *ryokan*. She stood. "More attackers?"

Ken shook his head. "No, I imagine that will be our friendly innkeeper. And boy is he going to shit when he sees this."

"Good to know I'll be helping improve America's image overseas," Annja said.

Ken pointed. "Well, you might want to get rid of that thing before he sees it. At least then we can claim self-defense."

Annja nodded, closed her eyes and the sword vanished. When she opened her eyes again, she saw Ken shake his head. "Wow."

The innkeeper appeared at what used to be their door.

24

"Who told you to attack them?"

Nezuma paused as he listened to the voice on the telephone. After a moment, he cleared his throat. "Of course I know you don't report to me. But I thought we had an understanding—"

The voice on the other end of the phone cut him off again. Nezuma closed his eyes and listened to the venom coming at him, vowing that he would very soon see this particular mission finished to his devious liking.

"Fine. Good day."

He clicked the phone off and turned to look at Shuko, who sat quietly eating some fruit on the *tatami* mats. "I swear they are the biggest fools on the planet."

Shuko said nothing but only looked up at him expectantly. Nezuma frowned. "They attacked Kennichi and the woman last night in their *ryokan*."

"Why?"

"I have no idea except that his young guns wanted vengeance for what Kennichi did to them back in Tokyo. It was a silly move and probably drew a great deal of unwanted attention to us. It also put them more on guard than they have been so far."

Shuko took another bite of her fruit and kept staring at Nezuma. "So now they know."

"They've known for sure that they have people watching them. But a full scale attack in the middle of the night borders on insane." Nezuma sat next to her and took her hand. "Shuko."

She looked at him. "Master."

He shook his head. "I did not want to do what I had to do last night. I hope you understand that."

"I understand."

He rested his head on her shoulder. "We are so close right now to finally gaining what we've been after—"

"What *you've* been after."

He looked at her. "This isn't just about me. It's about what the *dorje* can do for both of us."

She shook her head. "I've never cared about that."

"What do you mean?"

"I only care about what it can do for you, master. What it means to you—the value and glory you see in its recovery—means more to me than the item itself."

Nezuma bowed his head. "But it will give us the life we've always dreamed of."

Shuko shook her head. "But don't you see? I already have the life I've always dreamed of. You gave that to me years ago when you plucked me out of that slum. And every day since then I've thanked the gods for your appearance in my life."

Nezuma placed his finger under her chin and lifted it to meet his gaze. "You know I share your feelings."

"Do you?"

"How can you question me?"

Shuko took her hand and pulled at the neck of her kimono. The dark black-and-blue welts on her skin showed like an angry yoke around her neck, mottling the skin toward her collarbones.

"This," she said quietly, "is not what two people in love do to each other."

Nezuma covered her neck back up. "You know I have a violent temper."

"Yes. I know."

"And you know that I sometimes do things I don't mean."

"But I have never experienced any misdirected hatred from you. At least, not until last night."

Nezuma nodded. "Would you prefer to leave?"

Shuko looked at him. "Would you let me?"

He leaned back. "You think I would kill you?"

She said nothing.

Nezuma sighed. "I suppose you do after last night."

"Yes."

"You have every right to." He took a bite of the apple on the plate. "But my life would mean nothing without you in it."

"Do you really mean that? Truly?"

Nezuma swallowed. "Yes."

A small smile formed at the corners of her mouth. "Thank you."

Nezuma kissed her on the lips. "I'm sorry for hurting you."

She hugged him tightly, pressing her sobs into the folds of his robe. She shuddered and convulsed as he held on to her. When she was done, Nezuma could feel the wetness of her tears on his shoulder.

"You feel better now?"

She nodded, still with her face in his shoulder. He smoothed her hair back, running his fingers through the dark tresses as she sniffed and attempted to compose herself.

"My little beauty," he said softly.

She sighed and kissed him then, pleading with her lips, slowly and long. Nezuma kissed her back, laying her back on the *tatami* mats, taking his time to be gentle and soft with her.

As he nuzzled her, he thought about the timetable they would need to adhere to in order to pursue Kennichi and Annja Creed. At least they knew where to find them—that was if they stayed around long enough.

Shuko whimpered as he kissed her. Sex would take precious time away from them.

He frowned. But it was apparently necessary in order to reassure Shuko that he did truly love her. After all, he needed her badly by his side during the coming battles he felt sure would take place.

And afterward…

He smiled as Shuko's body tightened and then relaxed under his kisses.

Afterward, he could always dispose of her at his leisure.

"IT LOOKS DIFFERENT in the daylight."

They stood outside of Jiro's place, down the dank alleyway that just a few hours previously had been a home to wayward drunks and the smell of urine. Now, in the brightness of day, it looked like a run-down place, but the sense of danger was removed.

Ken pointed at the door. "It's been opened."

Annja followed his gaze. She could see the pry-bar marks by the hinges. "It looks like someone took it off and then put it back on when they were done with it."

Ken nodded. "Exactly."

"What does that mean?"

"Someone doesn't want anyone thinking there's something wrong inside." Ken moved closer to the door and pressed his ear against the steel and rust. After a moment, he stepped back. "We need to get in there."

"What for? Who knows how old these marks are? Knowing your friend, he's probably out somewhere or asleep. In either case, maybe we shouldn't bother him."

Ken shook his head. "I need to know if someone was asking about us. What if there's another party interested in us that we didn't know about before?"

"Ken, we're supposed to be in the mountains right now. Not down here looking for your pal."

"And if we don't know who is looking for us, we could walk into a trap," Ken said.

Annja pointed at the door. "Well, just how do you think you're going to get in there?"

Ken removed a small packet of something from his coat. "Stand back."

"What is that? Another special gift from Jiro?"

Ken looked at her. "What do you mean?"

"You could have told me about the gun."

Ken shrugged. "Didn't seem important at the time. Jiro always tosses in extras like that if he thinks I might need it. It wasn't something I asked for especially."

"But you knew he put it in the bag."

"I suspected."

Annja frowned. He certainly seemed perfectly comfortable reaching for it last night before the attack broke loose. "If you say so."

Ken unfolded a gray clayish substance from the packet and placed a small amount around each of the hinges. From another pocket he withdrew small cylindrical objects that Annja recognized as detonators.

Ken plugged them into each packet and then looked at Annja. "We should probably move away."

"You don't have to ask twice. I've seen this stuff blow before," Annja said.

They ducked around the corner and waited. In thirty seconds, there was a loud firecracker sound and when they looked back, bits of smoke wafted from the doorway.

"That wasn't as loud as I thought it would be," Annja said.

"Jiro gets good-quality stuff. Not your typical loud-bang explosive. It helps with avoiding unnecessary interest."

They examined the door. All the hinges had been blown off, but the door stayed where it was.

"Must be extremely heavy," Ken said. He reached into his coat and fished out a folding knife that he inserted in the gaps between the door and the frame. He exerted some pressure and the slab of the door started to come away from the jamb.

"Look out."

Annja moved and the door fell forward, clanging louder than the explosive in the alley. Ken glanced inside and all around the jamb.

"No booby traps."

"Did you really expect some?"

He shrugged. "You can never tell. And I always think it's better to be safe than sorry, as the old saying goes."

They stepped into the corridor and headed for the elevator at the end of the hallway. When they reached it, Ken repeated his examination and only after two full minutes did he proclaim it safe to ride.

They stepped in and closed the grate. The elevator groaned its way up to Jiro's loft. They could hear music playing, but at a much lower volume than it had been last night.

"Maybe he's asleep," Annja said.

"Impossible," Ken said. "When we took the door off, he would have been down here with guns blazing. He's got the place wired for alarms and intrusion sensors."

"Doesn't seem like they stopped the people who might have gotten in here last night."

"No," Ken said. "It sure doesn't."

The elevator stopped and Annja pulled back the grate. Ken took point as they moved closer to the doorway. Annja could see the stacks of crates and boxes pretty much as they had been last night when Jiro had been scouring and rummaging through them.

Ken stopped. "Maybe you should wait here."

"What for?"

"It might not be…safe inside."

Annja frowned. "Ken, we had a battle last night where I

killed several men. Do you really think that I'm going to stay out here like some sheltered dove while you go in there and face any possible dangers alone?"

He smiled. "I suppose not."

"Good. Now let's get on with this. The sooner we do, the sooner we can get going to find that *vajra* of yours."

Ken nodded. They stepped over one crate and then another. The deeper they got into the loft area, the more apparent it became that there had been a shoot-out.

Ken knelt and brushed his fingers across a part of a crate where the wood had been splintered. "Ricochet."

He stood. "I don't think this is going to turn out well."

"At least he appears to have tried to fight them off," Annja said quietly.

Ken sighed. "For all the good it did him."

"We might be wrong. He might be okay."

They turned a corner and saw the dark pools of blood. Annja knelt and used a scrap of wood to poke the liquid. It was thick and sticky. She looked up at Ken.

"It's a couple of hours old. Already congealed," she said.

He nodded and poked his head around another corner.

Annja heard him gasp.

"Ken?"

He ducked back around and faced her. "He's not okay."

Annja brushed past him and looked. Jiro was seated in a chair in a large tub that had been filled with water. A car battery sat nearby with leads running up to alligator clips that had been attached to Jiro at extremely intimate parts of his body.

Jiro's lifeless eyes stared at her.

Annja blinked and looked away.

Ken's hand was firm on her shoulder. "He didn't give us up easily."

"Who would do this?"

Ken shook his head. "I don't know. But when I find out, I'll kill them. If not for the *vajra*, then for Jiro."

25

"I'm sorry for your loss."

Ken nodded, bowing his head for a moment. "He was a good kid. A little on the dodgy side, but he sure didn't deserve this."

"No one does," Annja said. "And we'll make sure whoever did this doesn't get to do it to anyone else."

"It's my fight," Ken said. "It's not right for me to ask you to come along any further."

"Don't be ridiculous," Annja said.

Ken shook his head. "Between last night and this, no, I can't ask it of you. You've been great so far, but this is getting out of control. These people will apparently stop at nothing to get the *vajra*."

"If you think I'm backing out now—"

"Maybe Taka was right. Maybe the *vajra* shouldn't be disturbed at all. Maybe it should just be left alone where no one else can find it," Ken said.

"You really think it's safe anymore?" Annja asked. "After

all of this, these people are closer to it than ever before simply by virtue of tagging along on our coattails."

"What are you saying?"

"That you can't simply disengage from the hunt now. Because you started it, you've got to see it through to the end. Or else the wrong people will be able to find it. And I don't think you want that happening."

Ken nodded. "You're right, of course."

"Yes. I am."

He smiled. "Thanks for being so modest."

Annja touched his arm. "Enough of this. We need to get going or there's a chance—"

Ken stopped her. "Wait!"

Annja heard it, too. In the distance, the sound of wailing sirens broke the early-morning quiet.

"Think they're headed this way?"

"We can't stick around to find out," he said. He headed to the window and looked out. "They're already here!" He turned and ran to Annja. "Come on." He grabbed her by the hand and led her toward the elevator but stopped when he heard the clamor of footsteps and shouts from below.

Annja pulled up short. "They'll call the elevator."

Ken scrambled around looking for a stick. He found a ski pole and jammed it in the elevator winch. "That should stop them for a few minutes." He turned and ran back into Jiro's loft with Annja close on his heels.

"Is there a back way out of here?" she asked.

Ken nodded. "I thought Jiro to always have an escape hatch. I know he put one in place."

"Shame he couldn't have used it last night."

"I think they somehow caught him by surprise," Ken said. "But I'll find out when we catch up with them."

Annja could hear the groan and whine as the elevator call button was repeatedly pushed and the elevator strained against the ski pole.

The police officers were calling from down below.

"What are they shouting?" Annja said.

"Something about the building being surrounded," Ken said. "You know, the usual."

Annja smirked. At least he had his sense of humor intact. "You think they mean it?"

"I don't know. I'm not sure why they're even here unless someone spotted the door and called them about that. I don't think they'd mobilize the whole force for a simple breaking and entering."

"But again, we won't be around to find out."

"Right." Ken rummaged in a closet and after tossing a few boxes out of the way, he reemerged with a frown. "Where is it?"

Annja heard a sudden snap and a victorious shout from below. "Ken, the elevator!"

He nodded. "Come on!"

They ran toward the largest of the crates. Ken ran behind one and then came back out with a smile. "Found it."

They moved behind the crate and Annja saw the small metal grate open up as Ken jerked on it. A tiny set of stairs led up. But where?

"Pull it shut behind you," Ken said. "And let's hustle. They'll be up here any minute."

Annja stooped in and pulled the grate down behind her.

She felt the dusty stairs beneath her hands. They'd be filthy as sin when they got out, but they couldn't afford a run-in with the cops right now. Not when there was so much at stake.

And as much as Annja hated the idea of running like a guilty party, she didn't think the police would be all that warm and fuzzy toward her.

Ken shuffled quickly up the stairs and Annja heard him pop open the other end of the tunnel. Bright sunlight flooded the tunnel. He scampered out and put his hand back in to Annja. "Come on."

She grabbed it and he helped pull her out of the air-conditioning duct onto the roof. She glanced back. "You think they'll figure it out?"

"Don't know, don't care." Ken ran to the edge of the roof and glanced down. He moved back. "Not that way. Cops are all over the place."

He checked the opposite edge and saw the fire escape. "This will work."

Annja followed him. Ken helped her over the lip of the roof. "Start climbing down."

"I hope this doesn't go past Jiro's windows."

Ken shook his head. "It doesn't. We would have seen it, remember?"

"Yeah." Annja ducked down and let her feet descend as she gripped the rusted sides of the fire escape. She looked at the bolts securing it to the side of the building and frowned. This thing doesn't look like it's been used in years, she thought.

Above her Ken started climbing down. Annja looked beneath her and frowned. "Oh, no."

"What's the matter?" Ken asked.

"The fire escape isn't extended."

"Just keep climbing down. When you get to the final step, you'll have to trigger the release yourself. Can you do it?"

"I guess."

Annja climbed down farther. The last of the ladder rungs arrived too quickly and she was still at least fifty feet from the ground.

"See that hook? There's one on either side," Ken said. "Undo them and then you should drop down toward the ground."

Annja located the hooks and unsnapped them.

The fire escape didn't move. "Dammit!"

"Jump," Ken said.

Annja glanced back up. "What?"

He grinned. "Not down. Just jump up and down and see if that triggers the release."

Annja took a breath and jumped. She felt the other half of the fire escape start to give. But a bit of rust seemed to be hindering it from coming all the way undone and letting the fire escape continue down toward the ground.

"Jump again," Ken said. "Hurry!"

Annja jumped.

The ladder came free and Annja plummeted toward the ground. She grabbed the ladder with both hands as the building face shot past her. She glanced up at Ken who was now scampering toward her even as the distance between them increased.

The ladder jerked to a sudden halt, nearly toppling Annja from her perch as gravity pulled hard on her body. "Oof!"

Ken came streaking down the ladder. "You okay?"

"Shoulder," Annja said. "But yeah."

"They'll be on the roof soon. We've got to go now."

Annja slid down the last few rungs. The fire escape was still short of the ground by a good twenty feet.

"Now we'll have to jump," Ken said.

"That's concrete down there," Annja said. "Twenty feet and we'll have ourselves a couple of broken bones. If we're lucky."

"You trust me?"

"I guess."

"Thanks." Ken chuckled. "Listen to me. Drop down and when you hit the ground, tuck yourself into a ball and roll. Can you do that?"

"Do I have a choice?"

"Sure, you can spend years in prison when the cops catch you."

"What about you?"

"I'll take my own life in a fit of traditional duty." He grinned. "Just do it, Annja. You'll be fine if you do what I say."

The ground looked a long way away, but she knew Ken was right. There was no time left to dawdle. She took a breath and let go of the fire escape.

She exhaled and then the ground shot up for her. Her feet hit and she allowed herself to collapse, breathing out the last of her breath, and immediately sinking on her knees, tumbling and then rolling.

She stopped rolling and felt okay.

Ken hit the ground a second later. He rolled and was already up and moving even as Annja tried to get up. Her shoulder hurt like hell.

Ken's hand was on her arm. "Come on. You okay?"

"Shoulder."

"We'll get to it later. We've got to get out of here."

They ran down the neighboring street. When they'd cleared a block, they risked looking back. Only then did they see the heads of police officers peering over the edge of the building, scouring the streets below for signs of Ken and Annja.

"You don't think they know what we look like, do you?" Annja asked.

Ken shook his head. "Not a chance. Unless they had video cameras there, which they didn't. We're cool."

"Nice to know we won't end up on *Japan's Most Wanted* tonight."

"We need to get back to the *ryokan* and get our gear."

"Too bad you didn't get a chance to refill your ammunition supply while we were there," Annja said.

Ken grinned. "Says who?"

"You did?"

He lifted his jacket and Annja saw the spare magazines filled with fresh rounds. "You had time to grab that?"

"While I was looking, yeah."

"I don't suppose you found me a gun?"

"Unfortunately, no."

"Great."

"You can use mine, if it makes you feel better, but honestly, I didn't think you'd want a gun after that giant sword you used last night."

"Don't bring that up."

"I'm not." Ken smiled. "But it was an awfully big blade."

"And somehow I managed to handle it well."

"You did seem very well accustomed to handling it."

They crossed the street by the train station and Ken pointed at a noodle restaurant. "We'll grab some lunch here and then head back."

"At this rate it will be dark when we get into the mountains," Annja said.

"Probably."

"You're not concerned about that?"

Ken shrugged. "Day, night, it doesn't much matter to me. But I want to make sure you're okay. So we'll eat and give that shoulder a moment to rest. If it isn't better when we get back to the *ryokan*, then we'll see a doctor about it."

"I'm sure it'll be fine," Annja said. "And I'm not really a huge fan of doctors."

"You're scared of doctors?"

"I never said that."

"Okay."

He held open the split curtain and they entered the small stand. Ken pointed at the seating bar. "I'll order. You sit and pretend doctors don't scare you."

"Ken," Annja said. "Don't make me pull out my big sword."

He laughed. "I can't figure out if that's some sort of vague sexual innuendo or not."

"It's not," Annja said.

But she was smiling too.

26

Nezuma watched as Annja and Kennichi made their way into the noodle stand. Next to him, Shuko shook her head.

"The police certainly acted like idiots."

"They usually do," Nezuma said. "Even though they were told to be there shortly after Kennichi and Creed entered the building. Leave it to our bureaucratic morons to screw up something so simple."

"Why did you want to lay a trap like that? It seems rather counterproductive to me."

Nezuma smiled. "Because it would give us a bit more time to get ourselves in position. Plus, I have a contact on the police force here. Given a little time, I could have arranged to have him place a homing device on Kennichi or Creed. And that would have given us a great deal of luxury."

"Such as not having to sit here and do surveillance?"

"Exactly." Nezuma slid on his sunglasses. "There's nothing I abhor more than this mundane lack of action. Even now, they're having themselves a bite to eat while we're forced to sit out here and wait for them to finish."

"I could get us something," Shuko said.

"No." Nezuma shook his head. "We might miss them leaving while you're gone and I don't want to have to leave you behind."

"Thank you."

He smiled at her. "Of course."

"So we wait now, is that it?"

"Yes."

She leaned against the armrest of the black BMW they rode in. "Do you remember when you took me to Milan for my birthday?"

"What about it?"

"The fashion show we went to, the one where you said I was more beautiful than any of the women who walked the runway."

He nodded. "I remember. And it was the truth. You always take my breath away."

She touched the side of his face. "I never said thank you for that trip."

He smiled. "I thought you said thank you in other ways."

She turned away. "Well, yes, but I like to say it for real, too. You didn't have to take me anywhere for my birthday, but you did. And it meant the world to me. Spending time with you was the best gift of all."

"That dinner we had was amazing. The wine especially was incredible."

Shuko nodded. "The waiter said it was from a local winery. That the restaurant was one of the only places in the world where you could get a bottle of it. And how it was aged, the secret family recipe."

"We had some great times together, didn't we?"

She smiled at him. "Yes."

He patted her thigh. "And when we get the *dorje*, we'll have even more of them, just you wait."

"I am."

Nezuma looked back at the noodle shop. "I must admit I was a bit impressed by Creed's athletic ability with that fire escape. Part of me expected she would fall when it came to the sudden stop."

"As did I. But she managed to hold on. I think it's fair to assume she injured her shoulder, though. I saw her clutching it as they ran down the street," Shuko said.

Nezuma frowned. "Knowing the ninja, he'll have some sort of herbal remedy that will make her all better."

"Too bad."

Nezuma shrugged. "No matter. She's as good as dead anyway as soon as they locate the *dorje*."

Shuko checked her watch. "They really ought to be coming out any time now."

"You're going to estimate how long it takes them to eat?"

"These subway noodle stands don't make money if they don't keep the customer turnover high. Meals get served fast and customers know to eat just as quick. I should know—there were enough of them where I begged for food when I was younger."

"Before me," Nezuma said.

She smiled at him. "Yes. Before you."

He pointed. "It appears you were right."

In front of the car, Annja and Kennichi walked away from the noodle stand. Nezuma nodded. "She's not clutching her shoulder anymore."

"You think she's acting?" Shuko asked.

"Maybe."

Nezuma started the car and slid it into Drive. "This is the tough part. I've got to keep tabs on them, but without making this car an item of curiosity for them. That wouldn't be good."

"I'll go on foot," Shuko said. "That way we'll have me as point. You can trail behind at a safe distance."

Nezuma frowned. "You're sure?"

"Why not?"

"Because that man ahead is a ninja. And he's very well-trained. He's shown himself to be extremely capable at detecting surveillance."

"You think I can't stay concealed?"

"I didn't say that."

She smiled again. "I appreciate your concern, master, but I'll be fine."

"There's a risk of him seeing you. He might think we were the ones who killed his contact back at that warehouse. He might just take his anger out on you."

"I can handle myself."

Nezuma shrugged. "It's your call."

Shuko opened the door. "Then I choose this." She opened her cell phone. "I'll be in touch."

Nezuma watched her go and shook his head. He couldn't remember her being quite so stubborn before this. He wondered if the near choking he'd given her last night might have been just a bit too much.

He sighed. The hunt for the *dorje* had absorbed much of his life, from the time he was a young boy and had heard legends about it. And when he'd grown up and learned that the *ninjitsu* family that had been given the *dorje* had then entrusted it to mere monks, it had angered and infuriated him.

As the last remaining descendant of Shotoku Taishi, Nezuma took it personally that the gift his ancestor had given to the ninja had been so callously disregarded. And if the *dorje* was returned to the Taishi family, the legends spoke of untold wealth and power that would be theirs.

Nezuma had spent much of his family fortune trying to locate the *dorje*. And he had spent much of his time scouting for an assistant he could secure the *dorje* with.

Shuko was that person.

Or she had been until recently. Certainly Nezuma had feelings for her. He wouldn't deny himself the truth, and the truth was simply that he had affection for her.

But love?

No.

And that was precisely what she wanted.

From the way she spoke—the memories of past trips, the dinners, the wine and the vacations—all of it meant she was thinking far too much about what their time together meant to her.

She wasn't thinking about the mission.

And that was dangerous.

Nezuma sighed. He would definitely have to kill her.

He ruminated on the matter but then pushed it out of his mind. He'd killed others whom he'd cared for. He'd murdered his own mother when she'd threatened to cut him off from any financial support when he was just eighteen years old.

He would have expected it to be difficult to kill the woman

who had brought him into the world kicking and crying, who had suckled him at her breast while he grew.

But no.

In fact, Nezuma had relished the utter feeling of absolute power as he grasped her tiny throat in one hand and simply flexed his wrist the right way. The barely audible crack as her neck popped surprised him more.

It was so easy.

And he never had nightmares about it, either. But Nezuma wasn't sure he believed in an afterlife anyway. Or heaven and hell. But the promise of magic with regards to the *dorje* had been enough to make him sit up and buy into the superstition.

He grinned. Who wouldn't?

Ahead of the car, Nezuma watched Creed and Kennichi walk purposefully down the street as if they were headed right to their location.

"They're in a hurry," he said to himself.

Shuko lingered behind, on the opposite side of the street. She perused the sidewalk market stalls and only showed the vaguest sense of direction. Nezuma smiled and shook his head. She was the best at tailing someone on foot.

And in a car, she was pretty good, too.

Shuko moved down the street and then pressed the buttons on her cell phone. A second later, Nezuma's own purred on the seat.

"Yes?"

"You see them still?" Shuko asked.

"They're out of my range. I can see you."

"They look like they're grabbing a taxi. You'd better come and pick me up."

"Wait it out until that's confirmed. I don't want to risk burning you."

He could hear her impatience on the phone. "And if they get into a fast cab, it will take too long for you to pick me up. We could lose them again."

He frowned. "Your impatience almost cost us this yesterday. Let's not make that mistake again."

"Trust me."

Nezuma cut the phone off and slid the BMW into gear. He rolled down the street slowly and then pulled over by the corner, idling.

Behind him now, Shuko still showed no interest in either the party she was tailing or the car that Nezuma sat in. He glanced down the street and could see Kennichi and Creed hailing a taxi.

Shuko slid into the front seat. "There they go."

Nezuma pulled out and into the traffic slipstream. The taxi cut down a side street. Nezuma frowned. "I don't like this."

"You think he's directing the driver?"

"Wouldn't you?"

"Yes."

Nezuma pointed. "You see? He just had him pull over and idle for a moment." Nezuma drove past the street and then took the next option left.

"You know your way around Ueno?" Shuko seemed surprised.

Nezuma smiled. "I've been here a number of times. Each one ended worse than the previous trip. Nothing but endless frustration in my search for the *dorje*."

"So you suspected that it was hidden somewhere in Iga?"

"Suspicions," Nezuma said, "are at best worse than assumptions. But yes, I suspected it. And I spent long hours up in those mountains looking and trying to find anyone who could help me uncover where it might be."

"And now we're back here again."

Nezuma frowned. "This is not a sweet homecoming, either. Not by any stretch of the imagination. I abhor Iga and what it represents. The fact that ninja used to flourish in this geographical location leaves me nauseous."

"Why do you hate them so much?" Shuko asked.

"Because they are the antithesis of what true Bushido stands for. Ninja operate outside the law of moral conduct."

Shuko looked at him. "Master…"

Nezuma smiled. "I know, I'm stretching things a bit, aren't I?"

"Just a bit."

He nodded. "When my ancestor gave them the *dorje*, he was bestowing a tremendous honor upon them. And I feel like they spit it back in his face by relinquishing their responsibility to care for it properly. It's almost as if the ninja themselves knew what they were capable of and that the *dorje* couldn't be expected to survive their natural greed."

Shuko pointed. "The taxi has moved."

Nezuma waited for it to pass by. "It helps knowing the streets of the town, though."

"Does that knowledge extend into the mountains, as well?" Shuko asked.

"Yes. It does."

She smiled. "Good. Because I think that's where we're headed next."

27

"The air smells like incense here."

Ken nodded as they stood at the trailhead strapping on their packs. "I think it's hibiscus. But I'm not a horticulturalist."

Annja adjusted the shoulder straps and winced. "Hopefully this won't give me any trouble."

"It still hurts?"

"Somewhat. The massage you gave me in the cab made it feel better. But I'm not sure how it will hold up once we get moving."

"You should have let me talk you into seeing a doctor. Your health is more important than the *vajra*."

Annja smiled. "I appreciate the concern, Ken, but it's okay. Really. And who knows, the straps might restrict the blood flow enough that it actually dulls the pain."

"Only until you take the pack off later. At that point it might make the pain even more intense. You might not get any rest, and that will affect your ability to navigate the trail. Or…" His voice trailed off.

"Handle any trouble that happens to come our way?"

Ken started to say something but then just shook his head.

Annja shrugged. "I guess I'll have to wait and see what happens. But in case you were wondering, I can still get to the sword."

"I thought we weren't talking about that."

"We're not."

Ken finished lacing up his boots and stood. "Are you ready?"

Annja jumped once and settled the pack on her shoulders. "Yeah. Let's get going. I'm anxious to see the mountains."

Ken took the lead. Annja found the trail easy to follow, mostly having been cleared of obstructions and lined with gravel in places. Their boots crunched over the ground for about a mile, gradually sloping upward at twenty degrees.

Ken pointed. "We're bushwhacking from here. The trail is not what we want to follow beyond this point."

"Okay," Annja said uncertainly.

He glanced at her. "You okay?"

"Shoulder's great," Annja said, Even though she could feel it throbbing under the padded straps of her backpack.

Ken cocked an eyebrow but didn't say anything else.

Annja followed him into the brush. "Don't you want a compass?"

"Don't need one. The map that Taka showed us was extremely specific. We took the trail to this point and now I know where we're going for the rest of the way."

"I'm glad you do, because I already forgot," she said.

Ken nodded and held up a small piece of paper. "Yeah, well, I also made notes."

"Cheater."

"Absolutely."

They moved through the woods, dodging the upturned logs and the roots sticking out like prehistoric dinosaurs. Vines stretched across the forest floor, and twice Annja almost lost her footing, only to have to right herself with her bad arm. Each time, she winced but fought through the pain.

Ken kept a steady pace but it wasn't particularly taxing. Still, by the middle of the afternoon, it didn't feel to Annja as though they'd made much progress. The upward slope had been constant, though, and Annja could see they'd risen in altitude a fair amount.

"How high up are we now?"

Ken shook his head. "I'm not sure. But I'd guess we're a good way up. We'll still be in the tree line for the rest of the trip. It's not like we're scaling Everest or anything like that. And the map Taka showed us didn't indicate a mountaintop monastery."

"Caves," Annja said. "We're looking for caves."

They pressed on, skirting small mountain ponds and large boulders that seemed tossed up from the depths of the earth itself. They dipped into valleys and found a vague mist that enveloped them only to climb back out into the sunshine.

Overhead, clouds passed over the sun, darkening the entire mountain before slipping aside to let the late-afternoon sun warm them yet again. Annja felt entirely uncomfortable the whole time.

"Is the weather always like this?"

"Unpredictable is how the locals describe it," Ken said. "They're not surprised if it snows in the summer and hits eighty in the winter. What with the mountains being here, the temperature fluctuations alone are something of a peculiarity."

"That's not the only thing making me uncomfortable," Annja said.

Ken glanced back. "Your shoulder feeling worse?"

"Well, there's that, sure."

"Then you're talking about the people following us."

Annja stopped. "You know?"

"Of course. They've been with us since we arrived."

"You didn't say anything."

Ken scrambled back down the animal track they'd been walking on and looked at Annja. "I didn't think I had to, to be honest with you."

"Why not?"

Ken shrugged. "Because you've shown the level of awareness that I would expect keeps you informed about such things. Me saying anything just seemed sort of...redundant."

"Oh." Annja frowned. But he was right. She had known there were people following them on the trail. How they were managing to do it without making much noise and still staying on Annja and Ken, she didn't know, but they were apparently adept at it.

"You think they're our friends from Ueno Castle?" she asked.

"No doubt." Ken rubbed Annja's shoulder. "You sure you can do this?"

"Yes."

He nodded and turned around, heading back up the way he'd come. As he made his way, he stopped and looked back at Annja. "Have I said thank you yet?"

"For what?"

Ken spread his arms. "For this. You didn't have to do any of this. But you did anyway. I know it's a bit unlike some of your other relic quests, not as amazing. No dig site or any of that. But I appreciate you being here just the same. I mean that."

"You're welcome." Annja smiled. "Now let's keep going. I don't want our friends to get too close. I'm not sure if I feel like fighting them yet."

"No worries," Ken said. "We'll deal with them when we have to and not a minute before."

Their climb increased and Annja could feel the vague pressure on her lungs as they tried to compensate for the change in altitude. They weren't extremely high up, but the climbing alone was exhausting her more than she would have expected. She reasoned that with the shoulder injury, she wasn't in tip-top shape anyway.

The sun started to dip behind the horizon shortly after six. The shadows in the trees seemed to sink toward the ground, elongating on the slope as they climbed using an old trail long since forgotten by all but a select few.

Ken leaned against a giant boulder. "It's getting late. We'll need to stop soon. Make camp."

"What's your map say?"

He checked it and pointed. "There ought to be a glen of sorts over the next rise. You okay with going a bit more?"

"Sure."

"You're a good liar, Annja."

"Thanks."

Ken smiled and they moved off again. Annja's shoulder throbbed mercilessly against the strap of her pack. She could feel the sweat all along her hairline and dripping down her back, making her shirt wet with perspiration.

She pressed on and only after she'd managed to climb over a series of fallen tree trunks did the forest floor suddenly level out.

"At last."

Tall pines stretched overhead, and the ground was littered with the soft needles of their growth. Annja stumbled down into the glen, following after Ken, who was heading somewhere.

And then Annja heard it, too.

Water.

They'd been drinking throughout the hike, so they certainly weren't dehydrated. And yet Annja found herself drawn to the sound of the water, possibly because it seemed so out of place this high in the mountains.

"What is it?" she asked.

But Ken didn't seem to hear her. He kept walking toward the sound. And Annja chased after him, not sure if he would stop close by and she could dump her pack, even though she desperately wanted to.

"Hello?"

Ken vanished over a slight rise and Annja followed.

She stopped on the other side.

"My god."

A towering waterfall cascaded down from a height of

hundreds of feet above them. The water spilled out of the rock worn smooth by centuries of water pouring over it.

"I've heard the mountains up here held treasures like this," Ken said. "I don't know if I ever expected to see it firsthand."

"Are we camping here?"

He glanced at her. "Yes."

"Thank god." Annja slumped to the ground and released the tabs on her straps. Instantly, the weight vanished from her back and shoulders.

But the pain jumped into her shoulder, causing her to grimace. "Damn."

Ken noticed and squatted next to her. "Is it bad?"

"It's not good."

"Let me see it."

Annja frowned but unbuttoned her shirt and slid out of it. It felt strange not being dressed in front of him.

Ken's hands felt warm on her skin. He pressed in and she jumped.

"That hurts?" he asked.

"Yes."

He nodded. "It might be your rotator cuff. Something like this could really lay you up for a good bit of time. Are you sure you don't want to go see a doctor?"

Annja laughed. "Not exactly a good time for us to debate this, is it?"

"I suppose not."

"It'll be dark soon. Our best bet is to stay here and make camp like you said. I can get some food and sleep and see if things improve in the morning," she said.

"And if they don't?"

Annja laughed. "Knowing how stubborn I am, I'll probably insist I'm fine and that we should continue."

"And should we?"

She looked at him. "I know how much this means to you."

"You mean quite a bit to me, too, Annja."

His hands were still on her shoulder, kneading and massaging. She could feel their warmth seeping into her muscles. She closed her eyes and breathed in and out slowly. "That feels good."

"I'm glad I can help you," Ken said. His voice seemed thicker and closer now.

Annja suddenly snapped her eyes open and started putting her shirt back on. "I think that's good." She nodded. "Thanks. Thanks a lot."

Ken stood. "Are you sure?"

"Yeah. I'm good. Really good." She finished buttoning her shirt and then busied herself with her backpack. "So, do we get the tent up or what? What about the people following us?"

"They want the *vajra*," Ken said. "I don't think we need to worry about them for now."

Somehow, Annja had a sense that Ken was right. They were not in any imminent danger.

"We can do that," Ken said. "Or we could just sleep out under the stars. Seems like it might be a nice night for it."

"It might be a little cold."

"We'll have a nice fire," Ken said. "And we can pack the sleeping bags with pine needles for extra warmth."

"All right."

"You leave the cooking to me," Ken said. "I want you to rest. All right?"

"All right, but you should know something about me."

Ken stopped and looked at her. "What?"

"I'm really fussy about how I eat my canned ravioli."

28

"It really is beautiful here," Annja said after they'd eaten dinner. She sat on her sleeping bag, which was placed atop a thick bed of pine needles. The fire spit and hissed nearby, sending warmth out into the cool night. The combination of solid food, scent of pine and the radiating heat of the fire had dulled the pain in her shoulder. But only a little.

Ken looked at her in the twinkling firelight. "Places like this are very special when you find them, especially more or less by accident."

"How so?"

He shrugged. "Acolytes journey to areas like this to test themselves. The sheer power of the waterfall is enough to both inspire and terrify."

"What makes it scary?"

Ken smiled. "Would you take off your clothes, wade out into the freezing waters, and meditate while the waterfall crashed down on you?"

"I'm not an acolyte," Annja said.

"Perhaps," Ken replied. "But you don't necessarily have to take religious vows to seek spiritual enlightenment. Many people opt to find their own way to such ideals through processes similar to those following a traditional path. This waterfall might be one of them."

Annja looked at the wall of water cascading down from high above them. The bank they had chosen to camp on was a good two hundred yards away, and the resulting spray of water hitting the rocks below didn't reach them. But the constant roar echoed all around them. She realized they wouldn't hear anyone approaching their camp. But then again, no one would hear them over the din of the waterfall.

"I wonder how they stand it."

"The water?" Ken grinned. "I'm still trying to figure out how I did it."

"You've done it?" Annja eyed him. "You've actually meditated under a waterfall?"

"Well, not this waterfall, but yeah. I did. I took part in some *shugenja* endurance testings."

"*Shugenja?*"

"Another sect of ascetics seeking enlightenment. Their plan for ridding personal demons is pretty intense. One of them is to submerge in a freezing pool of cold water, or else endure the cold phase by meditating under a waterfall."

"And they just let you partake in that?"

Ken shrugged. "I'd been observing them and they asked if I wanted to join them in their 'fun,' I think the head guy called it."

"And you did."

"Well," Ken said, "his tone was very mocking."

Annja grinned. "What did you think?"

"Honestly? At first I thought my testicles were going to be the size of raisins when I was finished. And not good-sized raisins, either. I mean really tiny, tiny raisins."

Annja held up her hand. "I get it."

"But you know, after I was in there and trying to calm myself down, relax my heartbeat, breathe, meditate, that kind of thing, I actually found that it wasn't so bad. Somehow, my body adjusted itself because of how I controlled my mind." He frowned. "I think that's the thing so many people forget these days. The mind controls the body, not vice versa. Anything really is possible if you believe in it hard enough. We create our own reality every day, but most of us just don't realize it."

Annja leaned back on her good arm. "You might have another career as a New Age guru."

Ken shook his head. "I'm not interested in leading a group of people who are, by and large, already more lost than everyday people."

"Sounds like you just lost your flock there, buddy."

Ken smirked. "My flock." He shook his head. "That's the whole problem right there. People—doesn't matter who they are—for some reason seem to feel this unbelievable need to have others worship them or be seen in a position of power. It's all based in a terrible insecurity they have with themselves. And rather than face their insecurities head-on and actually transform themselves into someone capable of incredible power and potential, they run from the challenge.

They become supposed teachers more capable of pointing out everyone else's faults than they are at living a productive life fully in charge of themselves."

"You make it sound pretty bad."

"It is pretty bad," Ken said. "Go into any bookstore and look in the self-help section. There's a misnomer right there. None of those books help people help themselves. They all do the same thing—point out how lacking the reader's life is and then nudge them on a path of responsibility avoidance. The books give a laundry list of excuses as to why the reader's life is so utterly in chaos."

"Why don't you write one, then?" Annja said.

He laughed. "It wouldn't be long enough. I'd write a page about how people should be able to look into the mirror and see what is truly reflected back, not what they wish was reflected."

"That's it?"

Ken pointed overhead. "You see the moon?"

"Sure."

"And now look at the water below it. The moon's reflection is there, too, right?"

"Yeah."

"But you also see the ripples in the pool coming from the water hitting the rocks and all that stuff."

"Of course."

"So it that a true reflection of the moon, then?"

Annja frowned. "I'm not sure I follow you here, Ken."

Ken nodded. "I didn't mean to get so out there on you. I hope I'm not spoiling the evening."

"You're not."

"Good." He sighed. "Think of it this way—a lot of people would look at the sky and see the moon and then look at the reflection of the moon and say they were two completely different things. On one level, they'd be right. After all, one is, in fact, the actual moon, and one is but a reflection. But on another level, the one they're attempting to espouse, they're wrong. Yes, the moon's reflection does not look like the moon, but that doesn't make it a false representation."

"The reflecting surface shows what it is presented with."

"Yes, but with all the distortion and disturbances in place, as well. The reflection of the moon in the water shows how the moon truly appears in this time and place. The person looking at the moon—in other words, the person looking in the mirror—might want the refection to be perfect, the way they want to see themselves. But in reality, there is no perfection in the person looking in the mirror. There are faults and problems that need to be addressed. Only then will the reflecting surface be as peaceful and calm as what it reflects."

"So, that's the big truth?" Annja asked.

"One of them," Ken said. "But it's a big one. There's an epidemic of victimization in society as a whole these days. I thought it was just isolated to the United States and its support system of charlatans, talk-show hosts and early-morning-news idiots, but I've since seen that the rest of the world is rapidly acquiring the same lack of self-realization."

Annja nodded. "I've actually wondered about that. Everyone seems to be in such a hurry to blame someone else for their problems—"

"That the problems never get solved," Ken said. "That's exactly it."

Annja sighed. "I knew someone. A good friend of mine a long time ago who always tried to take the easy path. Instead of working harder, she would always look for the path of least resistance. She came from a broken home, abused, that sort of thing. All her life she blamed her failings on that past."

"What happened to her?"

Annja shook her head, chasing away the memory. "She took the path of least resistance off a rooftop in Chicago."

"I'm sorry."

Annja nodded. "Yeah, well, I hope she's at least happier now than she was in this life."

"You think she was right?"

"Of course not. God, using that line of thinking, I'd have just as much right to kill myself as the next idiot. I never knew my parents. I had problems growing up just like everyone else. But I dealt with it. I didn't let it be an anchor that would end up drowning me."

"You're a true warrior, Annja."

She looked at Ken and smiled. "Well, I appreciate the sentiment."

He shook his head. "It's not empty sentiment, but a statement of fact. What I've seen of you, you don't let adversity beat you. You rise above it. Look at how you've been today."

"How have I been today?"

"Your shoulder was killing you earlier. I could see the strain on your face. At times, it looked pretty bad and I thought we might really need to get you down to the hospital. But I could also see the determination in you. Your spirit commanded and your body obeyed. Even as you sit there right now, your pain has lessened, hasn't it?"

"Somewhat, yes."

"So you see that it does work. Your mind and spirit are more than capable of healing what ails you. You only need to get yourself out of the way in order for the process to be utter and complete."

Annja's eyes narrowed. "What are you driving at?"

Ken smiled. He pointed at her. "That's where you need to go."

Annja took a breath and closed her eyes. She replayed the words Ken had spoken and felt her gut pushing her in a direction that seemed unrealistic, but when she put aside her conscious thought, she realized it all made perfect sense.

She opened her eyes. "Well, that was interesting."

"Was it?"

"Yes." Annja smiled. "I didn't expect something so fast."

"It's amazing what we're capable of when we get out of our own way and let it happen naturally."

"Speaking of natural," Annja said. She stood up.

"Are you going somewhere?"

She smiled. "Don't you know already?"

He shook his head. "I told you before. I'm not a mind reader, although it might seem like that sometimes. I merely respond to the fluctuations I feel in nature and from other people. Sometimes that enables me to have an innate understanding of what people might be considering, but I would never call it mind reading or telepathy or any of that stuff. To me, those are traps along the way to true enlightenment."

Annja took a breath. "How would mind reading be a trap?"

"If you knew you had that power, what would your reaction be?"

"Amazement."

"Granted. But for most people, they would then focus on that power, to the exclusion of everything else they might accomplish. They'd become trapped in the lone manifestation of their potential rather than continuing the journey to see the even greater skills that await further down the path."

"You are an amazing person to talk to," Annja said. She started unbuttoning her shirt.

Ken's eyes opened wider. "Annja."

She shook her head. "It seemed crazy at first but now it seems like the most natural thing in the world, doesn't it?"

"I suppose, but—"

Annja shook her head. "I mean, I shouldn't even fight it any longer. It's right here in front of me and I've been trying to deny what I felt. But that's not the way to do it, is it? According to you, I should just go boldly forth and embrace what I feel, right?"

"I suppose so."

Annja pulled off her shirt and unhooked her bra. The cold air wrapped around her, making her teeth chatter. "Hey, it's a little cold out here."

Ken watched her with a strange look on his face. She smiled. "What?"

He shook his head. "Nothing. Please don't let me stand in the way of whatever it is you're about to do."

Annja slid out of her pants and panties and laid them on the ground. Then she stood before Ken completely naked, wearing only a smile.

"Don't you know, silly? I'm going under that waterfall."

29

Annja could feel Ken's eyes on her as she stepped into the frigid waters of the pond. Whatever vestiges of modesty she had left had vanished when her panties had come off.

For his part, Ken seemed unaffected by the sight of Annja standing naked before him, something that only disturbed Annja for a moment before she realized that he would not allow any emotion to show on his face when presented with that situation. Inside, he must have been one hormonally carbonated mess, she decided.

She stood on a small rock facing the deeper water. Her legs were already thundering with shakes brought on by the cold.

What in the world was she doing? She almost turned around and strode out of the water, but knew she couldn't. She knew she wouldn't.

Annja stepped off the rock and sank into the water.

It took her breath away like a kick to the chest.

She surfaced and sucked air. "God!"

Ken stood on the bank of the pond watching her but made no move to assist. Annja knew he'd come in if she needed him.

But she didn't need him.

At least not yet.

She made her way toward the waterfall. The closer she got, the colder the water became. She could see her breath misting in front of her face in stark contrast to the water.

There was a narrow ledge of stone directly beneath the main torrent of water.

Annja stepped onto it.

The sheer weight of the water almost crumbled her resolve. Combined with the freezing temperatures, just standing there would be a workout in and of itself. Annja wondered if her legs, after hiking for hours, would be able to stand the exertion.

She squatted and then stood up slowly.

Her entire body shook. She couldn't suck in breaths and exhale fast enough. The cold and the force of the water were making her shudder. If she didn't figure out how to get through this quickly, she was sure she would get hypothermia and die.

She thought about what Ken had talked about. She thought about the few times she'd seen other people trying to meditate and that sort of thing.

Isn't it really just breathing? she thought. I should try to count my breaths like I've seen them do in movies.

Without thinking, Annja brought her hands together in front of her stomach and tried tuning out the waterfall and the cold. She took a deep breath in and tried to exhale it slowly, drawing it out as long as she could.

She gasped and sputtered.

"Dammit!"

More water seemed to be crashing down on her, as if someone had turned on the faucet full bore way high up on the mountain. She was going to drown standing under a freezing waterfall trying to meditate, of all things.

If her friends could see her now.

She almost grinned, but her teeth were chattering far too much.

She tried blocking out the water and the cold again. Maybe if I think hard enough about other things, she decided. That might work.

She thought about Ken and the hunt for the *vajra* and the crazy things they'd been through so far on the trip.

But the water roared in her ears. And the cold sucked all the warmth from her body.

She shook her head. It wasn't working. How long was she expected to stay here under this onslaught? What was she trying to prove to herself? If this was where she was supposed to be, then why wasn't anything happening yet? Why wasn't she able to stand there in the freezing water while an avalanche of water dumped itself on top of her? It didn't make any sense, and Annja found herself getting angry that something as silly as a cold waterfall was going to kill her. The sheer idiocy of the thing drove her nuts. She was an accomplished archaeologist, someone who had put in her dirt time on digs that were anything but glamorous, and was now poised for a certain degree of fame and prestige. But she was standing beneath a frigid waterfall in the mountains of Japan trying to accomplish God knew what while a guy on shore that she just might have a serious crush on watched her attempt to figure out nature and the path to enlightenment.

She sighed.

I'm a dope.

She was about to move off the ledge when she noticed that the water didn't feel quite so cold anymore. And neither did the crushing weight of the water feel so suffocating.

Something had changed.

But what?

She started to try meditating again, blocking out the cold and the water. But as soon as she did, they both returned with full ferocity.

Annja frowned. When my mind wandered, I seemed to be able to withstand this better. So instead of concentrating and trying to block this out, I should simply accept this and move on.

The cold subsided.

Annja smiled.

She waved her arms about under the waterfall, enjoying how it felt when the heavy water surged over them. All the pain in her shoulder had vanished as well. Annja nodded, glad, but not silly enough to think that she had cured herself of a rotator cuff injury. It would still need to be looked at, but in the meantime, she could at least function with it as it was.

So this was the lesson? That she had to accept things in her life that had the appearance of a trap and only then would it cease to be one? She frowned. Somehow she expected the lesson would be a little bit more significant than this.

But she realized that her expectations had made it more than it was supposed to be. And like the waterfall, she should just simply accept it as it came to her and let it be what it was, with no distortions or disturbances.

Annja smiled. That was it.

She felt relaxed and calm. And strangely aware.

She looked up into the waterfall, seeing the roaring white and blue of water as it frothed and tried to chomp down on her body. But Annja knew how to beat it, by accepting it, and didn't fear the frigid waters any longer.

She frowned.

Something looked peculiar higher up. Splotches of darkness where there ought to have been light. The rock face behind the waterfall wasn't flat and solid.

But more like a honeycomb.

A honeycomb, she wondered, that might just be a series of caves?

She stepped off the ledge and found herself walking into Ken's arms.

"Hey."

He smiled at her. "I came to help you out of the waterfall."

She noticed immediately that his clothes were also gone. They stood naked together in the cold water.

"How did you know that I was done?"

"I knew. Let's leave it at that."

Annja smiled. "You knew I'd find the answer, didn't you?"

"For some people, the waterfall is a test they will never be able to surmount. For other people, it is but one more test along the path. You are a warrior, Annja. I've told you that before. And now you know it's true."

"It was amazing."

"What worked for you may not work for someone else. It's

important to realize that there are no paths that are perfectly identical. Beware of anyone who tells you there are. No person walks the path exactly the same way, and that's how it should be. We are all individual and unique, as are the routes to our own enlightenment. What you've done tonight will bring you that much closer to becoming invulnerable."

Annja looked around them. The trees swayed in the breezes. She could hear crickets now that she hadn't heard earlier. Even the moon overhead seemed more brilliant than it had prior to going into the water.

"I almost feel like Eve in the Garden of Eden," she said.

Ken kissed her then, his lips closing over her own. She pressed into him, kissing him and letting her lips part as they grew bolder with each breath.

When he pulled back, she said, "Wow."

He smiled. "Is that a good thing?"

"It's a horrible thing," Annja said. "Come here and do it again."

They moved out of the water, both of them almost dry by the time they got back to their sleeping bags. Annja sank into hers, feeling the material wrap around her in warmth.

The fire threw shadows across Ken's skin as he stood in front of Annja. She reached out to him and he sat down next to her.

"Kiss me again," she told him.

He did and Annja drew his sleeping bag over them both, nuzzled herself against the warmth of his skin, and accepted the natural progression of things with a great deal of happiness.

30

Annja stretched out in the sleeping bag. They'd made slow, leisurely love under the stars and the moon while the crickets and the waterfall serenaded them. It was one of the most utterly relaxing moments in Annja's recent life.

She got out of the sleeping bag and slid back into her clothes. Ken did the same. While Annja certainly didn't want the night to end, they did need sleep if they were going to find the mysterious temple where the *vajra* lay hidden.

She watched Ken pull on a turtleneck sweater. He had been one of the most considerate lovers she'd ever had. And more than ever before, she wanted to help him find the *vajra*.

"I saw something in the waterfall," she said.

He slid his socks on. "What was that?"

"I looked up into the water. I thought I saw something farther up."

"What?"

"It looked like it honeycombed inward. Maybe the caves are up there. That's what I was thinking."

Ken frowned. "Maybe. But you said you looked right into the water? Are you sure you'd be able to see that well considering it was dark and the rush of water might have distorted your vision?"

"Well, I saw it and then I felt a pull toward it."

"Okay," Ken said. "We can check it out in the morning. But right now I think we should get some sleep."

"It's been a long day," Annja said.

"Yes." Ken pulled his sleeping bag over toward Annja. "And a hard day, too."

Annja grinned again. "Well, the night was the hard part." She turned over and closed her eyes, feeling safe and secure in the small glen by the waterfall. She deepened her breathing and soon enough drifted off into sleep.

WHEN THE YOWL BROKE across the glen, it sounded like a banshee screeching mixed with the cries of a wounded animal.

Annja sat bolt upright.

Ken was already out of his sleeping bag with his pistol in hand.

"What was that noise?" she asked.

Ken shook his head. "I don't know."

Around them, the trees had gone still. The crickets no longer chirped. Even the roar of the waterfall seemed subdued. Annja searched the darkness for any sign of an enemy. As she did so, she gradually eased herself out of her sleeping bag. At least if they were attacked, she'd be able to defend herself.

Another yowl sounded, followed by a long, drawn-out moan that wafted through the glen. Annja had never heard any animal that sounded like this before. And she'd been close enough to many that she felt reasonably certain of what lived in the woods.

Then she remembered what Taka had told them at the temple in Osaka. Hadn't he told them about the legend of the *kappa* swamp vampire that supposedly guarded the mountain monastery?

"Ken."

"It's just a legend, Annja." Ken shook his head. "Taka was probably just having a little bit of fun at our expense."

"Yeah, well, he's not here right now to ask, and this thing is out there somewhere. And I, for one, am not feeling too good about things right now." She closed her eyes and saw the sword, but when she reached for it, she couldn't wrap her hands around the hilt.

What was going on?

She opened her eyes. "I can't get my sword."

Ken frowned. "Why not?"

"I don't know."

"That's not good." With a free hand, Ken rummaged in his backpack and then tossed Annja a hunting knife in its sheath. "Here."

She caught it and unsheathed the blade that shone in the fading moonlight.

Another yowl sounded.

"That was a lot closer."

Ken had adjusted himself to aim properly. "I think it came from over there." He pointed at a grove of trees on the farthest edge of the glen.

"Don't shoot unless you have a target."

Ken glanced at Annja. "Yeah, thanks."

"Sorry," she said.

"Forget it. Just stay alert."

It grew colder then, as a stiff wind blew from deep out in the forest. Along with it, a mist seeped into the outskirts of the glen.

"It's getting foggy in here," Annja said.

"Temperature change," Ken said. "Totally natural."

"Are you sure?"

Ken nodded, but his face looked grim. And Annja didn't think he looked particularly convinced of his own statements.

The hunting knife felt firm in her hand. She was puzzled, though. Why couldn't she draw the sword out? She needed it certainly. So what had she done wrong that she couldn't bring it out at her command?

She wondered if her experience in the waterfall had done something to her. Had it somehow made her unable to get the sword? What would she do now that she couldn't get to it anymore?

She frowned. That couldn't be it. What would make her unable to use the sword if she'd just meditated? It just didn't make any sense.

Her stomach sank.

What if making love to Ken had been the wrong thing to do? What if it had signaled some sort of lapse of moral judgment on her part? If the sword truly had once belonged to Joan of Arc, then was God mad at her for sleeping with Ken?

Well, she thought, it certainly felt like the right thing to do. And it had been a lot of fun to boot.

No, there had to be another reason. Annja had never aspired

to be Joan of Arc anyway. That was something she'd always maintained in the wake of discovering she could use the sword. She didn't put herself on a higher level than anyone else. And she really had no idea how the sword figured into her life.

It was more of an ongoing experiment than anything else.

It's probably something obvious, she thought. Something I'm overlooking.

Another yowl broke the silence, followed by two more.

"Problem," Ken said.

"What?"

"There seems to be more than one of them."

Annja swallowed. "Arc you sure?"

"The first one—" Ken pointed "—came from over there. But the next two sounded at the far end of the pond. And they weren't echoes, either. There are definitely more than one of whatever is out there."

"Wonderful."

"I'm thrilled, too."

Annja considered the hunting knife. "I don't think this is going to be much use against multiple attackers."

"There's something else."

Annja frowned. "You're just full of good news tonight."

Ken pointed at the ground. "The mist is getting thicker."

Annja looked and saw he was right. The mist that had seeped in a few minutes previously was expanding to envelop the entire breadth of the glen. Annja's lower torso was already covered.

"This still natural?" she asked.

Ken shrugged. "I haven't been out here enough at night to know if this is natural or not. I was saying that earlier to try to calm you down."

"It didn't work."

"It didn't work on me, either," Ken said. "But you can't blame a guy for trying."

"I can if something worse happens to us now," Annja said. The mist was billowing in, like a thick smoke hugging the ground but drifting higher. Already many of the tree trunks close by were impossible to see.

"Mist like this cannot be natural," Annja said.

She looked inside of herself again to see if she could get the sword. But as she reached her hands for it, it seemed as if an invisible force field was inhibiting her from getting close enough to wrap her hands around the hilt.

"Damn."

"Still no sword?"

"No."

"I won't have much of a shot with this gun," Ken said. "My line of sight sucks right now. Trying to pinpoint a fast-moving target will be crazy."

Two more yowls sounded. They were much closer now.

"The mist plays tricks with the sounds," Annja said. "Right?"

Ken shook his head. "They're in the glen with us now."

Annja gripped the knife harder.

Ken tapped her on the shoulder and held a finger to his lips. There'd be no talking now. No sense letting whatever was in the glen know exactly where they were. If they were going to be attacked, they'd at least have to work for it.

Another three yowls filled the air. To Annja it seemed as if they were only twenty feet away.

Her heart hammered in her chest. But she didn't really feel afraid. She frowned. Now, that was weird.

In every instance of combat before this night, she'd had some sense of danger in some way. She used to think it was natural to get butterflies like that, but in recent years she'd learned to rely on it more as instinct than mere anxiety.

She found it accurate, almost to a fault.

But now her warning system seemed to be faulty, as well. She couldn't draw the sword out and she couldn't rely on her instincts to protect her.

Everything was falling apart. And nothing made sense.

The mist drifted higher, up to their necks. Ken and Annja ducked beneath the opaqueness. Even being close to each other, they had trouble seeing anything.

Ken used his fingers to describe how he wanted Annja positioned. They would squat back-to-back in the event of an attack. At least that way they could know one definite thing in the mist of uncertainty.

Annja shifted around quietly, getting into position. Feeling the strength of Ken's back against hers made her feel a little bit better, but only a little.

Another yowl sounded.

Ten feet now, Annja thought. And the timbre had changed, as well. Like they're hunting for us in the mist.

And still, she wasn't afraid.

Are we safe here in the mist? she wondered. If we don't do anything to give away our position, is there a chance that whatever is out there won't be able to get a fix on our location and thereby attack?

It seemed too good to be true. And Annja didn't much feel like relying on mist for protection.

The hunting knife felt a little slippery in her grasp, and

she realized she was sweating a lot in response to the stress of the situation.

She heard a low growl that couldn't have been any farther than six feet away.

They're so close!

Annja wanted to shout and run into the mist, driving them off and just slashing and attacking, but Ken's back kept her where she was. She wouldn't leave him to be alone in this mess. She would stay with him and they would fight to the end.

The mist now enveloped everything around them. Annja could see nothing but white-gray, illuminated by the vague moonlight above. As far as she could tell, the mist simply went on forever.

She heard something to her right.

And then something else.

They're right there, she thought. Right there. They must hear us breathing. Any moment now they'll attack.

She closed her eyes and looked again for the sword, but nothing happened.

Why? She frowned. So much for going out swinging.

Behind her, she heard a sudden knock and then heard Ken moan. His back went slack.

"Ken?"

Something knocked her under her ear and the mist vanished as blackness dragged Annja under.

31

Nezuma rolled over on his side, perched on the cliff overlooking the glen. The ghillie suit he wore enabled him to blend in perfectly with the surrounding forest. The night-vision scope he had spent the previous hour looking through rested in his hand.

Next to him, wearing another ghillie suit but squatting against the trunk of a tree and armed with a Heckler & Koch G36 assault rifle, sat Shuko. She held a parabolic microphone and attached to a set of earplugs in. When she saw Nezuma roll over and look at her, she took out the plugs.

"That was interesting," he said.

"What happened after the fog came in?"

"A lot of confusion," said Shuko. "They had no idea what was going on. They seemed disoriented and completely unaware. You heard the animal howling, as did I, but just before the mist dissipated, I heard two sounds that could only have been people getting knocked out."

"You're sure about that?"

"Absolutely." Shuko pulled back the hood of the ghillie suit so she could lay down the parabolic microphone. "This thing is state-of-the-art technology. And I'm pretty good at identifying sounds like that."

Nezuma pondered this for a moment. "Once the fog rolled in, I couldn't see anything. The way it came, though, seemed rather bizarre. I thought it was a natural occurrence, but now I'm not so sure."

"You think they had a fog machine?"

"I don't know. What I do know is Kennichi and Creed are now missing from the glen where they were a few moments ago. Their gear is also missing. The whole thing seems rather strange to me."

"Looks like a snatch job," Shuko said.

Nezuma smiled. "That," he said, "is exactly what it looks like to me, too."

"You think someone beat us to the punch?"

Nezuma undid his hood and let it back so fresh air could circulate on his skin. "Possibly. But I don't know who."

"Your Yakuza friends," Shuko said.

Nezuma spit. "They're not friends, Shuko—you know that. As far as I'm concerned, they're idiots. And they certainly don't have the ability to pull off something like this in such an isolated area. It would require far too much planning and technical skill to bring it off successfully. Plus, they would need an intimate knowledge of this area."

"They don't have that knowledge."

"No," Nezuma said. "They don't."

"Which leaves us with what—two possibilities?" Shuko said.

Nezuma nodded. "A party we might know about or a party we have no idea about."

"I doubt we'll figure it out here."

"True. What did you hear before the mist came down?"

"The woman said something about the waterfall."

Nezuma sat up. "What did she say?"

"Something about it looking honeycombed. That she saw something while she was inside it."

"Interesting." Nezuma glanced at the waterfall. It fell from a soaring height, probably close to two hundred feet. It was a pure wall of water falling over rocks that had probably been there for hundreds of thousands of years.

"What are you thinking?" Shuko asked.

He glanced at Shuko, who was already pulling off her ghillie suit. "I am considering the possibility that Creed is actually a bit smarter than I recognized early on. That perhaps she did indeed see something when she was in the waterfall."

"The entrance to the caves?"

"Very possibly." Nezuma rolled his suit up and stowed it in his backpack. "Let's get going."

Shuko followed him down the side of the cliff. They'd positioned themselves there earlier after Nezuma had declared it one of the few areas from which they could comfortably observe the glen without fear of someone coming up behind them.

The trail down was steep, with bits of shale and gravel coming loose with every step. Nezuma and Shuko adjusted their footwork accordingly, using their body weight to slow their descent so they wouldn't accidentally fall.

At the bottom, they paused, squatting by the trail leading

up. Nezuma used hand signals to let Shuko know they should wait to see if anyone was around and reacted to their walk down from the cliff.

But after ten minutes of nothing but natural noises, Nezuma signaled it was time to move. He drew out his own gun, a smaller Heckler & Koch UMP that he could fire comfortably with one hand.

Shuko came behind him, cradling the heavier H&K. The bullets in her gun were much more powerful than Nezuma's. They moved to the glen. Nezuma approached first with Shuko braced by a tall pine scanning the area in case of an ambush.

Nezuma knelt where the camp fire had been only forty minutes before. The ground was damp and there remained only a patch of burned grass where there had been stones, logs and char from the fire.

He frowned. What could so utterly erase the presence of people in such a brief span of time?

Even the pine needles that Kennichi and Creed had used to make themselves more comfortable had been scattered around. In fact, he realized, someone coming through this glen would be hard-pressed to prove that there had been anyone camping there recently.

Nezuma shook his head. There was no way on earth this could have been carried out by anyone he knew of.

He turned and waved Shuko in. It went against his better judgment to bring his cover fire in, but he wanted her to see what they were dealing with.

Shuko knelt and brushed her hands along the ground. Nezuma knew she was looking for sign—tracks left by

Kennichi and Creed and possibly by whatever had grabbed them almost an hour before.

"There's nothing here," she whispered. "We saw them, clear as day, and we saw them vanish. But there's nothing here that would prove they even existed."

Nezuma nodded. That's what he was afraid of. He nodded to the waterfall. "Let's get in there."

Shuko stood and they moved to the pond. But rather than strip down, Nezuma and Shuko split up and each took a side, scanning the entire area.

Nezuma caught water spray in his face and he brushed it away, still alert for any possible indication that the mist and what it contained was coming back. He bent low and looked behind the waterfall as much as he could. But given its position, doing so was almost impossible.

He saw Shuko coming back. "Any luck?"

She shook her head. "It's too difficult getting a glimpse at it. I think we need to actually get into the water."

"I agree," Nezuma said.

Shuko hefted her G-36. "I'll get the dry bag."

Nezuma turned back to the waterfall. What was it about this that had produced such an odd occurrence? And if this really was the entrance to some sort of hidden monastery, then how did they access it?

Shuko returned and Nezuma slid his UMP into the bag. Shuko closed the zipper and then secured the overlap that would protect the guns from exposure to water. Shuko's would fire anyway even when submerged, but Nezuma wasn't sure about the performance of his UMP after being dunked. He didn't want to take any chances.

Shuko strapped her pack on again and hefted the dry bag, as well. From her belt, she drew out her knife and stepped into the water.

Nezuma also drew out his black-bladed tanto knife. At twelve inches, it was a wicked-looking blade capable of penetrating a car door or slicing a free-hanging rope in half. Nezuma had used this particular weapon numerous times to great effect.

He strode into the water, vaguely aware of how cold it was. If Annja Creed could withstand the water, then he was going to, as well. There would be no way he'd ever succumb to it when the American woman had already demonstrated her ability to withstand its temperatures.

They approached the waterfall.

"Shall I take point?" Shuko asked.

Nezuma looked at her. She'd dropped saying "master." It was another sign she was becoming complacent about their relationship. He shook his head. "No. I'll go up first."

He ducked under the falls and shuddered as the cold torrent hit him like a sack of bricks. The water came up to his thighs and he slogged through it, reaching the flat stone ledge where he'd seen Creed standing and doing some imitation of meditation.

Nezuma stood on it and looked up into the raging water. It blinded him for a moment until he adjusted his head position so the water hit only parts of his head and face, leaving his eyes alone.

About a hundred feet above him, he could see the dark outline of something oval. And above that, more similar-shaped entrances. That must be it.

He leaned out of the falls and saw Shuko. "It's here."

She came under with him and looked where he pointed. She nodded and had to shout over the roar of the water. "But how do we reach it?"

Nezuma shook his head. "I don't know."

Shuko moved toward the back of the waterfall and pressed her hands against the smooth slabs that ran from high overhead to the floor of the pond below. Nezuma watched her work with her eyes closed and smiled. She was truly a gifted woman and an apt pupil.

It would be a shame to kill her, he decided.

"Master."

He smiled. "Yes?"

"I think we can scale the wall."

Nezuma pursed his lips. "Are you sure? We don't have the gear necessary for that and the challenge of the water rushing over us."

"We've got enough rope. I can try it first and secure anchor points. You can climb up next."

Nezuma looked up. It was a long way to go. Any misstep would cost them their lives. The thought of departing this plane of existence without having recovered the *dorje* did not sit well with Nezuma. "I don't know," he said.

"It's the only way."

She was right. Nezuma could see no other way to access the caves above. They would have to climb.

"All right, but go slowly. I don't want anything to happen to you."

She smiled, looking like a beautiful mess as the water splashed down on her. "I'll be fine."

Nezuma tried to move out of her way. He'd still have to stay under the freezing water while she climbed so he could try to spot her in case something bad happened. He knew honestly, though, that if she fell, there'd be little chance of his catching her or otherwise saving her life.

Shuko must have known that, too. But the knowledge that she could die had never stopped her before, and Nezuma could see it wasn't about to give her pause now.

She slid her pack off and rummaged through the top pocket, drawing out a length of twisted nylon-and-hemp rope noted for its ability to withstand high weights and harsh conditions.

Nezuma frowned. This certainly qualified as harsh.

Shuko looped the rope around herself and then drew out a few anchors that she stowed on her belt. She looked at Nezuma.

"I don't know if I'll find anyplace to put these. Hammering them in could potentially alert whoever might be there."

Nezuma nodded. "Understood. Just do the best you can to show me how to follow your lead."

"Your life is in my hands," Shuko said smiling.

Nezuma grinned. "Try not to let that power go to your head."

Shuko gave him a quick peck on the lips and then felt her way to the back of the waterfall again. Nezuma watched as she found two footholds and then looked up, reaching for places to put her hands or fingers.

Nezuma had seen her climb enough times to know that if anyone was capable of scaling the back side of a waterfall, it was Shuko. Her name meant "claw," after all.

And if the universe willed it, they'd soon be in to those caves with the *dorje* at long last in sight.

32

Annja's head throbbed much the same way her shoulder did—as if someone were using her to pound out a drumbeat over and over again. Her eyes popped open and she moaned as she tried to sit up but found she couldn't.

Ken was already awake and he smiled at her. She noticed that he was bound in strange ropes and started to say something about it when she finally realized they were both gagged.

She glanced around the room. They were on a stone floor. The walls were plain except for torches embedded in the rock and a tapestry that hung nearby featuring hundreds of small but angry-looking deities.

Annja followed Ken's eyes as he pointed out that they were not alone. The room was filled with about a dozen monks dressed in dark-brown-and-blue kimono robes and split-skirt *hakama* that had been tied around their legs. They wore simple slippers, but what made them look ominous were the spears and swords they all carried.

A pair of hands found Annja's ropes, and the tightness disappeared, followed by a renewed sense of pain as the throbbing increased in her shoulder and head. The hands also cut away her gag, and Annja spit it out on the floor.

She looked up and saw a face she thought she recognized. It was the strange monk who had fought the schoolgirl assassins in Osaka. But this time, he wasn't smiling. His face looked severe and the baldness of his head did little to make him look jolly.

He said a few words in Japanese to her, but Annja just shook her head. He noted and then cleared his throat. "I thought perhaps you might speak Japanese considering who you're with and what you are looking for."

"Sorry, no," she said.

"No matter."

Annja glanced at Ken, who was still trussed up. She looked back at the monk. "What about my friend?"

He smiled. "We have to be sure that he won't try to kill us when we cut him free. We know that he is exceptionally skilled in martial arts."

Annja looked at Ken, who nodded once. "He'll be fine," Annja said.

The monk nodded to one of the others, and the man knelt to cut Ken free. Annja halfway expected him to come out of the ropes fighting, but instead, he simply took out his gag and then continued to sit quietly.

The older monk nodded, apparently satisfied that Ken wouldn't try anything. "Are you both all right?"

Ken looked at Annja. "Your shoulder can't be feeling too good right now," he said.

Annja nodded. "Hurts like hell. So does my head."

"I apologize for the need to render you unconscious, but our success as a sect has depended largely on our ability to remain hidden from society. If my people were a bit rough in their handling of you, I apologize. I didn't realize they hurt your shoulder, as well," the monk said.

"The shoulder was injured before your people took us," Ken said. "But it has been bothering her. It's the rotator cuff."

The monk nodded. "I will have an herbal remedy made that will dull the pain—both in your shoulder and in your head." He looked at Ken. "Do you require the same?"

"No. I'm fine."

"As I expected. How long have you trained in *ninjitsu*?"

"Almost twenty years."

"So you are aware of how to control your pain and discomfort."

Ken shrugged. "Yeah, I've used the skill any number of times."

"Please get up and follow me. We have several things to discuss, and I wish for this to be concluded as soon as possible. Your presence here is jeopardizing my people."

Annja started to protest, but then remembered that she and Ken had been followed everywhere they'd gone. Trying to argue they hadn't been would be foolish and grate on their new host's nerves.

They trailed behind him as he strode down the stone hallway. The flickering torches cast strange shadows. Here and there, they saw several doors carved into the rock of the walls. Where they led, Annja had no idea. "Where exactly are we?" she asked.

The old monk looked back. "You don't know?"

"No."

"You're in the mountain."

Annja stopped. "So, it *was* a series of caves I saw?"

"Yes. We use them to circulate fresh air into the caverns up here. But it's not a path I'd recommend using as a way in— the climb is far too dangerous for anyone to attempt."

They reached a room with a blazing hearth where thick planks of cedar had been turned into benches. A low table sat in the middle and the monk gestured for them to be seated at it.

From another area, a monk came in carrying a tray with a tea service. He set it down before them and then withdrew.

"My name," the old monk said as he reached into his robe and produced a small packet of something dark and leafy, "is Eiji. I am what you would call the abbot here at this particular monastery."

"So there really is a monastery here in the mountains of Iga," Annja said.

Eiji broke the dry black leaves into one of the tea cups and then poured the steaming hot water over it. Annja watched as the water turned dark brown and a peculiar scent wafted into the air. Eiji passed the cup to her and bowed.

"This will ease your pain," he said gently.

Annja took the cup and sniffed at it. It seemed too hot to drink, but she pursed her lips, blew across the surface and then sipped a bit of the tea. Surprisingly, it wasn't bitter, but quite sweet.

"It's delicious," Annja said. And as the warmth flowed down her throat, she could feel the deadening effects of it begin to work on her head and shoulder. "What do you call it?"

Eiji shook his head. "The herb is far too dangerous to discuss in detail. Someone without the proper training attempting to use it would undoubtedly kill themselves or the people they made the tea for."

Annja raised her eyebrows. "This is poisonous?"

"If given in the wrong dosage, absolutely." Eiji smiled. "Most medicines are both a curative and a poison to some extent anyway, so please don't be so shocked when I tell you that."

Annja took another sip. "Just so long as Ken here doesn't have to haul my corpse back down the mountain."

Eiji nodded. "Which brings us to the question of your traveling partner here who has thus far said very little." Eiji looked at Ken. "You have questions, no doubt."

"It's here, isn't it?" Ken asked.

Eiji smiled. "I like your candor." He sighed. "Over the years, we have found that those people who find their way to us are usually anything but honest. And when they attempt to recover the *vajra*, they inevitably fail. Simple honesty is always a good way to start out."

Ken bowed. "I have come a long way to find it."

"No doubt," Eiji said. "But why do you want it?"

"It belongs to my family."

Eiji looked at him. "Are you telling me that you are a member of the Yumegakure-ryu?"

Ken bowed again. "I am the last member of the family. My name is Kennichi Ogawa."

Eiji perked up. "If that is true…"

Ken stood and pulled off his shirt. He turned and in the firelight Annja saw the small tattoo over his left shoulder blade. It looked like some of the samurai family crests that she'd seen over the years.

Eiji peered closer and then leaned back. "You have the correct *mon* for the family. But then again, any artist could re-create that."

Ken put his shirt back on and shook his head. "There are so few people who know about the crest, let alone where to position it, such a theory holds no water. I am the last male heir to my family name, marked at birth using bamboo needles to deliver the ink under my skin. The tattoo has been with me since I was born."

Eiji clapped his hands and another monk appeared. Eiji said a few things to him, and he nodded and then vanished.

"Please sit down," Eiji said. "I apologize for my rudeness. But surely you would admit that we have had our fair share of imposters over the years. I find it difficult sometimes to remember that there are truly honest people still left in the world."

Ken smiled. "What you and your people have done for my family has been exhausting and invaluable for millennia. I certainly understand your readiness to suspect anyone who claims to be the rightful heir to the Yumegakure-ryu."

The monk reappeared with trays of fish and rice. He set it down and then left. Eiji gestured. "I'm afraid we don't indulge in a wide variety of diet here. But we can offer you the freshest fish and rice and vegetables. I'm sure you will be happy with how it is prepared."

Annja picked up a set of chopsticks and dived into the rice and fish, carefully plucking bits of meat and vegetables from the tray and chewing them. "I didn't realize how hungry I was," she said.

Eiji grinned. "That is another side effect of the tea you just drank. It makes you rather hungry."

Annja looked at him. "What the heck did I just drink—cannabis tea?"

"Of course not." Eiji watched her eat. "But it is a potent appetite stimulant. Such a thing is necessary anyway for you to recover."

Ken ate, as well, but Annja could see he wasn't very hungry. "You okay?"

He nodded. "How many people have come here pretending to be the rightful heir to my family's name?" he asked Eiji.

The monk sipped his tea. "Probably twenty since I've been here."

"That many?" Ken shook his head. "I never realized it would attract so many people."

"The lure of power is extremely strong," Eiji said. "The promise of wealth and fame is sometimes too much for someone to handle and they retreat to the lesser realms of deceit and greed."

"When did you get here?" Annja asked.

"A long time ago," Eiji said. "I came from Nepal."

"Nepal?"

Eiji nodded. "We are not without our own support systems. There are other monasteries like us scattered around the globe. In the remotest areas, we find homes and methods for preserving our particular traditions."

"What are those traditions?" Annja asked.

"We are warrior monks," Eiji said. "We do not follow the

same path as so many of our supposed brethren. We eat meat, and we practice martial arts. That alone makes us unique."

"And here in Japan, are you the only monastery?" she asked.

"North in Hokkaido there is another. Again, built within the mountains where we have access to fresh water and clean air. The monastery in Nepal is built near Everest. My brother Siben is the head monk there."

"It's fascinating," Annja said, "to think that there are still secret societies like this alive and functioning."

Eiji shrugged. "We make no attempts to influence the world. We are charged with merely preserving our own traditions." He glanced at Ken. "And sometimes, we are tasked with other things, like the protection of precious relics."

"How did that happen?" Annja asked.

"We weren't always isolated and remote like this. Far back in history, we were one of the oldest sects operating in Japan and elsewhere. Leaders looked to us for wisdom and guidance. But as Japan and other places fell apart through domestic and civil unrest, their reliance on us shifted to reliance on might and greed. We recognized what was coming and decided the best way to preserve our own destiny would be to simply disappear into the annals of history."

"And you've been here ever since?" Annja asked.

"Not here, per se. There have been other monasteries. But warlords and various other factions destroyed those. We retreated higher and higher and into more remote areas, until we at last found places that could protect us as much as we protected the places."

"You protect the places, too?"

Eiji's eyes twinkled. "The legend of the *kappa* swamp vampire is one of our finest. The howls you heard outside—they did a good job, did they not?"

Annja laughed. "Definitely."

"We are guardians of the land. This place is vital to our survival, and nowadays we are vital for its survival, as well."

Ken looked up. "What happened to all the people who claimed to be me?"

Eiji shrugged. "They died, of course."

"You killed them?" Annja asked.

Eiji laughed. "Of course not. We didn't have to kill them. We simply showed them how to get the *vajra*. Their greed and deceit took care of the rest."

"How so?" Ken asked.

Eiji leaned forward and patted his leg. "You'll find out soon enough."

33

Nezuma gritted his teeth and pulled himself farther up the rope as the waterfall crashed down on his shoulders. At the very top, he saw Shuko's hand reach for him and he grabbed it, finally hauling himself over the ledge and into the cave entrance.

"That was a challenge," he said around gulps of breath.

Shuko nodded. "It was probably the most difficult climb I've ever undertaken. I wasn't sure I could do it. But at least we're here now."

The cave they sat in was about four feet high, impossible to stand in, but easy enough to traverse by crawling. The rock walls seemed smooth. Nezuma ran his hand along the cool stone and shook his head. "Do you really think this is the way in?"

Shuko shrugged. "I haven't had a chance to explore farther in. My goal was to get here, find an anchor for the rope and then get you up here."

Nezuma watched her open the dry bag and check the weapons. She nodded and then handed Nezuma his UMP while she fixed the strap on the G-36. "They're fine. No trace of water damage at all."

Nezuma accepted the gun from her and smiled. "Excellent."

Shuko crawled forward a distance. "Seems okay. But you never know—No!" She screamed and Nezuma heard the sound of something zipping by his head. He ducked as blades shot past his head.

Shuko moaned from farther up. Nezuma eased himself forward as fast as he felt he was able to. The presence of what could only be booby traps frightened him.

Shuko lay on her side, gasping through her mouth. The sound of her breathing was high-pitched and rattled. Nezuma scrambled over her.

"What happened?"

She pointed. "Blade…it caught me in the top of my chest."

Nezuma looked at the injury. If she'd ducked her head, it might have caught her directly in the face, but since she was looking up, it had sliced into her chest and embedded itself into her lung.

Already, her breathing rasped and sputtered. Pinkish red foam bubbled out of her mouth. Shuko gripped Nezuma's hands.

"I'm sorry, master."

Nezuma frowned. "No more master."

"I love you," she gasped.

He gritted his teeth. "I know."

Her eyes pleaded with him. He knew what she wanted him to say, but he just couldn't say it. He'd never honestly loved her. He had cared for her. But love? No. And saying it now just because she wanted to hear it was unnecessary.

She sucked breath in. The bleeding would kill her soon enough, Nezuma decided.

"I...know...you...would have...killed me...anyway," she whispered.

He was startled. "What?"

"When you found it. You would have killed me."

He frowned. He thought he'd managed to conceal his intentions, but somehow she'd known.

"Do it."

He shook his head. "No. There's no need."

"You would have anyway. Don't let me die like this." Shuko gripped his hand hard.

"If you aren't man enough to love me, then at least be man enough to kill me."

Nezuma unholstered the UMP and brought it up to Shuko's heart. He looked into her eyes but found only contempt staring back. Her lips parted one more time.

"Please."

Nezuma's finger tightened around the trigger, but he wouldn't shoot. She'll be dead soon anyway, he thought.

He watched her face for another moment before reholstering his UMP and moving on. No sense wasting good bullets on her. There'd be plenty of other people to kill soon enough.

Nezuma scampered forward. This complicated things, though—he would have to deal with Kennichi and Creed on his own, rather than have the backup that Shuko had provided.

He thought about going back and taking her weapon, as well, but disregarded it. The G-36 was too big. And dragging a bag of worthless gear might weigh him down.

He moved on, careful now because of the booby traps.

He didn't want to end up like Shuko.

"WHAT EXACTLY DID YOU MEAN when you said we'd find out?" Annja asked as Eiji led them down yet another corridor that seemed to take them farther into the mountain. The air seemed still, almost as if very little of the fresh air they circulated into the mountain made it this far in.

"It's why you are here," Eiji said. "And it's where you're destined to go. Everyone who seeks the *vajra* must seek it in the same way. There are no shortcuts."

"Too bad," Ken said. "I was hoping I'd show you the tattoo and maybe you would roll it out here for me."

Eiji looked at him. "That was a joke, correct?"

"Apparently not a very good one," Ken said.

Eiji pointed down the corridor to a door. "That is where you must go now if you truly seek the *vajra*."

"Through the door?" Annja asked. "That's it?"

"The door," Eiji said, "will lead you to a series of caves and a labyrinth built into the mountain. There are numerous options and only by choosing wisely will you find the *vajra* at the end of it."

Ken sighed. "Have you ever been in there?"

Eiji smirked. "You aren't the first person to think that putting a weapon to my skull and forcing me to reveal the path to the *vajra* would save a lot of time and energy."

"You haven't," Annja said. "The *vajra* was placed inside

long before you were born. And to safeguard it properly, there's no way they'd reveal how to get to it."

Eiji nodded. "The secret died many, many years ago. And none are alive who would know how to get past the various obstacles. I can only tell you the same thing I've told the others who came here—be careful."

"Great," Ken said. He looked at Annja. "Are you ready for this?"

Annja felt her shoulder, which seemed much better since she'd had Eiji's tea. "Yeah, I think so," she said, feeling excited by the challenge.

Eiji bowed once more to them. "Weapons are not allowed inside. Otherwise I would return your supplies to you. They will be here for when you return. If you return."

"Thanks for the vote of confidence," Annja said.

Eiji bowed a final time and then strode off, leaving Annja and Ken alone in the silent corridor. The torches flickered and cast shadows that leaped from the wall to the floor and back again. Each time the light illuminated a different section of the rock wall, revealing the many facets of it.

Ken took a deep breath. "I guess there's not much more to do, is there?"

"Except to go in and get it," Annja said. "We've come this far. To turn back now—"

"I can't turn back," Ken said. "This is where my destiny lies. My search either ends here or else it opens up a whole new world for me."

"I'm hoping for option two myself," Annja said.

He smiled. "As am I."

They walked down the hall to the door. Like all the other

doors in the mountain monastery, this one was also made of stone. Ken looked at the hinge work and shook his head. "I wouldn't even know how to imagine creating a working hinge made out of stone like this. It's amazing."

"The whole concept of this place is amazing," Annja said. "Who would ever believe that such places existed? With all the technology we have and all the places we've explored, there are things still right beneath our noses that we don't know anything about."

"Live and learn," Ken said. "Here we go."

He grasped the latch and pulled back the door. Annja expected to see him have to pull hard to get the door to open, but it swung back easily, revealing a gaping maw of darkness that seemed ready to devour them whole.

Ken peered inside. "Smells musty."

Annja got two torches from the brackets on the walls and handed one to Ken. "This might help."

The torches immediately lit up the area beyond the door. But rather than anything remarkable, the only thing they found waiting for them was yet another corridor.

"This place is built like a pyramid," Annja said. "Miles and miles of corridors with very few real rooms. You could get lost and never know how to get out if you were in here alone."

Ken ducked inside with her. The roof was lower and the smoke from the torches billowed up and spilled across the stone above them.

"It looks like it runs about a hundred feet before there's a wall farther down," he said

Annja followed his gaze and nodded. "Shall we?"

Ken stopped her. "You don't think there'd be any booby traps at this stage, do you?"

Annja halted. "Honestly, no. I don't think this is the official start of anything. Eiji said this door would take us to a place where there was a series of caves that would then lead us to a labyrinth, right?"

"Yes," Ken said.

"Then I think we're safe here."

Ken sighed. "Nothing ventured."

They walked down the corridor. As they did, Annja hoped that she hadn't been wrong, that she wouldn't suddenly hear some sort of rushing air that might signal poison darts or hidden scythes swooping down to kill them.

They made their way slowly and carefully. But nothing surprised them.

They reached the end of the corridor and saw that it turned to the left and sloped upward.

"I guess we go up," Ken said.

Annja followed him up the hallway, discovering that they both had to duck as they rose in height since the roof seemed to get lower and lower as they progressed.

"Who built this?" Annja said. "A drunk engineer?"

Ken pointed. "Look."

Annja held her torch higher and could see farther ahead. "Looks like it levels off."

Ken nodded. "Yes. And beyond that, I see dark openings."

Annja's heart quickened. Finally, it seemed as if they were close to the final stage of their search. If they could make it past the traps and obstacles and actually retrieve the *vajra*, all would be good. Then they'd only have to figure out a way to take care of the people waiting to take it from them.

She shivered, thinking about the voice in her ear back at the hotel room. He'd sounded so utterly evil, as if he knew just what he would do before he killed her if she didn't give him what he wanted.

"You okay?"

She snapped back to reality. Ken was staring at her. "Annja?"

"Yeah. Yeah, I'm fine. Just daydreaming for a second there. Sorry."

Ken nodded. "As long as it's out of your system now. From here on out, things are going to get tricky. We need total concentration."

They arrived at the end of the corridor and stood on a level patch of stonework in front of three cave entrances. Ken and Annja examined all of them, looking for any obvious signs that one would be a better choice than the others.

They could find nothing.

"Each one seems identical to the other," Annja said after another examination of all three.

"I suppose they'd have to be," Ken replied. "No sense bothering if they couldn't make the very first obstacle a challenge."

Annja nodded. "This is an obstacle, isn't it?"

"Sure," Ken said. "Not in the traditional sense, but choosing the wrong path could quite obviously kill us. This may actually be the toughest part of the entire search to get the *vajra*."

"You really think so?"

Ken shrugged. "Nah, there are probably worse things inside."

Annja smiled. "Great."

"You have any thoughts on this?" he asked.

"Would tossing a coin be bad form?"

Ken held up his hands. "It might not do wonders for your career if people found out you'd chosen something based on a coin toss rather than exhaustive scientific analysis and historical perspective, but it's fine by me."

"Great," Annja said. She held up a coin. "Heads or tails?"

34

"Annja?"

Annja held up the coin. "Yes?"

"There are three cave entrances here," Ken said.

"I know that."

"Your coin only has two sides."

"I—" She frowned. "Nuts, I forgot about that." She slid the coin back into her pocket and leaned against the wall. "So much for that idea."

Ken stepped away from the entrances and frowned. "Any thoughts from a historical perspective you think might be important here?"

Annja sighed. "I wish I had my laptop. I could punch this whole situation in and see what comes up."

Ken stood in front of the first entrance and closed his eyes. Annja watched at him.

"What are you doing?"

He motioned her over. "Stand here and close your eyes.

Remember what we were talking about at the waterfall? Go inside and check yourself against using this as the way in."

Annja closed her eyes and saw herself walking into the cave. Almost immediately, she felt a vague stab of pain in her stomach. "No," she said, almost shouting.

She opened her eyes. "Sorry, I didn't mean—"

Ken shook his head. "Don't apologize. I got the same feeling. This is not the one to use."

They moved down to the next entrance and repeated the process. Again they both got a bad feeling.

At the entrance to the third, Annja smiled. "Do we even need to do this with this one? It's the only one left."

Ken nodded. "Just to be sure."

Annja closed her eyes again and walked into the entrance in her mind. This time she found it perfectly comfortable. She opened her eyes to tell Ken this was definitely the one to use.

"Ken—hey!"

She was already standing in the cave entrance with her torch. Ken stood next to her smiling.

"Cool, huh?"

"How did that happen?"

Ken shrugged. "The only way I could explain that is that our bodies took over and moved us in there in order to show it was safe. Much of this next stage might be a willingness on our part to almost switch off our conscious minds and let our instincts take over."

Annja frowned. "I wish I could do that easily. But honestly, I don't know if I can turn it off."

Ken put a hand on her shoulder. "The fact that you're standing in the cave with me right now proves that you can.

Just relax and pay attention to how you feel physically as we proceed. That will be the best source of answers, I think."

They moved deeper into the cave, walking slowly. The walls closed in as they advanced, forcing them to switch to single file.

"I'll go first," Ken said. "No sense in making you trip any traps. This is my family's relic, after all."

"We'll swap it out every so often," Annja said. "I knew the risks going into this thing. It's not fair for you to take them all."

He nodded and then continued along. The cave walls suddenly opened up, and then in front of them, they saw a huge chasm. Swirling air rushed around them, emanating from somewhere far below and continuing up for hundreds of feet.

"Looks like we've arrived at our first challenge," Annja said.

"Second," Ken said. "The first was getting in here, remember?"

Annja stood near the lip of the chasm. "It's too far to jump to the other side. We'd never make it."

Ken looked at the rim. "Our ledge ends just down there. There's no way to skirt across to the other side. And we don't have climbing gear to attempt the walls."

"They look pretty smooth, anyway," Annja said. "Probably worn that way by the air and water over the years."

Ken crossed his arms. "I guess we'll have to think of something else, then."

"Or not think about it at all," Annja said.

Without hesitating, she walked off the ledge into the chasm.

NEZUMA SQUIRMED his way deeper into the mountain. He was rather surprised that Shuko's death hadn't affected him all that much. He smirked. I must be even more coldhearted than I thought.

He heard movement ahead of him. The cave had narrowed significantly as he got farther in, forcing him to keep his arms pinned by his sides and use his torso to do all the work.

But up ahead, he could see flickering lights. Torches, judging by the smell. And he heard people talking, too.

Guards?

He frowned. Taking them out in his current position would prove suicidal if he even attempted it. He'd need to get himself into better position in order to do it and live.

But as he was trying to figure out how to do that, the voices dwindled. Nezuma could hear footsteps and realized he was most likely nearing a corridor of some sort.

All he'd need to do was make sure it was clear before he exited.

Then he could track down the *dorje*. And kill Kennichi and Annja Creed.

He still wished he had backup with him. Shuko would have easily held her own against either one of them, freeing Nezuma to enjoy himself rather than leave him to do all the work.

Still, he was satisfied with how the events seemed to be unfolding. If the gods smiled on him, he'd recover the *dorje* and be back home within the next few hours.

And tomorrow, he could go out searching for a suitable candidate to replace Shuko.

Life was about to get good.

"ANNJA!"

Ken ran to the edge of the chasm and looked down, expecting to see nothing but blackness. Instead, he saw Annja staring back up at him.

"Hey," she said, smiling.

He shook his head. "How the hell did you know to do that?"

She shrugged. "It was the only thing that made sense. I closed my eyes and just walked forward. It's a rock bridge of some sort, but it's wide enough to allow the air current to come up on either side, helping the overall appearance look like one giant bottomless pit."

Ken hopped down. "You're amazing."

"You taught me how to do it."

Ken looked toward the other side. "You sure this goes all the way across?"

"Nope, but I guess we'll find out."

Ken stopped her. "You're closing your eyes?"

Annja smiled. "It's worked so far." She shut her eyes and started walking. She heard Ken sigh and knew he had done the same thing.

Each step she took made her feel more amazed than the last. Who would believe that her instincts could guide her like this? They were facing certain death if they made the wrong choice, and yet twice her instincts now had saved her.

There's probably more than that, she thought, but I'm only really becoming aware of it now.

She stopped suddenly. Annja opened her eyes. Ken stood beside her in exactly the same position.

"What happened?" she asked.

Ken shook his head. "I don't know. I just stopped suddenly. Like my body didn't want to go on anymore."

Annja knelt and felt the ground in front of her.

She nearly toppled off the edge into the pit.

Ken grabbed her and pulled her back.

Annja breathed out. "So much for the bridge going all the way across. I guess it ends there."

"It's a trap," Ken said. "To lull us into a sense of complacency. If we got to this point, we might not have trusted our instincts to stop us and simply walked over the edge."

Annja nodded. "Incredible. I wonder who built this thing."

"Someone keenly interested in making sure the *vajra* was well protected, apparently," Ken said. "Maybe a crazy old monk, maybe a samurai, maybe a ninja. Who knows?"

Annja sat down. "Now what?"

Ken sat down, too. "I wish I knew."

NEZUMA SLID OUT of the narrow duct and dropped to the floor twelve feet below. He immediately brought the UMP out and kept it at the ready. The last thing he wanted was to start a gun battle with anyone. But he couldn't afford to let anyone know he was inside the mountain.

Not yet.

He moved quickly down the corridor, making sure his shadow never fell in front of him. This necessitated his moving from one side of the hall to the other in order to keep the torches and their flames from betraying his presence.

At the end of the corridor, he had two options—left or right.

He chose left.

Down at the far end of the corridor, he saw another door. He headed straight for it.

"How far away do you think it is?"

Ken shrugged. "It looks like it's maybe ten feet or so."

"You think we could jump it?" Annja asked.

"Maybe. But what if it's another optical illusion? We run and try to make a ten-foot jump only to find ourselves flying off into the great void. Not exactly how I saw myself going out, you know?"

"I don't know what else to do," Annja said. "I've tried closing my eyes and I'm not getting anything. I don't see any clear indication as to how we're supposed to proceed."

"Neither do I," Ken said. "And for some reason, I can't figure out why it would end like this. There has to be a way across. A way to continue forward. But how? And where?"

Annja frowned. "Wait," she said.

"What?"

"What did you just say? About going forward."

Ken held up his hands. "I said there must be a way to go forward. What else would the point of this be?"

Annja smiled. And turned.

"That's it."

Ken frowned. "What?"

"We don't go forward at all," Annja said.

Ken shook his head. "I'm not walking backward to my death, Annja."

"No. We don't take this bridge at all. We never had to. But

this was built to protect the *vajra,* and that protection seems to rely on using people's preconceptions against them."

"Explain," Ken said.

"So, you manage to make it into the right cave, maybe by instinct, maybe by blind luck. Then you get to the chasm, and perhaps you find out that there's a cleverly disguised bridge across. You think that's it. You can see the other side and skip right across and fall to your death midway."

"Okay."

"But maybe if you find the bridge, you're not supposed to go forward." She dragged Ken back to the edge of the chasm where they'd started. "Look!"

Ken squinted and then barely saw what Annja was pointing at. A small crawl space made to blend into the rock. He glanced back at Annja.

"I guess we go this way," he said.

Annja nodded. "I think so."

35

Annja led the way as the crawl space opened down at a sharp angle. "Hold my ankles," she called back to Ken. "It drops off farther ahead."

"Don't get complacent, Annja," Ken said. "That's what has probably killed everyone else."

· That and the fact they weren't legitimate heirs to your family, Annja thought. But she kept her wits about her and moved slowly. Every few feet she would stop and close her eyes. Every time she felt a pull to keep going.

The crawl space emptied out into a large room. Annja didn't step down onto the floor until she'd tested it both physically and using her instincts. Both proved sound, so she slid all the way out of the crawl space and waited for Ken to join her.

He slid out and shook his head. "I don't know how earthworms do it."

Ahead of them a single door awaited. Annja frowned. "Not much of a choice here, it would seem."

Ken held her back. "Let's exhaust every other possibility before we take the obvious choice."

They spent the next twenty minutes going over every inch of the simple room. They both reached the same conclusion that the door was the only way to proceed, or as Annja reminded them, go backward.

Ken pulled the door open, and a strong updraft greeted them, extinguishing both of their torches and plunging them into absolute darkness.

"Uh-oh," Annja said.

Ken cleared his throat. "Well, I don't suppose you have any matches, do you?"

"Eiji and his boys cleaned my pockets out before we came into the labyrinth. I don't have a scrap to work with here," she replied.

Ken dumped his torch. "No sense carrying it along with us if we can't rely on it."

Annja dropped hers, as well. "I guess this is the real test, huh?"

"Yeah. The entire thing has been designed to whittle away at what we use and take for granted on a daily basis. Now we're deprived of the one thing that really makes our conscious mind work against us—our eyesight. If we're to continue on, it will have to be by using our other senses."

"And instincts," Annja said.

"Exactly."

They both paused. Finally, Ken said, "Did you still want to take point?"

Annja laughed and felt Ken brush against her. "What are you doing?"

"Looking for a point of reference."

"That was my butt."

"Seemed like a good enough point for me." He chuckled. "Actually, that was an accident. I was looking for the door frame, so at least I know which way we came in." He paused. "You, uh, didn't turn around when you came in, did you?"

"No."

"Good, I'd hate to get started going in the wrong direction."

"You wouldn't get far," Annja said. "You'd run into the walls of the room we came into from the crawl space."

"Good point."

Annja felt him brush past her again. "You got that reference point?"

"I think I'm ready. But we're going to crawl if that's all right with you."

"Absolutely." Annja got down on her hands and knees.

"Take my ankle," Ken said. "We'll do this the way they do in search-and-rescue situations."

Annja grabbed for his ankle. "Okay."

"Go ahead."

"I just did."

Ken paused. "Annja, hurry up and grab my ankle so we can get going."

Annja squeezed harder. "I have your ankle."

"No," Ken said. "You don't."

NEZUMA STOPPED just short of the door.

He could hear breathing on the side of it. Two distinct breathing patterns, he decided after another minute.

Guards?

Or meditating monks?

He frowned. It didn't really matter. They would have to be killed. They prohibited his access and that simply wouldn't do.

The question was how to get them to open the door.

Nezuma slid back and to the side of the door, checking the entire perimeter of it. It didn't seem to have a lock.

So why not just open it?

He grinned. The two monks on the other side were about to get the surprise of their lives.

He gripped the door handle and pulled.

"ANNJA?"

She felt higher and found skin. Searching for the inside of the ankle, she tried to palpate the skin and detect a pulse.

There was none.

"I think I just found another seeker who didn't quite make it."

Ken scrambled back and bumped into her. "You okay?"

"Just a bit startled. I was going to comment on how cold your leg felt, but then when I realized it was a corpse, I felt better, if you can imagine that."

"Probably better than finding another live person in here with us," Ken said, sounding shaken.

"Yeah."

Ken sniffed. "He hasn't decomposed. Is it stiff?"

Annja nudged the body. "Yeah, definitely rigor mortis but not decomposition. Is that even possible?"

"I don't know. I'm not used to being around the dead."

"Let's move," Annja said. "Staying in the room with a dead body doesn't do much for me."

"Good thing," Ken said. He scrambled back up but not before taking Annja's hand and placing it on his ankle. "You ready?"

"Now I am."

Ken started crawling and Annja followed.

NEZUMA KNELT in the darkness of the room. On either side of him, the bodies of the two monks lay with their necks snapped. He'd decided it wouldn't be good to shoot or stab them. Too much noise and too much blood.

By snapping their necks, they could still be positioned in such a way that they looked as if they were meditating.

Provided no one examined them too closely.

It ought to buy him some more time.

That was all he needed.

Nezuma stood and stole down the new corridor.

"I'VE HIT A WALL."

Annja came up alongside Ken. She let her hands travel up and over the surface, but she found nothing but solid stone. "Weird."

"How far do you think we crawled?"

"Felt like it had to be at least two hundred feet."

"That's what I thought, too."

Annja sighed. "Have you been checking your internal compass?"

Ken chuckled. "Good phrase for it. Yeah, I have. And everything seems to indicate this is where we need to be."

"I agree."

"But what is here?" Ken asked.

"Let's check all over the walls and see if we can find something that we'd be able to see immediately if we had light."

She felt Ken's hands on her. "Something's been bothering me," he said.

"What?"

"How did the person back in the room die? We haven't seen anything that I'd say is dangerous for a while now. So what made him die like that? And why hasn't he decomposed?"

"Maybe he's the swamp vampire," Annja said.

"I'm being serious."

"I know. I've been wondering about that, too."

"The only thing I can think of," Ken said, "is that there must be something in here that killed him."

"There's a comforting thought."

"I think maybe he crawled back there when he realized he was dying."

"Which means whatever killed him is still in here."

"Yes."

"Swell."

Ken sighed. "Just one more thing to think about as we explore."

NEZUMA STOPPED and frowned.

He could hear voices. The sound of lots of voices was coming from behind the door down the hall.

They were excited about something. And from the numbers he heard, there was no way Nezuma could successfully take down all of them without the risk of injury or death to himself.

He did what made the most tactical sense to him.

He waited.

"I FOUND SOMETHING."

Annja followed the sound of Ken's voice to another wall. "What is it?"

"A series of three holes in a horizontal line, spaced about twelve inches from each other."

"How big are the holes?" Annja asked.

"Only big enough to get my hand into."

Annja took a deep breath. "Why is it I'm having flashbacks to when I went scuba diving and the dive masters told us to never stick our hands into the holes in coral because of the moray eels that lived there?"

"I was thinking there might be spiders up here," Ken said. "But I understand what you're saying."

"You think there's any other way to do this?" Annja asked.

"Have you found anything else?"

"No."

"Neither have I." Ken sighed. "Yes, I think this must be it."

"I don't suppose you can see anything by looking in?"

Ken chuckled in the darkness. "I didn't stick my eye right up to the opening but I tried to squint and see. Nothing."

"Figures."

"I'm going to do it, Annja. I have to stick my hand in one of these holes and see what happens."

Annja heard him breathing deeply and knew he'd be closing his eyes to check with his instincts about which hole might be the safe one.

"Okay," he whispered.

"You know which one you're going to choose?"

"The middle one," he said.

"Good luck, Ken."

"Thanks. Here I go."

Annja held her breath. She heard the rustle of skin against stone as Ken stuck his hand in.

"It's deep."

Annja waited.

Ken breathed out in a rush. "There's something in here."

"Pull your hand out, Ken!"

She heard him bringing his hand back. He was breathing fast. What could have bitten him? Annja wondered. Would they be able to get help? Where were those stupid monks?

"Annja." Ken's voice sounded like a faint whisper.

"Yes?"

"I think I have the *vajra*."

As soon as the words registered, Annja felt like screaming. But she didn't because the next thing she knew, the entire room was filled with brilliant golden white light.

Annja couldn't see a thing.

36

When she finally managed to blink her way back to full vision, Annja saw that they were in a large room surrounded by roughly twenty monks including Eiji. All of the monks smiled, but Eiji's smile was larger than any other.

"You found it," he said.

Ken held it aloft. "Yes."

Annja looked at the golden *vajra*. Ken handed it to her. "I couldn't have found it without your help."

Annja took the *vajra* and found it heavier than she'd expected. It lay across her palm, roughly six inches long with five prongs at either end curving in toward the center. Ornate metalwork adorned the length of it. Just holding it, Annja felt as though she might be powerful enough to rule the world.

She handed it back to Ken. "This belongs to you and the Yumegakure-ryu."

He accepted it and stood facing Eiji and his monks. "Thank you all very much for your service in the protection of this relic. My family and I thank you most sincerely for your time and devotion to its protection." He bowed low and Eiji and his monks returned the bow.

Ken helped Annja to her feet.

Eiji regarded them both. "You found it without too much hardship?"

Annja smiled. "There were a few times I thought we might not reach it."

"Ah, thought," said Eiji. "That devious little inclination we all have to reason things out can often cause us more harm than good. Imagine if our prehistoric ancestors had stopped to consider a rational solution to the sudden appearance of a saber-toothed tiger?"

"We wouldn't be here today," Annja said.

"The labyrinth was designed to only let those through who could trust their instincts and know that they would be safe no matter what appearances presented themselves," Ken said.

"Not an easy lesson," Eiji said.

"As evidenced by the dead who have tried before," Annja said. "Speaking of which—"

"Yes?" Eiji asked.

"There's a corpse back in the room before this one. You might want to take care of it."

Ken frowned. "One thing before you do that."

Eiji smiled. "You want to know if I lied to you when you asked if I knew how to defeat the labyrinth?"

"You could have just brought us to this room and we could have gotten it much more easily than we did."

"I did know about the existence of this room," said Eiji.

"We all do. But it would do no good for you to have forced me here. The *vajra* can only be retrieved going the route you traveled. Trying to force it out the back way would have had terrible consequences."

"Like what?" Annja asked.

"This monastery is built over a fault line, and whoever designed the labyrinth made sure that any fraudulent attempts to get it would result in a massive cave-in that would kill everyone in the mountain and forever trap the *vajra* under tons of rock."

Ken nodded. "Sounds fair."

Eiji turned and spoke quietly to two of his monks and then turned back to Ken and Annja. "They will take care of the body." His eyes twinkled. "I imagine that must have been a big surprise."

"Something like that," Annja said.

Eiji nodded. "You must be tired and hungry. We will celebrate the return of the heir to the Yumegakure-ryu with a feast."

"I don't think so," a voice said.

Annja turned and jumped. "What the hell are you doing here?"

Nezuma stood in the doorway, holding a gun in his hands. Judging by how he held it, Annja guessed he knew precisely how to use it if he needed to.

Nezuma grinned at her. "Nice to see you again, Miss Creed."

Annja frowned. "You didn't get enough of me at the *budokan* tournament?"

"Oh, I had plenty of you there. I imagine you're healed up nicely now? Your ribs all better?"

"Still sore."

"Ah, pity." Nezuma shrugged. "Couldn't be helped, though. I'm sure you understand. Just a friendly match and all."

"That doesn't explain you being here, though."

"Doesn't it?"

Annja glared at him. "I assume you want the *vajra*."

Nezuma nodded. "How quickly you forget our arrangement."

"What arrangement?"

"If you like," Nezuma said, "I can come over there and whisper in your ear the way I did in your hotel room."

"That was you?"

"Of course."

Annja gritted her teeth. "If you weren't holding that gun, I'd knock your teeth down the back of your throat."

Nezuma smirked. "No. You'd try to do that. And of course, you'd end up getting your ass handed to you the way I did it back at the *budokan*."

"I drew blood, too, Nezuma. Don't forget that," Annja said.

"Every dog has their day. You were bound to get lucky once or twice. I wouldn't bank on that saving your life today."

Annja caught a subtle movement out of the corner of her eye. One of Eiji's monks moved.

Nezuma's gun swiveled and spit two rounds into the monk's head. It happened so quickly that the sudden explosion of bullets caught Annja completely unaware. She clapped her hands over her ears and cried out.

The young monk slumped to the floor, already dead.

Nezuma shook his head and looked at Eiji. "That was a very stupid thing to do, old man."

Eiji simply looked at him with no hatred or animosity in his eyes. "My fate has already been decided. It makes no difference what you do."

"Is that so?" Nezuma's gun barked again, putting a single round directly between Eiji's eyes. The abbot of the monastery crumpled to the floor at the feet of the other monks.

Ken held up the *vajra*. "Enough! Isn't this what you want?"

Nezuma regarded him coolly. "Give that to me, ninja."

Ken smiled. "You spit that word like it's an insult."

"It is. Your kind have no honor."

Ken's eyes danced. "There's honor in killing unarmed monks and old men?"

"And lots of other people, too," Nezuma said. "I'm very good at it."

"Proud, too," Ken said. He raised the *vajra*. "What's so special about this that you would come here and cause so much destruction?"

"The *dorje* was given to your family by my family."

Ken's eyes narrowed. "I don't believe you."

"I don't care," Nezuma said. "It's the truth. I am the last in the Taishi family line. And that *dorje* belongs to me."

"If it was a gift to the Yumegakure-ryu for the service they rendered to your family, what makes you think you have the right to reclaim it?"

"Because you relinquished it to these monks. You took what was an incredibly potent gift and hid it in a mountain."

Ken nodded. "For the good of mankind."

"Rubbish! You hid it here because you were afraid of using it. You knew you didn't have the honor and power to wield such a magnificent thing. And rather than give it back, you couldn't admit your weakness and chose to hide it here instead."

Ken shrugged. "I have no idea what my ancestors might have thought except that they believed it might be used for evil purposes."

"Cowards."

Ken looked at Nezuma. "And what would you do with this?"

"That's none of your concern."

Ken shook his head. "That's not quite true. Since I hold the *vajra*, it's in my best interests to know what you'd do with it."

"It is in your best interest to hand that over to me right now before I kill you," Nezuma said. "There is nothing else you should be concerned with."

"And I'm to believe that you'll let us all live if I hand it over?" Ken smiled. "I think we both know that's not going to happen."

"I never said I wouldn't kill you," Nezuma said. "But I'll make it quick and relatively painless if you hand it over right now."

"I can't do that," Ken said.

Annja closed her eyes for a second. She could see the sword. She reached for it and felt her hands close around the hilt.

In the instant when Nezuma leveled his gun and fired at Ken, Annja tore the sword free and swung it down, causing the bullet to bounce off the blade and ricochet off the cave wall.

Annja swung the sword horizontally and caught the barrel

of Nezuma's gun, knocking it off target. She swept up and tried to cut back down, but Nezuma deflected the blade and redirected it away from him.

He backhanded Annja in the face with the gun, causing her to stagger and drop the sword.

As it clanged to the ground, it simply vanished.

Nezuma stopped and aimed his gun at Annja. "Now, what exactly just happened there?"

"Nothing. It was an optical illusion," she said.

Nezuma's eyes sparkled. "Could it be that I'll gain not one but two magical items today to help me in my conquests? How amazing."

"I don't know what you're talking about," Annja said.

Nezuma put the gun barrel against her temple. "If I were you, I would somehow find a way to get that sword back right now. Or else I will shoot you dead and not care about the sword at all. After all, once I get the *vajra*, I won't need anything else."

Annja closed her eyes. She could see the sword back where it belonged. She wrapped her hands around it but it wouldn't move.

She opened her eyes. "I can't get it out now."

"Why not?"

"I don't know."

Nezuma sighed. "In that case, I don't really have much use for you anymore, do I?"

"Nezuma."

Annja heard Ken's voice and looked over. Ken flicked his wrist, and Annja saw a blur of metal go whipping past her head.

It caught Nezuma's hand and he cried out, backing away as he tore the *shuriken* out of his skin and bone and tossed it aside.

"Enough of this. You're all dead." Nezuma raised his gun.

Annja closed her eyes and tried to get to the sword again. But it still wouldn't budge. Why not? I need it now more than I ever have before. Why won't it come out?

Ken dropped and rolled forward as Nezuma's gun fired. Ken came up and flicked his wrist again. The two *shuriken* he threw at Nezuma made the huge man jump to avoid them.

Annja marveled at how fast Nezuma was for his size and she had flashbacks to how he'd fought back at the *budokan*.

Ken closed the distance and kicked out at Nezuma's leg, using it to bridge the distance and come in, bringing the *vajra* down hard on the bridge of Nezuma's nose.

Annja heard a sharp crack as Nezuma's nose was crushed. Blood ran out of his nose.

Ken followed up with a chop to the side of Nezuma's neck that made the bleeding fighter stagger.

But he swept back, ducking as Ken attempted to gain an arm bar on Nezuma. Nezuma righted himself and jerked his gun up, trying to aim it at Ken's head.

Annja could see his finger already starting to squeeze the trigger.

"Ken!"

Two gunshots rang out. Annja winced.

Ken rolled to the floor.

Nezuma sank on his knees.

Ken got to his feet.

Nezuma looked down at his chest and the blossoming crimson stain on his shirt. He brought his hand over his chest and looked at it in disbelief when it came away red.

"Who?"

"Me."

Annja looked at the door. A woman stood there caked in dark blood and grime. But the terrible gun she held looked deadly enough.

Nezuma frowned. "Shuko?"

"Hello...*master*."

37

Annja watched the shock wash over Nezuma's face. Despite the gunshot wound, he still managed to pull himself up. "I thought you were—"

"Dead?" Shuko smiled. "I'm sure you wish I was. But fortunately, I took some precautions back in the circulation caves to ensure my own survival. A little body armor and some latex makeup can work wonders. Not that you cared to try to help me even if it had been real."

"I would have—"

"Please," Shuko snapped. "You left me for dead willingly. And it's been apparent for a while now that you've been planning to kill me anyway. You almost did at the *ryokan*."

"You let us fail," Nezuma said.

"Deliberately," Shuko said. "If Kennichi and the woman spotted us, then they might just get complacent enough to not spot the real team I had in place. The one that allowed me to stage the attack on their *ryokan*."

Nezuma shook his head. "This makes no sense. That attack was carried out by the Onigawa-gumi."

Ken looked up. "It was?"

Shuko nodded. "Of course it was. I needed to make it look like we wanted you both dead. I sacrificed several good men in the process. But sometimes, that is the price you must pay."

Ken leaned back. "My god."

Shuko smiled.

"What is it?" Annja asked.

"All this time…I'd heard the rumors but I never believed them, of course. Who would?" Ken looked at Shuko. "It was you."

She nodded. "Yes."

"Who is she?" Annja asked.

Ken pointed at her. "She's the *oyabun*—the head—of the Onigawa-gumi Yakuza clan."

Nezuma sniffed. "Utterly ridiculous. She is merely my pupil—albeit a fine one. She had nevertheless betrayed me. An *oyabun*? Nonsense."

Shuko glanced at him. Disdain shadowed her face. "You were always far too concerned with appearances and tradition to allow yourself to see what was truly happening after you plucked me from the slums. As I learned, I also schemed."

"I should have let the rats eat you," Nezuma spit.

Shuko smiled. "Maybe. But I used my training and resources to start what will soon be the most powerful crime syndicate on the planet. Already my emissaries are reaching out to like-minded organizations all over the world. Soon we will use our networks to rule crime like never before."

Annja closed her eyes and saw the sword resting there.

"But you," Shuko continued, "you would never have let me live to see my own destiny. That's why I took matters into my own hands."

"I might have killed you at the *ryokan*," Nezuma said. "Where would your grandiose plans have been then?"

"You would have died in another second had you not released me," Shuko said. "There was a sniper resting his crosshairs on your head just waiting for me to give him the signal."

Nezuma closed his mouth.

Shuko turned to Annja. "I must say it's been a pleasure seeing you travel with Ken and help him in his quest for the *vajra*. It's not often I feel admiration toward another woman, but you have certainly earned my respect."

"Uh…thanks," Annja said.

Shuko shrugged. "It's a shame I'll have to kill you."

"Couldn't we talk this over?" Annja inched her way toward Ken.

Shuko gestured with the gun. "Don't do that. It might make my trigger finger jump before I'm ready."

Annja stopped moving. Shuko looked at Ken. "So, you heard the rumors, then?"

He nodded. "People said the *oyabun* was a woman, but I didn't believe it. My own stupidity, I suppose."

"Would it have changed anything?" Shuko asked.

"No. The *vajra* belongs to the Yumegakure-ryu and no one else."

Shuko frowned. "Pity. I thought we might make an alliance. I could use someone to train my men in the ways of the ninja."

Nezuma groaned. "Kill me now, Shuko. I want to hear no more of this dishonorable talk."

Shuko shook her head. "Such hypocrisy. You claim to hold the traditions of Japan sacred. That you wish for the old-world Bushido ways, and yet you would use the *vajra* to further your own criminal agenda." She sighed. "But have it your way."

Her gun barked twice and the rounds caught Nezuma in his chest. He dropped to the floor dead.

Shuko turned her attention back to the monks. "Go. I have no quarrel with you. You're free to leave."

The monks filed out of the room, leaving Annja and Ken behind. Ken shifted slightly, palming the *vajra*.

Shuko looked at her watch.

"Waiting for something?" Annja asked.

Shuko smiled as the sound of gunfire broke out. Sustained bursts of automatic fire caromed around the monastery along with screams and moans of the dying.

Ken frowned. "You sent them to their deaths."

Shuko shrugged. "My men were anxious to kill after the harsh beating you two put on them the other night. To say they're anxious to meet you and avenge their comrades is a bit of an understatement."

"Just what do you think the *vajra* will do for you?" Ken asked. "Do you know anything about it?"

"Do you?"

Ken smiled. "Not a damned thing. I was looking forward to seeing what it could do."

Shuko shook her head. "Well, unfortunately for you, I'll be taking that now."

The gunfire had stopped elsewhere. Annja felt sick thinking about all the monks who had just been slaughtered. She felt waves of rage wash over her and she closed her eyes.

The sword rested in front of her.

All she had to do was grab it.

"I don't think so," Shuko said.

She opened her eyes and saw Ken holding the *vajra* aloft. He looked different somehow.

Shuko brought her gun up to bear, but as she did so, Ken started chanting in some weird monotone that Annja had never heard before.

Shuko froze.

Annja snapped her eyes shut and grabbed the sword. She opened her eyes and threw the sword across the room.

The blade hissed through the air as beams of light shot out of the *vajra* and into Shuko at the same time the sword slammed into her midsection, shoving her back into the wall.

Bright red blood shot out of her mouth, and her eyes went wide and white almost immediately. The beams of light cut into her body like lasers.

Shuko threw her head back and screamed.

Annja brought her hand up to shield herself from the intense light exploding across the room.

Ken kept chanting.

The light vanished and Ken stopped his mantra.

Shuko stood transfixed at the rear wall. Her gun lay on the floor.

She looked down at Annja's sword jutting out of her chest. She slumped over.

Dead.

Annja breathed out. "Wow."

Ken brought his hand down with the *vajra* in it and turned it over in his hand. "That was certainly something."

"How did you do that?"

He shook his head. "I have no idea. I just…I don't know… made it happen, I guess."

"Well, whatever you did, it certainly worked. It distracted her and I was able to reach for the sword."

"Look," Ken said.

Annja turned and saw one of the monks standing in the door frame. He bowed low and smiled. "You are all right?"

Ken nodded. "It's good to see you and your brothers intact."

"When she let us go, it seemed fairly obvious what would be waiting for us out there. Her men stood no chance. And staging the massacre seemed like a good idea."

"She certainly fell for it," Ken said.

"What will you do now?" the monk asked.

Ken smiled. "Honestly, I'd like to go home. Is there an easier way out of here than how we came in?"

He glanced at Annja. "Are you ready to get going?"

"Just one second." She walked over to Shuko and slid her sword out of Shuko's corpse. Holding it in both hands, she closed her eyes and returned the sword to its resting place.

When she opened her eyes again, both Ken and the monk were staring.

"Some day," Ken said, "you'll have to teach me how you do that."

Annja laughed. "Just as soon as I figure the whole thing out myself."

38

The monks showed them how to best exit the mountain, but kept Annja and Ken blindfolded the entire time, telling them that secrecy of the monastery was paramount and this way they'd never be able to reveal its actual location.

On the walk back down the mountain, Annja kept looking at Ken. She could see the happiness in his gait and spirit. Throughout the hike, he stayed fairly quiet, seemingly preferring to stay inside his own head.

Annja had a great deal to think about, as well. A lot had happened on this trip, and she had to process it all. She'd been concerned about how she was unable to bring the sword out to protect herself when she and Ken had been in the midst of the fog. But she guessed that it wouldn't come out because the monks hadn't meant her harm, despite giving the appearance of that. Had she been able to draw the sword, she definitely would have killed some of them.

So did the sword know when the danger was real as

opposed to imagined? And if there was no true danger, would she be able to pull it out anymore and examine it? Or had that time passed?

There was little doubt that things were evolving. Annja just wasn't sure where she fit into the whole picture. In some ways she felt like a tool to be used by the sword. And other times it seemed that the sword was the tool.

She still didn't feel that they were unified in body and spirit. That, she supposed, would take many years.

"Are you all right?" Ken asked.

She smiled. "I think so, yes."

Ken stepped over a thick tree root and grinned. "Some trip we've had ourselves, Annja Creed."

"It certainly has been something."

"What will you do now?"

Annja shrugged. "The same thing I always do—go home, get myself stuck in the middle of something new, exciting and potentially dangerous."

Ken laughed. "You enjoy that, don't you?"

Annja thought about it. "I suppose I do. Remember when you spoke about the moon's reflection on the water? And how we have a tendency as humans to see what we desperately want to see, not how things actually are?"

"I remember," Ken said. "It took me years to learn that lesson. Years to become comfortable with who I was—the man I'd become. It is not an easy thing to do, stare into the mirror of pure truth and be comfortable with what is reflected back at you."

"I can see how it wouldn't be." Annja shrugged. "But I guess I'm starting to feel a bit more comfortable with who I am now. And I do enjoy taking risks. I have to accept that part of myself if I am to understand fully what it means to have this sword that I've got."

Ken's eyes danced. "I thought we weren't going to talk about that."

Annja laughed. "Is this going to be our special phrase from now on?"

Ken stopped. "I didn't know there was going to be a *from now on*."

"Well, there's not," Annja replied, momentarily taken aback. "I mean, I just thought that, you know, if we ever run into each other again. It's a small world and all. And you know, you had been following me all over the place prior to this."

Ken smiled. "Then it will be our phrase. And maybe when we've both had some time to figure out our own personal destinies, maybe we'll see each other again."

"I'd like that," Annja admitted.

"As would I."

They passed the remainder of the trip in silence. Part of Annja hated the idea of leaving Ken. She'd had a lot of fun being with him. But she also knew that while it might be fun to hang out for a while, she'd grow restless. She had adventures to undertake. She had places to visit.

And evil to stop.

She frowned. Now where had that thought come from?

Ken reached the trailhead first and waited for Annja to come through the bush. "You think our car is still there?" he asked.

Annja stopped. "You don't think someone stole it?"

Ken shrugged. "Hey, we're not immune to car theft over here, you know."

"I am not walking back to Ueno," Annja said. "If the car is missing, you'll have to carry me back."

"Deal."

But the car was right where they'd left it. Annja was a bit surprised that none of Shuko's Yakuza thugs had demolished it on the way in.

"So, the Onigawa-gumi is all destroyed, right?" Annja asked.

Ken nodded. "I'd certainly think so. The monks took care of them. Despite Shuko's insistence that they were going global, I don't think they were. One reason I chose to approach the Onigawa-gumi in the first place was they were smaller than other clans. I felt I could deal with them reasonably." He laughed. "Well, as reasonably as you can with Yakuza."

"What if there are some left?" Annja asked.

Ken shrugged. "I'll take care of them."

Annja raised her eyebrows. "You'll kill them?"

Ken fished the car keys out of his backpack. "Annja, I don't ever look for a reason to kill. Neither would you. But if there's one thing I've learned it's that the universe has a scheme of totality to it. And places and events and people all fall into that scheme. Our destinies are designed so that we all intersect how we're supposed to intersect. It may be that I'm not supposed to kill them or it may be that I am."

"But how will you know what the universe or God or whatever wants you to do?"

Ken pointed back toward the mountain. "The same way we figured out what we were supposed to do in the labyrinth."

"Instinct?"

"Sure."

"I guess I'm not all that comfortable yet with the idea of using my instinct to guide me entirely through life," Annja said.

"No one's saying to exclude your logical, rational mind. You've got that for a reason, as well. But use it as part of your entire arsenal, not as the single guiding compass. The more tools you have and know how to use, the better and more fulfilling your life will be," Ken said.

"I guess that makes sense."

They ditched their bags in the trunk and then got into the car.

Ken slid the key into the ignition. "Think anyone planted a bomb on this?"

Annja frowned. "I hope not."

"Better check." Ken closed his eyes and then reopened them. "We're fine." He turned the key and the engine caught immediately.

Annja exhaled. "That's a relief."

Ken put the car into gear and they backed up on the gravel bed, listening to the tires crunch the stones underneath. Ken eased out onto the road and they drove back toward Ueno.

"You'll come back to Tokyo with me?" Annja asked.

"Sure. I have to go back there anyway. No sense staying out here anymore. I've got what I came for."

"I can book a return flight to the States for tomorrow."

"Which would leave us...tonight?"

Annja smiled. "A nice dinner?"

Ken nodded. "That sounds good to me."

Annja watched the scenery whip past the windows. "What did the *vajra* do to Shuko in the monastery?"

Ken frowned. "I'm not really sure. Traditionally, the *vajra* was used as something to remind the wielder of their incredible personal power. But I have no idea if the same thing applies to this particular *vajra*. After all, it was given to my family for very specific reasons."

"It looked like she'd been hit with laser beams or something."

Ken nodded. "Yes."

"Maybe the light of truth?"

"It's an interesting idea," Ken said. "You mean the *vajra* showed Shuko exactly who she was in a split second of time and the illumination of her true spirit was simply too intense for her to bear?"

"Something like that, I guess. I don't know. All this talk about truth and its reflections and that stuff has me thinking along those lines, but I don't know if I'm making any sense of it all," Annja said.

"You're doing fine." Ken rested one hand on the steering wheel. "And you might be right, who knows? As I said, I've got a lot of work to do in order to discover its secrets. Just as, I'm sure, you have to with your particular situation."

"Seems like we've each got our crosses to bear, huh?"

Ken smiled. "Looks that way."

"It's kind of nice, actually," Annja said.

"What is?"

They were on the outskirts of Ueno. Farmhouses gave way to apartment buildings. "Knowing that there's someone else in the world who's got something incredibly powerful that they need to figure out. I don't feel so alone anymore. Before this, I felt like some weird almost messiah."

"A reluctant messiah," Ken said. "I could see it in you when I first saw laid eyes upon you."

"I never asked for it."

"I know that. I think that's exactly why you might have been chosen to carry this particular responsibility. Most other people would go out of their way to seek the very thing you struggle with."

Annja frowned. "You sought your *vajra*. Does that make you less worthy than me?"

"I hope not," Ken said. "But only time will tell."

"I don't envy you."

Ken smiled. "I'm not sure I envy either of us."

"You promise to stay in touch? Let me know how you're progressing? It might be nice to bounce some ideas off of me now and then."

"Only if you do the same."

"I will."

"I'll tell you this," Ken said. "I'm glad I don't have to carry that sword."

"Why not?"

"It's far too large for me to handle. The *vajra* is nice and small."

"Size isn't everything," Annja said.

"It's what you do with it," Ken said. "Isn't that right?"

"Absolutely."

Ken chuckled. "The next time we get together, we've got to make sure we continue this awful string of innuendo."

"Oh, definitely."

"I feel so enlightened when we talk like this."

Annja smiled. "Don't you know that's the secret to all of this stuff?"

"What is?"

"Not taking it too seriously. I don't think either of us is a candidate for sitting on a mountaintop dispensing wisdom to the acolytes who traipse after us."

"Probably not." Ken shrugged. "So we're both reluctant messiahs."

"As long as we remember that the true path to enlightenment comes from living in the moment and embracing life, rather than retreating from it in some remote monastery or cave."

"I couldn't live in a cave," Ken said.

"Why not?"

"I'd miss my high-def television far too much."

Annja pointed. "You see? That's surely the sign of someone destined for great things."

"You think?"

"I know. Only the wisest people know that true happiness is found in a giant-screen TV."

"Keep that up and you'll be hawking electronic goods when you get back to the States," Ken said, laughing.

"I hear the money's good," Annja replied.

Ken frowned suddenly. Annja watched him tense up.

And then she felt it, too.

She spun around in her seat—

"If you two don't stop this inane chatter, I may just vomit all over the both of you."

"You!" Annja couldn't believe her eyes.

Garin sat in the back seat of the car.

Aiming a pistol at them.

39

"Hello, Annja. Nice to see you again."

Annja frowned. "I'm not so sure I can say the same thing about you."

Garin shrugged. "Well, that's to be expected, I suppose. After all, I am holding a gun and aiming at you."

"Who is this man?" Ken asked.

"Just keep driving, pal. Don't try anything funny. I'm not like the other people you've been dealing with lately." He glanced at Annja. "No offense, sweetheart."

"Go to hell, Garin," Annja said.

He shook his head. "Is that any way to treat an old friend? Really. So rude and the tone of your voice is completely uncalled-for."

"What's uncalled-for is you hiding in the back seat of this car. How long have you been here?"

Garin shrugged. "An hour or two. Ever since you left the

monastery. I just took a quicker way down. Got here first and hid out. I didn't think you'd mind."

"Oh, but I do."

Ken looked at Annja. "Is this your boyfriend?"

Garin exploded into laughter. "Please. Stop. How rich!"

Annja scowled. "He's not my boyfriend."

"Much as she'd love having a roll in the hay with me," Garin said, "the truth is we are not lovers."

"I don't want to sleep with you," Annja said.

Garin wiped the tears from his eyes. "Oh, sure. Keep telling yourself that, kid. You might believe it some day."

Ken glanced at Garin in the rearview mirror. "So what can we do for you, exactly? Are you looking for a ride into town?"

"Actually, no."

"Seems such a waste to come all the way out here just to talk to Annja," Ken said calmly.

Garin smiled. "I want the *vajra*."

Annja looked at Garin. "It's not yours."

"Obviously." He held up the gun. "Hence the pistol. I find it helps separate people from their belongings when they are reluctant to do so otherwise."

"He won't give it to you," Annja said. "It belongs to his family."

Garin leaned forward. "Let me put it this way—ever since you found that sword, I've been wondering what my worth is and what will happen to me now that you're around." He leaned back. "And you know what I came up with?"

"No idea. But I'm sure you'll tell me," Annja said.

"I came to the conclusion that it would behoove me to have other things I might fall back on in case it does come to pass that I find my strength waning. As a result of this epiphany, and really, it was a fabulous one over the most exquisite Italian food I've ever had— But I digress. As a result, I've been looking to acquire other items of antiquity that might help me preserve my current state, so to speak."

"Try a bottle of formaldehyde," Annja said. "That's what works for most old farts."

Garin chuckled. "I love it when you get that barb in your tongue. It's quite refreshing to see you still have it."

"I've still got the sword, as well."

Garin frowned. "Yes, well, we won't be pulling that out anytime soon, will we? After all, if I get one indication that you are, I'll put several bullets into your new paramour here."

"We're not lovers," Annja said.

"Oh? And that dalliance by the waterfall? What was that?"

Had everyone in the world seen her make love to Ken? Annja sighed. "I think we're still trying to work out exactly what that was. But neither of us is getting hung up on it."

"Exactly," Ken said.

"How nice you've got that understood," Garin said. "But I'll still kill him if you pull that blade out."

"I'm not pulling it out. It's been acting funny anyway lately."

Garin blanched. "It has?"

"Yes."

"I don't suppose you'd care to elaborate on how it's been acting funny, would you?"

Annja pointed. "I don't suppose you'd care to toss the gun out of the window and act like a civilized person for a change?"

"I don't think so."

Annja nodded. "So, I guess this will be something I talk

over with Roux, then. I'm sure he'll be most interested. Even more so when he finds out that he's got valuable information that you don't have."

Garin frowned. "That's not fair, Annja. I helped you acquire that sword."

"I never wanted the sword. I was simply there at the right moment and you and Roux didn't have a chance to get your greedy mitts on it."

"You're punishing me."

"Yes. And you're not going to get Ken's *vajra*."

Garin chewed his lip. "You could be lying. Making the whole thing up. Just to protect your boyfriend here."

"Yep," Annja said. "I could be. But you won't ever know, will you?"

Garin stayed quiet for a moment. Annja shook her head. "Is this why you approached me in the hotel? When you tried to warn me about Ken? Planting all that stuff in my mind that he might not be who he said he was? Was it all for this? Just to get the *vajra*?"

"Will you be mad if I say yes?"

Annja smirked. "No. I'll chalk it up to you just being you. And to think I thought you were actually concerned about me. Well, at least until you went after that waitress."

"I have needs," Garin said. "Don't begrudge me my primal desires."

"Whatever." Annja saw they were approaching the heart of Ueno. "Were you on our tail ever since the hotel?"

"Yes."

"And you saw, presumably, everything that happened?"

Garin shrugged. "There were a few instances where you

went to ground and I couldn't locate you. But I tagged your other interested parties, knowing they'd lead me back to you, and here I am now."

"Thanks for all the help."

"My pleasure." Garin cleared his throat. "You really won't tell me what's been going on, will you?"

"Not one word of information as long as you think about stealing the *vajra* from Ken."

"And if I play nice and let him keep it?"

"I might think about sitting you and Roux down and having a chat about what's been going on," Annja said.

"It would have to be neutral ground. The crazy fool still wants to kill me even though he claims he doesn't."

"Neutral ground is fine."

Garin sighed. "I'd really like that *vajra*."

"So take it," Annja said. "Enjoy it. But it probably won't help you when it comes time to deal with Roux or your own destiny."

Garin shook his head. "All right, fine. Whatever. You win. I won't take it."

Annja looked at him. "I want your word of honor or whatever it is you hold dearest to your soul."

Garin held up his hand. "You have my word as a master of the horizontal tango that I will never endeavor to steal Ken's precious *vajra*. Are we done now?"

Ken pulled over to the curb, got out and went to the trunk. He took out his backpack and Annja's and then walked over to Annja's door.

"Ready?"

Annja got out of the car and shouldered her pack. Garin looked out from the back seat.

Ken tossed him the keys. "The rental agency is down the road about a mile. You'd better get it gassed up first, though, or they'll charge you."

"Charge me? Now wait a minute, this is your car—"

Ken shook his head. "No, it's registered under your name. You see, I took the liberty of shadowing Annja, too. And when I saw you taking such an interest in her, I decided it might be a good idea to know who you were. Not an easy task—you're quite the interesting fellow."

Garin said nothing.

"But," Ken continued, "I managed to dig up some stuff on you. Nothing too big, but a usable credit card number and a nifty passport photo. Anyway, I charged our entire trip to your credit card, so expect that bill to be coming in soon."

"You son of a bitch," Garin shouted.

Ken shook his head. "Nope. I was legit, but thanks for asking."

Annja waved to him. "Goodbye, Garin."

He got out of the car. "I'll expect to hear from you, Annja."

"You will."

Garin tossed the keys into his other hand. He grinned at Ken. "Nice meeting you, pal."

Ken bowed. "The pleasure, as they, was all mine."

Annja looped her arm in Ken's and nudged him. "Come on, we've got a train to catch."

As they walked to the station, Ken glanced back in time to see Garin drive off. "You think he'll be okay?" he asked.

"He's managed for many years," Annja said. "I don't think he'll have too much trouble."

Ken stopped. "Maybe I should have told him about the explosives I stowed in the trunk."

"You didn't," Annja said laughing.

Ken shrugged. "It's the stuff we got from Jiro. I needed to put it somewhere." He sighed. "That just might delay your friend and give us enough time to put some distance between us."

Annja dragged Ken toward the train station. "Good. Now let's talk about that dinner you owe me."